LOW DOWN
AND DERBY

OHIO RIVER VALLEY CHAPTER
SISTERS IN CRIME

COMPILED BY SANDRA CEROW LEONARD

An Imprint of The Overmountain Press
JOHNSON CITY, TENNESSEE

This book is a work of fiction. All names, characters, places, and events are either the product of the authors' imaginations or are used fictitiously. Any resemblance to actual events or persons, living or dead, is entirely coincidental and beyond the intent of either the authors or the publisher.

ISBN 1-57072-312-5
Copyright © 2006 by Ohio River Valley Chapter Sisters in Crime
Printed in the United States of America
All Rights Reserved

1 2 3 4 5 6 7 8 9 0

To all of the members of the Ohio River Valley Chapter of Sisters in Crime, especially Jeffrey Marks, whose encouragement and effort have led us to this anthology.

ACKNOWLEDGMENTS

Low Down and Derby is the second anthology of mystery stories with a Kentucky Derby theme by authors in the Ohio River Valley Chapter of Sisters in Crime. Our first anthology, *Derby Rotten Scoundrels*, was a wonderful experience for our members in so many ways.

Everyone worked hard, and we thank each one: Deborah Alvord, Daryll Anderson, Jerilyn Anderson, Laurel Louise Anderson, Linda Atkins, Edmund August, Barbara Blackburn, Dorothy Burks, Michael Bradford, Gina Campbell, Marlis Day, Virginia Dulworth, Donna Elkins, Kit Erhman, Carmelita Everheart, Teesue Fields, Pamela Fischer, Sara Frommer, Sarah Glenn, Laura Guetig, Tamera Huber, Josephine Jacovino, A. R. Kearney, Elizabeth Kutak, Sandra Leonard, Jeffrey Marks, Gwen Mayo, Margaret Ann McCarthy, Richard McMahan, Elaine Munsch, Beverle Myers, Anthony Perona, Pat Robertson, Deborah Schenck, Sheila Shumate, Brenda Stewart, Cheryl Stuck, Elaine Thomas, Ann Waterman, Carl Yates, and Foul Play Bookstore.

Many thanks to Beth Wright, Sherry Lewis, and Karin O'Brien with Silver Dagger Mysteries for guiding us through the book publishing, editing, and marketing process.

Bob Hill, Mary Welk, Michael Embry, Steve Flairty, Anita Oldham, Lucie Blodgett, Carla Sue Broecker, Jason Mullis, and Jacob Glassner are some of the journalists who wrote kind stories about our efforts. An interview on WAVE-TV gave us regional coverage.

Our regular meetings are held in the Barnes & Noble at 801 South Hurstbourne Parkway in Louisville, Kentucky. Marty Gaddis, the manager, and Elaine Munch, the assistant manager, have been very helpful to our chapter. We would not have our wonderful speakers program without them. They also are generous in teaching us the complicated ins and outs of book selling.

We are grateful to Tony Terry, director of publicity for Churchill Downs, for helping us create more realistic racetrack scenes. He gave us a terrific tour of the Churchill Downs track, backside, and grandstands. Through it all, he patiently answered our many questions.

Our initial book launch was a great success because of Laura Guetig, who made our press kits, and Ann Payne, who hosted our launch party at the Pendennis Club.

And, finally, thank you to Sandra Cerow Leonard who compiled this book and learned the incredible need for everyone to master computer technology.

TABLE OF CONTENTS

Derby Parties

by Mike Bradford

The actual attendance at the Kentucky Derby is dwarfed by the vast multitude of those attending derby parties leading up to that first Saturday afternoon in May. From stellar red-carpet events for the rich and famous to the untold thousands of backyard cookouts, for the people of the Louisville area and the vast lands beyond, an annual derby party is the event of the year.

Some say the granddaddy of all derby parties is the one thrown by the former Doublemint twins, Priscilla Barnstable and Patricia Barnstable Brown. A recent Barnstable event is said to have been a real winner because the twins held a great hand: a King, a Strait, and two perfect tens. That's Larry King, George Strait, and Pamela Anderson and Bo Derek, along with twelve hundred of their closest friends. As for entertainment at the Barnstable Bash, think KISS, think Guns N' Roses, think Meat Loaf. Also think generosity. Since 1988 the Barnstable event has raised over five million dollars for charitable causes. So, double your pleasure, double your fun, by gum, with the Barnstable twins.

A derby party can be a coast-to-coast event. One major university conducts an annual derby bash as part of their Program for Equine Health. A party in Arizona features dozens of White Castle hamburgers flown in from Louisville and steam heated for the event!

To properly prepare for the derby party, one must buy the right recipe book and also pick up a book on the cocktails to serve. So go to it. Learn how to whip up burgoo, hot browns, Benedictine sandwiches, grits casserole, Derby-Pie, and just the right barbeque. By the way, in Kentucky, *barbeque* is a noun—never a verb.

You may find the following Web sites helpful:

www.atasteofkentucky.com/derby

www.nagsheadsoft.com/nhsweb19.htm

www.cocktailtimes.com/indepth/derby

Diamonds Glitter, Blood Stains

by Mike Bradford

Mike Bradford is a retired minister and eldercare executive. He and his wife, Julie, live and work in Kentucky. He has written two books in the Winthorpe Mysteries: Under the Bridge and Back Again *and* The Hole in the Bottom of the Sea. *Book three in the series,* While Searching for Air, *should release in 2006. To learn more about Davis and Kitty Winthorpe, visit* www.thewinthorpemysteries.com.

2:36 p.m. April 1:

I lounged in comfort when it all began. My wife was out shopping, and I had sunk into the soft leather of my big couch. As I napped peacefully, the doorbell rang. I fought off the sound, finally yielding to the intrusion.

Honestly, I speak the truth. A jockey stood at my door, wearing brown boots, with green-and-gold silks. At the curb stood a liveried groom holding the reins of a genuine Thoroughbred racehorse.

"Mr. Winthorpe?" the jockey said.

"Uh, yes, may I help you?

He bowed, presenting an envelope. "This is for you."

A crooked grin crossed my face. "Well, yeah—right!" The envelope bore one word: *Winthorpe.*

"Please enjoy," he said.

I stood dumbfounded as the jockey mounted and rode away, groom following. I wished my dear wife Kitty had seen that. Kitty is one hot number—Italian. She came to me with the maiden name of Servideo.

4:08 p.m. April 1:

I placed the envelope on my desk. I wanted Kitty and me to open the invitation together.

Soon she was home.

"Kitty!" I shouted. "You've got to see this!"

She gave me a funny look. "What?"

"Look at this."

She took the envelope. "Do I open it?"

"Give it a go."

She ripped the seam and removed a card. She read for a moment without expression, then she giggled. "You figure it out," she said, handing me the card.

Felicitations

Jasper and Mavis Crowe cordially invite you to
The Rookery
For the Fourth Annual Old Louisville

Derby Shebang

6:00 p.m. April 23rd to Midnight April 25th

Dress for the game

Eight thousand to play

Regrets only

"What's this all about?" Kitty asked.

I told her the story of the jockey.

She flopped onto the couch. "Incredible! We're going, of course."

"Eight thousand what?" I said.

"Well, dollars, I'm sure!"

I exclaimed, "For what?"

"Does it make a difference?"

"Well, yeah! Doesn't it?"

"Davis, it's an adventure. It's a party. That's the weekend before the Derby. It's a Derby party, no big deal. Who knows what the money's for?"

"Would it be too tacky to call and ask?"

"Davis, tacky has never stopped you before. Make the call. I'm getting ready for dinner."

I wish now I had thrown the thing away. I wish I had never shown the stupid envelope to Kitty. I should have known this involved insanity when the horse left a pile of manure in front of my house. Like a fool, I got the phone book.

4:27 p.m. April 1:

"The Rookery," a woman answered. "How may I help you?"

"Uh, this is Mr. Davis Winthorpe calling for Mr. Jasper Crowe."

I waited a short time.

"Jasper here. Winthorpe is it? Aha. May I call you Davis? How may I help you?" His strangely affected speech was punctuated with tiny bursts of laughter, seldom appropriate. Actually, his affectation sounded more like an effort to hock a bad oyster.

"Mr. Crowe—rather Jasper—yes, please call me Davis. I received your invitation. . . ."

"Aha, yes . . . delighted, delighted! Surely you will attend?"

"I must! Curiosity has me. Can you tell me more about whole shebang, so to speak?"

"Yes, certainly, five or six of us old-timers in Old Louisville have this little Derby Do one week before the main event. We invite new participants each year. You and your lovely wife represent those somewhat newly arrived in our part of town, and have bit of a reputation for adventure. Our little self-styled committee voted unanimously for the Winthorpes to be invited this year, you see."

Well, I failed to see. Actually, he implied we represented newly moneyed objects of curiosity with a reputation for monkey business. I waited for Jasper to speak.

"Well, yes, to say more. Our little bash is a scavenger hunt. Perfectly simple, but not perfectly decent, aha."

"Scavenger hunt?"

"Exactly!"

Bluntly I said, "And the eight thousand?" I waited through a long silence.

"Ahmmm, yes . . . I rather prefer that the use of the money be a surprise. And really, Davis, if you have to ask about the money, then what's the fun of the game?"

"Who else is attending?"

"My secret! Part of the game. Does it make a difference?"

"Oh, no, not at all. Why do you say we should dress for the game?"

"The game lasts the weekend, Davis. You will be our houseguests. There will be dining and dancing, evening wear expected. The rest is dirty work. I suggest you bring clothes fit for speed!"

"Well, okay! I'll see you April twenty-third."

"Yes, aha, ta, and all that!"

There it was. We had a date with who knows whom. I had no idea what to make of the eight thousand. I still remembered when 8K constituted a fortune, aha.

5:50 p.m. April 23:

I wore a white dinner jacket and black bow tie. My outfit represented vintage Palm Beach wear. I can't resist a consignment store. Kitty wore a knee-length, sequined, royal blue sheath, highly accessorized and set off by a lovely bodice—ruffled, pleated, puckered, or something like that.

We loaded a suitcase into Kitty's Town Car, and Karl, our driver, took us the three blocks to the home of Jasper and Mavis Crowe. We arrived at six, straight up.

The Rookery stands out as one of the more substantial mansions on South Third Street. Old Louisville offers the largest collection of Victorian mansions in America. The home of Jasper and Mavis represents this tradition well. A huge limestone edifice, it sports turrets, gables, keystones, stone lions—it has it all. The guidebooks refer to it as the Dobbs House, built by Ezra and Iris Whitley Dobbs nearly a century ago. A uniformed butler graced the porch. Get the picture?

We followed the butler into the grand hall, which was slightly smaller than a tennis court. I stood, gaping at the room and the eclectic collection of persons gathered there.

6:03 p.m. April 23:

Jasper, mid-fifties, made his entrance with a loud "Huzzah! Aha, huzzah, all!" Wearing a tuxedo, and standing over six feet tall, he loomed above my five foot ten. He appeared gaunt to the point of absurdity. Pinch-faced, with a long beak of a nose, he sported a bald spot at the crown of his head. What remained of his wispy salt-and-pepper hair exploded in disarray.

His wife followed. She had not aged well. She presented a round face with pale, splotched skin and flushed cheeks. Mavis, short of waist, had a potbelly that protruded farther than her breasts. Blue eyes twinkled beneath a frizz of curly hair only slightly better organized than her husband's.

"Welcome, all," Jasper said. "Welcome to our home, aha. Let the Shebang begin! Your tables bear your names. Please take your places. Now, friends! We waste time! Oh, yes, let me do the introductions."

Kitty gave a yank, dragging me to an elegantly decorated six-by-six table with our name printed neatly on a placard.

"First the intros and then the rules," he said. "Let me begin. . . ."

Let me butt in with a narrative. I had to do a little digging, but I will provide you with the names of those in our little flock. I also found some dirt on most, should you care to hear. Alphabetically:

Avery and Margaret Abernathy—*Permanent members of the Shebang. An architect without peer, he put together a first-class sticks-and-bricks concern known nationally. Avery took Margaret as wife number three. He cheated on the other two. Somehow Margaret keeps him on a short leash. She owns a multi-office real estate company, and she manages people and husbands very well.*

Maynard Bollinger and wife, Rita—*Maynard shares a business with Jasper Crowe. Maynard supplies both brains and labor. Jasper represents the dough. Rita, a very good-looking redhead, runs the office at Bollinger and Crowe Art and Artifacts. They helped found the Shebang.*

The Honorable Bennett and Lillian Hostettler—*Come from bourbon money. As the story goes, Bennett descends from Elijah Craig, the renowned minister who invented bourbon. In Kentucky, one can come no closer to royalty. Bennett formerly served as a Kentucky state senator. Lillian served as his mistress while in office. After defeat by a cagey Republican, the senator divorced his wife for Lillian.*

Rachel Malone—*Author of the nursery rhyme murder mysteries,* One Two Buckle My Shoe *and* Three Four Open the Door. *Her third novel occupied her attention at the time. She's a Louisville gal, living in Arizona. Comes home for Derby and other meaningful events. She represents new money—tolerated, not respected. Invited for need of celebrity impact.*

Allen Mason and Jimmy McDowell—*A couple, perhaps. They dressed alike and acted alike. Kitty called them the Twins. They sing with a rockabilly band that goes by the name of What If. Rachel Malone bankrolls and promotes this group. In order to get Rachel to attend, the Shebang had to invite the Twins.*

The Misters Lewis and Clark Tannowitz—*Bachelor brothers who still share the family mansion on Belgravia Court. Their family ran a chain of Louisville department stores for three generations before the boys sold out to a major chain. They got millions plus five percent of gross sales for ten years. That's a nice way to go. They invented the Derby Shebang.*

And that brings us to **Miles Davis and Katherine Servideo Winthorpe**. *Kitty got her money from the Mob. I got mine from the President of the United States. That's enough said. If I tell you more, I'll have to kill you. I believe the Winthorpes also provided amusement value. What's a party without a little Mob money?*

After introductions Jasper put the Shebang into gear. "My home is your home for the next fifty-four hours," he said. "There will be food, live music, and drink at all times. You may do whatever touches your fancy, aha. If you wish, you may play the game. If you choose to sleep or need to freshen up, we have provided a private bedroom upstairs for each couple. Identical lists for the scavenger hunt lie face down on your tables. I will sound a gong, and the hunt will be on! Oh, yes, aha, under each table you will find a Polaroid camera. Questions?"

I said, "What about the eight thousand?"

"Yes, I quite forgot! On the table in the center of the room, you see a set of keys. They belong to the gold Cadillac parked on the front lawn. Now would be a good time for each couple to deposit eight thousand dollars on the same table. We will retain ten thousand to kick off next year's Shebang. The winner may take either the money or the car. Enough said? As to you newcomers, let me inform you that, as winners of the Shebang last year, Mavis and I cannot participate."

Maynard lifted a glass and shouted hoarsely, "To our hosts!" He already appeared to be a bit tipsy.

Jasper grinned his silly grin and continued, "The winners this year will serve as hosts for next year. That's the tradition. Is there more?"

Silence.

"Oh, yes," he continued. "Mavis and I will remain here at all times to manage the proceedings. Also, Mr. Eric Berringer of Berringer and Settles Accounting will be present Sunday evening to verify your collections. Once on a table, no item may be removed. I believe that's it. Other than that, there are no rules! You may look at your lists now!"

The Derby Shebang
Objects of Our Attention ~ one point per item ensnared

The Signature of a Governor of Kentucky
dead or alive, you decide

Polaroid Photo of One Well Known
local notables not acceptable

A Speeding Ticket with Current Date
where's a cop when you need one?

Gold from a Church

A Dog, Stolen

Evidence from a Real Crime

Diamonds that Glitter
nothing purchased, not your own

Bloodstains
human, not your own
(no fair pricking other contestants)

Something Removed from Churchill Downs

Please document your activities. Items will be returned with apologies by the Founding Committee of the Derby Shebang.

For several seconds murmuring broke the silence.

One of the Twins shouted, "Does this mean we're supposed to break in and steal stuff?"

"Ethics, Jimmy boy? That's up to you."

"Do we bring the mutts here?" the other Twin asked.

"Only if you intend to win."

Silence.

Producing a tiny cymbal suspended on a gold chain, Jasper held up a tiny mallet. With the most ridiculous expression, he struck, producing a tiny *ting*. "Dinner is at eight," he said.

6:25 p.m. April 23:

Some sauntered to the bar. Most headed for the door. Maynard Bollinger led the charge, slurring the words, "And they're off!"

Rita showed no concern that he raced off without her. She asked for a whiskey sour.

Kitty embraced the game. She took charge as she slid into the Town Car. "Fourth Street, north. Go! Go!"

I said, "Kitty, we need a plan."

"Stop the car!" She whirled around. "What plan?"

"Let's split up and cover more ground."

"We'll need a copy of the list!"

I withdrew our copy from my jacket pocket and tore it in half. "Bingo!"

Karl stared at me through the rearview mirror. "What's next, Boss?"

I handed the bottom half of the list to Kitty. "Karl, take me to the airport.

Drop me off near the car rentals. I'm going to rent something red and racy!"

Karl floored the limo as we raced down I-65. On the way we told him all we knew about the Shebang, as we put our plan together.

I slid out at the terminal and said, "See you at eight!" I told Kitty to go back to our home and take the framed Kentucky Colonel's certificate off the wall in the den. It bore the signature of former Governor John Y. Brown.

She blew me a kiss and we parted.

The closest Budget could come to red and racy was a Mustang convertible. I put the top down and got on the Interstate, hell-bent for trouble.

7:00 p.m. April 23:

I spotted blue lights up ahead as I drove south. I pressed the accelerator and took aim. The officer was strolling back to his unit after ticketing an SUV. I flew by close enough to blow air up his undershorts. Yup, he got me! I apologized profusely, begging for mercy. The ticket came to $121.23.

Climbing over the fence at the County Pound off Manslick Road presented only a small challenge. Escaping with a beagle under my arm about killed me. I gasped for breath as I used my cell phone to tell Kitty I had secured the pooch.

8:10 p.m. April 23:

Arriving back on Third Street, I found Kitty earnestly guarding a *No Admittance* sign from the paddock area at Churchill Downs. She had hidden the Colonel's certificate underneath. Knowing that some guests had puzzled over how to get a governor's signature, she didn't want to tip them off to how she did the deed. We had four items in hand and the lead.

Rita Bollinger stormed about. Maynard had returned empty-handed and smashed. "The old fool is upstairs out cold," she moaned, sipping on a whiskey sour.

I overheard Clark Tannowitz whisper to his brother, "Good riddance of bad company."

Ah, well, a long night remained, and we had two days to go. I figured we could take time to dine, dance, and drink the evening away. Maynard could croak, for all I cared.

8:00 p.m. April 25:

When we gathered on Sunday for our final meal, The Rookery had gone to the dogs. Seven teams had nabbed assorted canines. The dogs seemed to have the run of the house. Baying loudly, my beagle led the pack.

Most of the regular Shebangers had given up the chase, worrying themselves silly because Maynard had escaped and could not be found. Rita was inconsolable. Jasper ran his mouth constantly, offering sympathy. I had no worries about Maynard. The hunt possessed the old boy. I knew he was out seeking victory.

I still did not have diamonds or bloodstains, but the Twins, who now led, celebrated cheap earrings they had shoplifted from Wal-Mart. I balked at stooping that low. I refused to steal from Wal-Mart.

Rachel Malone had teamed up with the Twins, making a threesome. I laughed because they languished over how to secure a governor's signature. Rachel played the game well, though. She spent most of her time at The Rookery embellishing on the tales she spun. She diverted others from the hunt while the Twins kept a frenzied pace. Celebrity hath its rewards.

Kitty showed up late, fretting over how to come up with evidence from a crime.

I had never experienced coconut-flavored rum, and Jasper served up buckets of it, mixed with 7UP. I liked the sweet brew, and soon I just skipped the 7UP.

"The stuff sneaks up on you," Jasper said.

"Yeah, right." My world wobbled with the booze. I couldn't think.

Kitty left during the meal. Remembering a cop friend of ours, she said she would search for him and beg.

8:50 p.m. April 25:

Refusing to drive in my condition, I found my way to the backyard at The Rookery. I needed the night air to clear my head.

Jasper's backyard sported a swimming pool and excellent landscaping. A large pile of landscaping stones occupied one side. It appeared that the Crowes were planning a new water garden. I wandered over for a closer look. Earthen terraces led my eye up to a wall of mortared Kentucky stone. A heavy plastic membrane covered a dug-out area beneath in preparation for filling with water. An impressive looking waterfall would soon grace the premises.

I studied some footprints around the area. To one side a shovel had been thrust into a mound of earth. Around the mound and on the plastic I saw more footprints—footprints from smooth-soled shoes. Now that seemed odd. I stepped into the area to nose around. I slipped the toe of my shoe underneath the plastic and lifted.

Then, behind me, I heard the voice—a very familiar voice. "I believe poor Maynard is under there."

I jerked upright, eyes wide. I once knew a man who took a whack on the head and lost a couple of days, but I remember everything. I heard the swoosh and the whang as metal hit my head. I remember the sound of my skull crack-ing. I felt myself floating forward in slow motion. I remember crashing face-first into the dirt. Then the lights went out.

Nine something or the other, April 25:

My world roared as I awoke. The surface beneath me rumbled. What could this be? I squeezed my eyes tight to clear my head. Surprised, I realized that I lay in the bottom of a boat! I found myself bound hand and foot. I twisted to gain comfort. My shoulders and wrists throbbed with pain.

The roar of the motor lessened, and the boat slowed. As my head cleared I could see that I lay between the twin consoles of a bow rider. I looked up and stared ahead, into the dark. The motor was still now, and the boat drifted on the smooth water.

"I'm so sorry to involve you. I didn't intend for things to come to this."

Jasper!

"Stay still, please!"

"The hell, you say!"

Jasper handled the controls while pointing a small, pearl-handled revolver at me.

"Jasper, what's going on?"

"Do we have to go into that?"

"Well . . . yes!"

"I'm going to throw you into the Ohio River and let you drown."

"What about Bollinger? What happened to him?"

"A necessity, Davis. No matter to you."

"I'm not going to drown in this stupid river without knowing why! Now talk!"

"I really need to get back to the Shebang. It's almost over, you know."

I knew the man had to be nuts. "Jasper, why did you kill Bollinger?"

"Pity, that. I rather liked Maynard." He took a long breath. "No one knows this, not even Maynard."

"Knows what? Make some sense!"

Jasper shifted the gun nervously in his hand. "The family money is in a trust. There is a clause that requires me to earn my own fortune by age fifty-five. Since I have no heirs and I'm the last of the line, all the principal will now go to charity."

"Fifty-five?" I said.

"Yes, next week, actually."

"So . . . what's the big deal?"

"Rita and I have been taking money out of our business. We sell art and antiques, you know, but business ain't what it used to be. We've been skimming to have a nest egg when the trust expires."

"How's Rita figure into this? She's Bollinger's wife."

"Sweet Rita and I have been lovers since our adolescence. We've bought a house on a small island in a small part of the world where a couple of million can set one up very nicely."

"So what happened? Your plan blew up? What about Mavis?"

"Mavis knows nothing. She's quite unattractive, you know."

"Maynard found out, right?"

"Exactly! He planned to go to the police after the Shebang. *Embezzlement* is such an unpleasant word, don't you think?"

Now I had the picture. I struggled to my feet, ignoring his gun. The time had come to get shot or get drowned.

"Turn around," he ordered.

I didn't move. "Jasper, you know you won't get away with this."

"Oh, I think I will. By daylight Rita and I will be safely away. I did in poor Maynard and used the Shebang as cover. Rita is putting on a big act. She is such a whiz at that sort of thing. I fear they'll never find poor Maynard's body. Monday they fill the pond."

"What about me? I'll wash up somewhere."

"Oh, I don't care if they find you. You're just a drunk on a scavenger hunt. By the time they find you, I'll be long gone. Turn around now."

If I had to go, this fool would go with me. I rocked the boat from side to side.

"Stop that!" he screeched.

I bounded forward. I rammed my shoulder into skinny ribs, and the air went out of him. The gun went off. I felt no pain. *He missed me! Wait, maybe I never knew what hit me. I'm dead! I feel nothing! I'm dead.* Then we plunged into the cold water of the Ohio River.

Jasper thrashed wildly beneath me. I felt him climbing up my body. He planted a foot in my gut and shoved himself toward the surface. Now I found myself alone, sinking into the deep. I struggled, not knowing up from down. My shoulder plowed into muck. I twisted about, bouncing my fanny against the bottom. Slowly I rose. I saw little bursts of light, as consciousness slipped away. Then my head broke the surface. I took one huge gulp and slowly sank toward the bottom again. Flailing my bound legs, I tried to swim like a porpoise. For a while, I felt hope rising, but exhaustion prevailed. I took a deep breath, letting myself sink. I had hit bottom once. Maybe I could again. The Ohio runs wide, but not always deep. Aah! I felt a pebbled surface beneath my bare feet and pushed upwards. I kept this up. Again exhaustion took over.

I took a deep breath and relaxed. I floated for a moment. Then I let myself sink again. Not much strength left. I wondered about Kitty. Then I felt muck beneath my feet. *Not as deep!* I shoved again and then fell flat on my face into the debris along the shore. The river had not killed me, but I was lost. No one else on the earth knew my whereabouts.

I lay still for a moment. The chill from the water racked my bones. My lethargy came as much from hypothermia as from booze and a whack on the head. I had to get out of that water quick! To my right I heard a powerboat start up. *That has to be Jasper. Dear God, help me! The man has gotten back to the boat and will find me!* The motor noise faded into the distance. *The bastard thinks he's killed me. I've been left for dead!*

Late, dark, and wet, April 25:

I butt-walked through the debris and muck, muttering obscenities, till I arrived at a massive, old tree trunk. Good! Snags protruding from the trunk gave me solid tools to attack my ropes. I gouged away, tearing both hands and sleeves. At last I could rip the ropes from my wrists and feet. Free—now what?

I waded back into the river and peered through darkness. Cold, weak, and lost, Davis Winthorpe needed help.

Then I saw the light. Literally, I saw the light. A towboat rumbled out of the night, pushing barges downstream. The searchlight swept by me.

I shouted with desperation and tears. "Hey! Please, over here!" I knew I could not be heard.

The light slowly swept back, stopping full on me. I waved my arms, shouting like a fool.

Words came, sounding like a blast from heaven, "Ahoy the shore. You got trouble?"

I made great sweeping motions. *Come get me. Come get me.*

The huge rig slowed to a stop. The night grew still.

Then I heard the sound of a small engine. *A boat! They've put a boat over the side!*

10:46 p.m. April 25:

"Damn, that was weird," the captain, said. "I saw this big white post on the shore. Didn't remember seeing that before. I thought I saw it move! So I brought the light back real slow and there stands this dude in a tuxedo. Now that's funny."

"Thank God for this white jacket!" I said as the crew tossed a blanket around my shoulders. I passed up the offered shot of Jim Beam for hot coffee!

"What happened?" the captain asked.

"Two drunk fools out in a boat. I doubt my buddy even knows I fell out."

"The devil, you say!"

I didn't want to tell about Maynard's body or the attempt on my life. I wanted to get ashore and get back to The Rookery before some other damn fool event took place. I said, "Could you put me ashore somewhere along the River Park at Louisville? I'm okay. I just want to get home and get dry."

"Tell you what, when we go through the McAlpin Locks, you can get off and call the authorities from there."

That would do it, but I didn't want to call the cops. I borrowed a cell phone from the captain and called my driver. "Karl, I need you! Where are you?"

"Parked, Boss, across from the Crowe place. Mrs. Winthorpe is right upset with you. You haven't checked in for a while."

"Come get me. Don't tell Kitty!"

11:38 p.m. April 25:

Karl let me out in the alley. I stumbled over a shovel as I crossed the yard. That had to be what Jasper beaned me with. I entered through the back door and took the servants stairs. All I had on my mind when I stepped into our room was the clean clothes in my suitcase.

Jasper stood fresh and dry near the middle of the room. He said, "I rather feared you would show up here."

Kitty sat on a little chair across the bed from the loon.

"Jasper, have you told Kitty your story?"

"Oh, certainly, no. I've been consoling your dear wife. She's simply beside herself. All the while I've been so hoping that you had died."

Kitty's jaw dropped.

Jasper pulled a small automatic from his jacket pocket.

I took a step toward him.

"That's enough," he said. "We've done that once already. Fool me once, shame on you. Fool me twice, shame on me, aha."

I moved toward the fireplace, where gas logs burned warmly, and pretended to warm my hands.

"Careful!" he shouted, turning to keep the gun on me.

There's much about Kitty that I could tell you. I simply don't have time or space. Let me sum it up with these words: *Never turn your back on a Servideo.*

She emitted a piercing shout and bounded across the bed. Using the bed as a springboard, she launched herself at Jasper. He crashed into the mantel over the fireplace, whacking his forehead. He flopped onto the floor, blood oozing from a welt across his brow.

"Maybe you could explain this," Kitty said.

"Crazy fool killed Maynard Bollinger—tried to kill me too. Maynard is buried out back. Rita is in on it!"

"Holy mother!"

"Get the gun. We're going downstairs. When we get in the grand hall, hold the gun on Rita. Don't even let her squirm!"

"Davis, wait!"

"Hell, no!"

I yanked the addled Jasper to his feet. I dragged him forward by his lapel and kicked the bedroom door open.

11:51 p.m. April 25:

The band sawed to a ragged stop as I pulled Jasper into the grand hall. Judging from the size of the crowd, all were present. A collective gasp filled the room. Then came silence.

"Kitty," I shouted. "Do we have all our items for the Shebang."

"N-n-no," she stuttered.

"What's missing?"

"Well, diamonds that glitter. And, uh, bloodstains."

I wrenched the Kentucky cluster from Jasper's pinky—about a dozen glittering stones. I slammed the ring down on our table. I took him by the ears and dragged his forehead across the remains of my Palm Beach jacket. "And there's your bloodstains! What else, Kitty?" I said, still shouting.

"I got worried about you. I forgot to get evidence of a crime."

I let Jasper slump onto the table. "Jasper killed Maynard Bollinger and buried him under the water garden out back. There's your evidence. Now . . . do we win?"

Eric Berringer of Berringer and Settles Accounting said, "I'm sorry, Mr. Winthorpe. Mr. Mason and Mr. McDowell presented a complete collection about eight minutes ago."

Those blasted twins!

And that's the whole Shebang. . . .

The Thoroughbred Horse

by Din Obrecht Dulworth

Ninety percent of all racehorse pedigrees can trace their lineage back to the Darley Arabian imported to England from Aleppo in 1704. He, the Byerly Turk, and the Godolphin Arabian are the three foundation sires of the Thoroughbred horse.

English colonists in Virginia brought the first Thoroughbreds to America. Bulle Rock, a son of the Darley Arabian, was the first of these. But it was the great and legendary Eclipse, foaled in 1764, who solidified the Darley Arabian's place as the most significant of the three foundation sires.

Diomed, a good race horse in England but unsuccessful at stud, was exported to Virginia at the age of 20. Something about Virginia's climate, or perhaps its mares, must have suited old Diomed, because he founded a "potent dynasty." His most successful progeny was Sir Archy (foaled 1805), whose line led to the great Lexington. Diomed was so well loved by Virginians that his death, at 31, was treated as a national tragedy.

By 1840, Kentucky had superceded Virginia as the leading state for the breeding of Thoroughbred horses.

Though much credit is rightly given to sires of famous horses, one must not forget the contributions of well-bred mares. The pedigrees of eleven Kentucky Derby winners can be traced to one of two mares given to Henry Clay in 1845 as political gifts: Magnolia and Margaret Wood. Three of those Derby winners are Regret, Middle Ground, and Sunny's Halo. Magnolia also produced the great Kentucky, at one time considered the best race horse ever foaled in the state.

Man O'War, who led the American sires list in 1926, was a successful broodmare sire as well. His daughters were much inclined to throw classic winners, also.

Arrivederci, Abigail

by Din Obrecht Dulworth

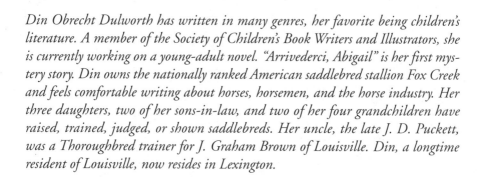

Din Obrecht Dulworth has written in many genres, her favorite being children's literature. A member of the Society of Children's Book Writers and Illustrators, she is currently working on a young-adult novel. "Arrivederci, Abigail" is her first mystery story. Din owns the nationally ranked American saddlebred stallion Fox Creek and feels comfortable writing about horses, horsemen, and the horse industry. Her three daughters, two of her sons-in-law, and two of her four grandchildren have raised, trained, judged, or shown saddlebreds. Her uncle, the late J. D. Puckett, was a Thoroughbred trainer for J. Graham Brown of Louisville. Din, a longtime resident of Louisville, now resides in Lexington.

Abigail Barclay stood on the porch of her three-story antebellum home. From that hilltop in Nelson County, Kentucky, she could observe the activity around the main barn two pastures away. The Barclays' signature gray and green horse van was being loaded with the Thoroughbreds headed for Churchill Downs: a filly for the Kentucky Oaks and a colt entered in the Derby. Their Derby hopeful, Lancelot, had proved to be a worthy contender, capable of winning "the most exciting two minutes in sports."

A cool breeze, wafting across the creek and up the long drive to the house, caressed Abigail's shoulder-length graying brown hair as she waited for the van to pass the wrought-iron gates at the bottom of the drive. *A good day to ship the horses*, she thought. *They'll be comfortable during the ride to Louisville.*

She had told her husband, Lance, that she would join him in Louisville the following day, though she knew she wouldn't. They were to have stayed with Dolly Tolliver again. Dolly would be giving her usual round of parties, and they would share the clubhouse box that Sam Tolliver's family had held on to for generations.

Dolly, older than Abigail by ten years, never admitted being over forty-nine. Abigail was forty-six and said so.

A red-tailed hawk flying overhead brought her thoughts back to the lush green 300 acres of pastoral charm before her. Then the van's engine started up, and the behemoth moved from the barn area. She watched it cross the old bridge, turn onto the farm's main road, and slow down as it approached the entrance gates.

Lance had insisted on going in the van with the driver this time, saying it would "be like old times." He waved to Abigail from the passenger side of the van's cab. She forced a smile and waved, remembering those early years when she and Lance had shared the cab of a secondhand pickup truck, hauling the only horse they owned in a rusting two-horse trailer.

Suddenly she spotted the farm's dark blue Chevrolet coupe following the van. She wondered why they were taking that car until she recognized the blonde-haired driver behind the steering wheel. *So that's how it's going to be,* she thought, angrily stomping her foot and hurrying back inside the house.

She was about to enter the library when her maid, Flora, called down to her from upstairs. "Mrs. Barclay, shall I pack your navy St. John knit or the Valentino silk?"

"Pack everything."

"*Everything,* ma'am?"

"Yes, Flora. Everything."

Abigail entered the library, closed the door, and walked briskly to the desk she and Lance had purchased in New York to celebrate a major win at Saratoga. Their house held several museum-quality pieces, but this 18th-century Boulle desk was her favorite. It constantly reminded her how far she and Lance had come in their twenty-six years of life together. She traced the desk's bronze ormolu mounts with her fingertips. Then she closed her eyes to recall the feel of the chrome-edged kitchen table she had used as a desk on old Mr. Hopkins's Sand Dollar Farm.

Lance, who at that time had been assistant trainer for Hiram Hopkins in Florida, grew up around horses and possessed the skill and necessary patience to bring a talented colt along. When he produced two stakes winners for Hopkins, the man showed his gratitude by making Lance the manager/trainer of Sand Dollar's Thoroughbred operation.

Abigail and Lance spent fifteen years working for him, and at his death, Hopkins—a bachelor and prudent businessman—surprised them both by leaving them his finest young stallion, his best broodmares, and enough money to begin an equine venture of their own.

Now, ten years later, the Barclays' Mist O'Morn Farm in Kentucky stood as a culmination of that dream. They had acquired the property at public auction and spent three years restoring the main house to its former opulence.

Abigail took a deep breath, opened the desk, and withdrew a key from a hidden compartment. The key felt cold in the palm of her hand as she rose and walked to the gun cabinet standing in a corner of the room. She unlocked its beveled-glass door, removed a shotgun, and expertly loaded the weapon with a double-0 buck shell. She racked the shotgun, lodging the shell in its chamber, before stuffing a shopping list and some cash into her pocket. Then she walked out the side door and behind the house to the garage that contained Lance's fleet of vintage automobiles. He made sure his favorite, the 1939 Lincoln convertible, stayed in pristine condition.

Abigail covered the shotgun with her jacket and slid behind the steering wheel of the antique. She started the car, put it in reverse, and backed out. She shifted again, drove forward down the hill, and turned left onto the paved road that led to the main barn.

Everyone at the barn was gone except Austin. "Good morning, Mrs. Barclay," he said. "You look nice in that convertible. It drives like a dream, doesn't it. You taking it to Louisville?"

"No. You here by yourself?"

"Yes, ma'am. Just me and those horses that aren't going. But they've all been fed and watered."

"Good. Then do me a favor? I need some things from town. Here's the list and some money. And . . . uh . . . here's a little something for you, too."

Austin's eyes widened as he reached for the crisp bills. "Why, *thank* you, ma'am."

"Take your time in town, Austin. I'm in no hurry."

He tipped his cap and climbed into his pickup truck. Turning the key in the ignition, he leaned out of the cab and said, "Don't you worry none about the farm, ma'am. Have a good time in Louisville. Things will be fine here. I've seen to it. I've taken care of everything."

"I'm sure you have," she replied. "You always do."

Abigail had a soft spot in her heart for Austin. Roughly her age, he had appeared at the farm, seeking a job, about the time she and Lance had acquired it. They hired him on the spot, and he proved himself to be a great jack-of-all-trades. They were particularly impressed with his knowledge of automobiles. He was almost a mechanical genius, keeping Lance's vintage fleet and the farm vehicles in superb running condition.

When Austin and the truck were gone, Abigail parked the convertible behind the barn, grabbed the shotgun, and headed for the mobile home about fifty yards away. She had made the same trek the night before, but then she had been armed with an ultimatum, not a shotgun. Now as she approached Mandy Morgan's trailer, the events of the night before came back to her.

"Why, Mrs. Barclay," Mandy had said, opening the door, "what on earth are you doing over here at this hour of night? Why, it must be—"

"Eleven o'clock," Abigail interjected. "May I come in?"

"Why, of course," replied the girl, pushing long strands of straight blonde hair behind her ears and stepping out of the way. "But please excuse the place. It's such a mess. Here. I'll just move these things out of the chair and you can sit down."

"Don't bother, Mandy. I prefer to stand."

Mandy seemed perplexed. "Well, then, what can I do for you, ma'am?"

"I want you packed and off the farm by noon tomorrow."

"Wh-what did you say?"

"You heard what I said, Mandy. I want you off this farm. And as soon as possible." Abigail produced a check from her coat pocket. "This should more than cover your wages for the rest of the season."

The girl stared with disbelief at the check being extended to her. "Mrs. Barclay," she said, "I don't understand. We're getting the horses ready for Louisville. We're leaving for Churchill Downs tomorrow morning. What have I done wrong?"

Abigail paused before answering. "Let's just say that your services at the barn are no longer needed," she said, her eyes fixed on Mandy's. "I think you've mucked out stall nine long enough."

The girl paled. Her blue eyes flashed and then narrowed before she said, "Does Lance know you're here?"

Lance! She had called him *Lance*. Abigail's face grew red with anger. "No," she said, "*Mr.* Barclay does not know I am here. But, young lady, I own as much of this farm as he does. I can hire and I can fire. And I want you gone."

Mandy stood with fists clenched and stared contemptuously at Abigail.

There was an arrogance about the girl that Abigail found disconcerting, but she kept her composure. Placing the check on the kitchen table, she said, "You have your things packed and yourself away from here by noon tomorrow, understand?"

Now it *was* the next morning, and as Abigail stood at Mandy's door again, she could hear what sounded like a television set playing somewhere inside the trailer. When her knock went unanswered, she tried the door. It was unlocked, so she let herself in. An old black-and-white TV, sitting atop the counter, was on, its picture rolling upward. *How typical of Mandy to leave it on and unattended*, she thought, *but then she doesn't have to pay the bills.*

Abigail had hoped to find the trailer cleared of the girl's possessions. It had not been. She put the shotgun down. "Looks like I'll have to pack *for* you, Mandy dear," she said aloud as she threw clothes from the closet, towels from the bathroom, and pictures from the wall onto Mandy's bed. "I gaveth and I can taketh away," she said as she wrapped sheets over the things and carried them all out to the Dumpster. She could just imagine the joyous expressions on the garbagemen's faces when they unloaded the trash on Monday.

She returned to the trailer, picked up the shotgun, and sat down on the chair she had refused to sit on the night before. She leaned over to adjust the picture on the television set. "Star Trek" was on, and Captain Kirk was about to be beamed up to the *Enterprise*. Abigail rose from the chair, backed a few feet, and buried the stock of the shotgun in her shoulder. She released the safety and aimed the weapon at the television. She liked Captain Kirk, so she waited for the commercial before pulling the trigger and beaming up the set.

The result surprised, shocked, and then amused Abigail. She sank, slack-jawed, onto the floor as the glass screen shattered and miniature fireworks erupted in the set's interior. She put her hand to her mouth as the set sputtered. The noise finally subsided as a puff of gray smoke belched from its eviscerated depths. Oh, how she wished Mandy had been in her sights. But the girl wasn't anywhere near the trailer. She was, as Abigail well knew, in the farm's blue Chevrolet coupe, following the van, and Lance Barclay, to Louisville.

When the smoke cleared, Abigail discovered that she had inadvertently blown a large hole in the trailer as well. She took solace, however, in knowing that she had rid Mandy's mobile home of most everything she had given her. The blown-out TV would be left as a visual reminder of a shattered friendship and a broken trust. But she wasn't finished. Not by a long shot.

She retrieved the shotgun from the floor, left the trailer, and walked back to the main barn. Entering it meant reliving the moment when she'd discovered Lance and Mandy in stall nine just the day before. Not as farm owner and employee, but as a fifty-two-year-old man and an eighteen-year-old girl engaged in more horseplay than horse business.

They had not expected her visit to the barn, nor had they been aware of her presence as she looked down at them through the upper stall bars. She had backed away on the aisle's soft sawdust and stumbled to her car in shock. She had rushed home to her private study and had wept uncontrollably.

Abigail had no children to take her mind off her grief. She and Lance had consciously planned a life together where she would always be free to travel with him from one racetrack to another. To their peers in the horse industry, they were a well-suited, much admired, inseparable couple.

Their private life had been as compatible as their public one. Their sex life had been great, but not for the past two years. Indeed, it had become almost nonexistent in the past few months, with Lance too tired for it, turning over, turning away. Why, she wondered, had she not recognized the danger signals?

Now, as she forced herself to look inside that hated stall, she recalled how she and Lance had worked side by side—and, yes, played—in such stalls as this. She remembered the nights they had spent in such enclosures with mares about to foal and how they grieved when a mare died giving birth or a foal was stillborn. She thought of the good times, too, recalling the joys they had shared with the young colts that showed promise, those that went on to win major races across the country.

Now, with years of hard work behind them, and Mist O'Morn Farm a success, along had come one Mandy Morgan, a wistful little waif, on a rainy day looking for a job. And it had been Abigail herself who had cajoled Lance into hiring her as a groom. She shook her head in despair. For, in time, Mandy had become like the daughter she never had, and Abigail had taken a maternal interest in her.

She wiped her eyes and strode to the tack room, where she removed the saddle she had special ordered for Mandy. She carried it to the lounge and draped it over the divan. Then she went behind the bar and mixed herself a drink. She settled in a recliner, took a sip from the glass, and telephoned her friend Dolly Tolliver.

When Dolly answered, Abigail sobbed and said, "I'm not coming to Louisville." When asked why not, Abigail spent an hour telling her.

Finally Dolly got a word in. "You through?" she asked.

Abigail nodded her head as though her friend could see through the phone.

"Well," said Dolly, "Welcome to the club. Sam did the same thing to me."

Abigail was stunned. She reached for a tissue to blow her nose. "Sam? *Your* Sam? When?"

"Not long before he died. I wouldn't have known about it had Hortense Pendergast not told me."

"Hortense *told* you? Oh, how awful of her."

"Well, Hortense didn't intend for me to know who she was. She'd disguised her voice, saying she was a 'well meaning friend' who thought I should know that my Sam was 'having a to-do' with a young girl in his office." Dolly laughed. "Abby," she said, "Hortense is the only one in our crowd who has ever referred to an affair as a to-do. So I knew it was her."

Abigail blinked in disbelief. "What did you do about it?"

"I got even."

Abigail swallowed hard. "How?" she asked, her voice barely above a whisper, her eyes round as quarters.

"*I* had a to-do . . . with Hortense's husband."

Abigail nearly dropped the phone. "Dolly! How *could* you? Atwater Pendergast has to be the ugliest man in Louisville."

Dolly sighed. "Darling, I wasn't interested in his face. I only wanted to get even."

Abigail found herself sitting on the edge of her chair. "Well, how did going to bed with Atwater get even with Sam?"

"It didn't," Dolly said matter-of-factly. "I wasn't half as mad at Sam as I was at Hortense. I got even with her for knowing about it and telling me. I would rather not have known."

Abigail shook her head. "Well, was your to-do really worth it?"

Dolly laughed heartily. "Atwater thought so. You know that gold horse-head bracelet you like so much?"

"You mean that gorgeous thing with the emerald eyes, sapphire nostrils, and diamond-studded mane?"

"That's the one," said Dolly.

Abigail scooted back in her chair. "I'm impressed. But I just can't . . . well . . . Lance has been the only man in my life, and. . . ."

"Sam was the only one in *mine* before Atwater," said Dolly. "I loved my Sam. Always will. But as you have found out, something happens to men when they get past middle age. Sam was fifty-nine when he had that affair. How old is Lance?"

"Fifty-two. Six years older than I am."

"Oh!" wailed Dolly. "When *are* you going to stop telling your age? Now, you listen to me. Lance has probably reached that stage in his life where he's afraid of 'losing it.' His infatuation with Mandy will probably pass. Then he'll be himself again."

"But I'm not sure *I* will be," replied Abigail. "Was Sam?"

Dolly hesitated a moment. "He tried to be. But then he died two months after he broke off the affair."

"I am so sorry."

"Well, I go on. You will, too."

"Dolly, I'm glad I called you. I do feel better. But when I think of Lance and Mandy in that stall, my blood boils." She reached for the shotgun. "If they were here now, I'd shoot them both."

"For heaven's sake, don't even *think* of doing such a thing," said Dolly. "*You'd* end up in jail. Besides, I cannot imagine you in one of those horrible orange jumpsuits. Orange is not your color, dear."

"What, then, should I do?"

"If you really want Lance back, talk it all out with him. But if he won't give up Miss Mandy, or listen to reason, then remember this: Half that farm and everything on it is yours. You helped make it the success it is. You really don't need Lance," she said. "You could run the farm without him. If what you tell me about that Austin person is true, you two could run the farm efficiently together. And with the reputation Mist O'Morn Farm has, you could always find a good trainer to take Lance's place. But right now, you and Lance have a horse that everyone believes will win the Derby. Lancelot is the favorite. And you have earned the right to stand with your husband in the winner's circle next to that marvelous animal you *both* worked so hard to raise and train. Lance Barclay may not deserve you, my dear, but *you* deserve that moment."

Abigail sighed. "Oh, I guess I do, but—"

"You *guess*? Where's your gumption? When these kinds of things happened to our mothers, they shut their mouths and swallowed their pride. But today, we women don't have to put up with that stuff. You and I have a life to live, Abby, and we should live it."

"I wish I had your confidence, Dolly. What makes you so sure of yourself?"

"Abby, two months ago, bored, I flew to Chicago and joined a group destined to tour European art museums. I didn't know a soul in that group. But it didn't matter. Something wonderful happened to me in Italy, and I came home rejuvenated."

"What happened?"

"Well, we were in Rome, and our group was getting a private tour of the Museo e Galleria Borghese. I was standing by the statue of Apollo and Daphne, feeling as mired down as she was. Looking at Daphne got me so depressed that I left my group in the museum and walked outside. There was music coming from the nearby gardens. That's when I saw him."

"Who?"

"A modern-day version of Michelangelo's David, only clothed and breathing. He was as beautiful a young man in body and spirit as I have ever seen. I was drawn to that boy's smile like a bee to a blossom, and I was not the only one. He attracted quite a crowd."

"Who was he?" Abigail asked. "An Italian movie star? A count? A gigolo?"

"No. An organ-grinder."

Abigail tried to stifle a giggle. "An organ-grinder?"

"Oh, I know it sounds ridiculous that a young man making music with a monkey on his shoulder and a cup in his hand could have such an effect on me," Dolly said, "but the sheer joy he exuded in pleasing all those people was wonderful to behold. Then that gorgeous boy locked his eyes onto mine, and I could not look away. I found myself moving toward him, my eyes dropping to his right hand as he ground that handle round and round."

Abigail gulped. "Then what?"

"Well, to make a long story short, my tour group didn't see me for four days. The organ-grinder, the monkey, and I took a tour of our own. Filippo—that was his name—was a university student studying Greek history. An organ-grinder only on weekends, it seems. Anyway, he wanted me to see the village he came from and meet his relatives. They were so proud of him and fascinated with the rich Kentucky woman who had taken such a liking to him. The villagers feted us with food and wine. The village priest blessed us when we left. Abby, I found my fountain of youth in Filippo and came home a changed woman."

Abigail sank back in her chair. "You planning another trip soon?"

"I'm going to Spain next. Wonder what adventure awaits me there?"

"Tell me when you get back. Then you ought to write a book."

Dolly laughed. "If I did, I can just imagine Atwater Pendergast trying to explain that bracelet for an afternoon to-do to his prune-faced Hortense, can't you?"

Abigail laughed, said good-bye, and got up from the recliner. She walked to the bar and raised her glass to the mirror behind it. "Here's to us, Dolly," she said. "Write the book and put me and this day in it."

She poured the rest of her drink into the sink, draped Mandy's saddle over her arm, and walked outside to the convertible. She placed the shotgun on the floor and the saddle over the back of the passenger seat, then drove toward the sinkhole at the other end of the farm.

Halfway there, she spotted a young man standing by the old bridge at the creek edge. He waved for her to stop. As she did, she noted the company name embroidered on his jacket and the heavy machinery behind him.

"What are you doing here on Sunday?" she demanded. "You people weren't supposed to start working on this bridge until tomorrow."

"Those may have been the original orders, lady, but my boss said Mr. Barclay wanted it done today."

"He wants it done today, does he?" said Abigail as she watched the fat drum turning atop the huge yellow truck behind him.

"Yes, ma'am. But I've got a problem. I was supposed to call my boss when I got here, but my two-way radio isn't working. Is there a phone close by that I could use?"

"Why, yes," said Abigail. "In the main barn. In the lounge. It's not far from here. Just over that rise," she said, pointing.

"Thanks," he said and sprinted down the road.

My, but he has a nice physique, thought Abigail, watching the young man through her rear-view mirror. Then she studied the equipment sitting by the bridge and flushed with a rush of inspiration. She spun the car around and parked it next to the huge yellow truck. She left the window partially down on her side of the car and raised the window on the passenger side. She closed and locked the convertible's cloth top before grabbing her jacket and getting out.

She raised her limber self easily into the cab of the monstrous ready-mixed concrete truck. Earlier that week, she had watched the men pour the bridge at the end of the drive leading up to the main house. Curious, she had asked the workmen how they operated the chute and the flow of the wet concrete. Thus it was a confident Abigail who sat on the driver's seat and grasped the joystick with her right hand, guiding the chute first forward, then to the side, then down, until its open end was jutting inside the convertible's window.

She pressed the pedal on the floor to release the flow of the wet concrete and watched, with fascination, as the thick gray substance oozed its way into the car's interior. The lava-like movement reminded her of The Blob, in the horror movie, as the concrete crawled into crevices, sheathed the shotgun, settled on the leather seats, rose above the dashboard, straddled the saddle, and eventually bulged the thick canvas top.

Abigail brought the pedal to its middle position to stop the flow. She jumped from the cab, clapping her hands, as the convertible settled on tires flattened from the weight of their grossly obese and solidifying passenger. Then she wrote, "Guess who?" in the concrete that pooled by the car.

She took a less-traveled path back to her house to avoid meeting the young man when he returned to his truck. Her trek seemed of little interest to the cattle on one side of the road and the broodmares on the other. One old mare, however, saw her coming and ambled over to the fence to await her. That mare expected, and usually got, a treat when Abigail came near. Abigail wouldn't disappoint her this day. She reached into her skirt pocket, brought out some mints, placed them in the palm of her hand, and offered them to the matron mare, now twenty-six years old and barren. Abigail hugged the mare's neck and kissed her muzzle.

The stallions usually got credit for the great progenies they sired. But Abigail knew that this was the mare who had often made the winning difference on their farm. It was she who had given many of her winning offspring so much heart, stamina, and drive. For that she had been awarded retirement on the farm.

Abigail patted the mare's flank and said, "We have a lot in common, old girl. Seems we've both been put out to pasture."

As she approached her house, Abigail saw Austin's truck in the circular driveway. She stepped onto the porch just as he emerged from the front door.

"Oh, there you are," he said, removing his cap. "Been looking for you. I just came by to tell you about the accident."

"Accident? What accident?" She felt suddenly unsteady on her feet.

Austin reached out to take her hand. "There was a bad accident on the way to Louisville, ma'am."

Abigail clutched her chest, and tears began filling her eyes. "Oh, no! Austin, has anything happened to Lance? Is . . . is he okay? Are the horses hurt?" She grabbed his arm. "Tell me . . . please!"

"Lance is fine," he said, placing a comforting hand on her shoulder. "And nothing happened to the van or the horses. It was the blue Chevy coupe. Seems the Morgan girl lost control of it. The car swerved off the highway, plunged over an embankment, and burst into flames. She's dead, ma'am."

Abigail sank down on one of the steps and put her head in her hands. She wanted Mandy out of the picture but was horrified at what had happened to her. She looked up at Austin, who seemed so calm about it all. "I don't understand," she said.

"No one can," he replied, leaning over. "Witnesses said the car just sped up all of a sudden. She apparently tried to stop it, couldn't, and lost control. But frankly, ma'am, I can't say I'm sorry it happened."

Abigail was shocked. "Wh-what did you say, Austin?"

He rose and put his cap back on. "I said, ma'am, that I'm not sorry it happened. That young lady was a troublemaker. Maybe, with her gone, things will get back to the way they were before she came here."

He helped Abigail to her feet and walked back to his truck. He was about to enter the cab when Abigail wiped her eyes and said, "Austin, didn't you tell me you had checked out all the cars a few days ago?"

He turned around. "Yes, ma'am." His steely gray eyes looked steadily at her. "In fact, I double checked that Chevrolet this morning before Miss Mandy drove off in it. It was in perfect shape for her trip to Louisville, ma'am." Then he raised himself into the cab of his truck and drove off.

Abigail mounted the porch steps, stunned by what she had heard and what she was thinking. When she entered the foyer of her home, she looked up to see her maid rushing out of the upstairs master bedroom. Flora's apron was down around her hips and her cap was askew as she leaned over the banister, her face a portrait of consternation.

"Mrs. Barclay," she said, "you haven't luggage enough for all the clothes you're taking to Louisville. If I didn't know better, I'd swear you were going to Europe . . . to Italy, or someplace like that."

"Why, Flora," said Abigail, smiling broadly as she ascended the stairs, suddenly aware of her opportunities, "I may do that very thing. But first I have to go to Louisville. We're going to win the Kentucky Derby, Flora. Which outfit do you think I should wear in the winner's circle?"

"I like the Valentino," said Flora, laughing.

"So do I," said Abigail. "It's so . . . so Italian."

Bloodlines

by Teesue Herring Fields

Like most sporting events, horse races are divided into classes to separate the very best athletes—the horses—from those of lesser ability. The Kentucky Derby is a Grade I stakes race, the highest level of competition and comparable to Division I of the NCAA.

The majority of horses in Grade I stakes have very good bloodlines, meaning that their parents were winners or related to winners of stakes races. Bloodlines are considered so important that the names of each horse's mother, father, and grandfather are printed in the program. When a horse with good bloodlines starts racing, he or she usually starts off at a higher class race. However, horses that consistently fail to win are moved to lower class races. Conversely, a horse that starts low and wins could be moved to a higher level. This is known as moving up or down in class and is something the smart bettor watches closely when analyzing a race.

Why would a winning horse be moved up in class? Well, horse races are no different than other sports. Higher classes carry not only more prestige, but more money for the winner. In 2005 the Kentucky Derby's guaranteed $2,000,000 purse grew to $2,399,600, and the winner, Giacomo, received $1,639,600 for around two minutes of work.

Moving Up in Class

by Teesue Herring Fields

Teesue Herring Fields has lived in the Louisville area for thirty years. She attended her first Derby in 1974—the one hundredth Run for the Roses—and got trampled by the masses in the infield. Since then, she watches the race on TV and attends the Kentucky Oaks on the Friday before Derby, a day often called "Louisville's Day at the Races." When not reading and writing mysteries, she has a day job as a professor of counseling at an area university.

Sara could not believe her good fortune. She was sitting by Matt in his parents' box at Churchill Downs the day before the Kentucky Derby.

"Glad you came?" he asked, squeezing her arm.

"Oh, yes," she said. "It's amazing that you do this every year."

"Some years my parents do need the box both days to entertain their out-of-town clients. But this time their guests aren't arriving until tonight, so they turned it over to me."

"And instead of keeping all this luxury to himself," added David, "he shared it with his friends." David was Matt's best friend and conveniently had asked Grace, Sara's best friend, to be his date.

"Hey, watch the mocking tone, there, Dave," Matt said. "I'll have you know, we pay big money to have these plush accommodations for two days each year. I probably could have sold today's tickets for a couple of thousand if I hadn't decided to invite you guys."

Sara was shocked. "Is that really true?"

Matt shrugged. "Probably. A Derby box on the clubhouse turn, even for Oaks Day, is still worth a lot. You can't just stand in line and buy one. My dad's company has had a box for forty years."

Sara surveyed her surroundings. The "box" was really just six uncushioned, metal folding chairs in a closet-sized rectangle marked off by pipe railing. There were similar boxes of chairs and railings in every direction, most of them filled with men wearing smart-looking suits and women wearing jewel-toned party clothes and glamorous Derby hats. Everyone was drinking mint juleps from the souvenir Derby glasses that listed all the previous winners.

Sara didn't know the final couple in their group, Bitsy and her date, Hal, but Matt had grown up with them. Bitsy fit in perfectly with the highfalutin women around her, right down to her elaborate pocketbook the exact shade of her plum colored dress.

"Next year," she said, "I'm going to be sure my parents let us have their table in the Sky Terrace for the Oaks. Then we won't have to sit out here in the sun and roast."

"Sorry the accommodations aren't up to your usual standards," said Matt. "You didn't have to come."

"Oh, Matt, you know I wanted to be here." Sara could swear Bitsy's Southern drawl had just gotten thicker. "I mean, I hardly ever get to see you since you went away to school."

"Shhh, no mention of school, please," said David. "Exams are over, and I have a few days of grace until grades are posted. The racing form is all I want to study right now."

Sara, too, was relieved that she had a weekend reprieve before grades were posted. She was pretty sure she had kept the B+ average that would allow her to keep her scholarship. If somehow she hadn't, it would be impossible for her to return to the private college she had come to love. Her divorced mother barely scraped together the few hundred dollars Sara needed for books each year. And Sara paid for all her clothes and other personal expenses by working on campus. But only Grace knew how tight Sara's budget really was.

Tightening her fingers around the mint julep glass that Matt had bought her, Sara tried to ignore the barbs Bitsy threw her way. It was clear that Bitsy was more interested in Matt than her own date. When finally Bitsy and Hal left to make some bets, Sara's shoulders relaxed.

"Sorry about Bitsy," said Matt. "She's an old family friend, and she's usually more fun than this. I don't know what burr got under her saddle."

Sara could have told him that she was the burr as far as Bitsy was concerned, but that would serve no real purpose.

"Let's go over to the paddock," said Matt. "We can watch them get the horses ready for the next race."

He took Sara's hand and pulled her through the crowd. They wound their way over the uneven brick floors under the clubhouse stands, past long lines of bettors at the pari-mutuel windows. Suddenly they emerged from the darkness under the stands into a sunlit area that reminded Sara of a brick patio. Surrounded on three sides by buildings, it was crammed with people.

Matt guided them to a place along the iron fence that bordered a grass-and-dirt oval with horse stalls at the back. Pushing Sara in front of him so she could see, he said, "The paddock is where the horses will be saddled before going out on the track. It gives us a chance to see them up close and study them a little."

The area pulsed with horses and men and women who led them in and carried their gear. In the grassy space in the center of the oval, well-dressed men and women stood in small clumps talking to each other.

Sara leaned back into Matt but had to shout because the noisy crowd around them was now standing three deep along the entire railing. "Who are the people in the middle?"

"Those are the owners and trainers of the horses and their guests. This is one of the perks of owning a horse, having a pass to get into the paddock before your horse goes to the track. For the Oaks and Derby, these are usually some of the most important people in the horse business. Most of them have been racing for generations."

Sara examined the people inside the fence. Yes, their clothes looked expensive, and the women were wearing flashy jewelry that probably didn't come from a department store. She looked down at her own clothes, a combination of consignment-shop selections and loans from Grace. How out of place did she look to Matt?

Just then, he slipped his hands around her waist and kept them there while he identified some of the people for her. She rested her head against his shoulder as she listened. She would concentrate on being with Matt and try not to worry about the rest.

He hugged her a little closer and pointed out the jockeys in their colorful silk shirts and caps as they emerged from their dressing room and walked over to their horses. After a few minutes, somebody called, "Riders up," and the trainers helped the jockeys mount their horses. Then the horses made their way to the tunnel that led out to the track, passing right by Sara and Matt. Straining against their reins, the horses high-stepped and shook their heads as they went by.

"It's so beautiful, Matt," said Sara. "Is it always this beautiful?"

He nuzzled her neck, sending shivers in all her corners. "Always. That's why I wanted to share it with you."

The crowd drifted away to follow the horses, and the noise dissipated. Sara could easily hear Matt, but she was glad he didn't let go of her as he spoke. "Those horses have been carefully culled through generations of breeding to be here today," he explained. "It takes a lot of money to buy good horses and breed them. Hundreds of thousands, maybe even millions of dollars are at stake when the owner buys or breeds a horse."

She shuddered. "That's the kind of gamble I could never understand."

"It's not that different from people. That's why smart people marry other smart people, so their children will be smart. That's making a bet, in a way. And in some ways, it's even more high stakes than buying a racehorse. Trying to influence what your kids will be like. Your parents must have been attracted to each other because they liked some of the same books or music. Mine met in law school and are interested in the same things."

"Maybe you're right." Sara decided to change the subject. How could she tell him that her honor-roll-student mother had dropped out of college to marry her truck-driver father because she was pregnant? It was chemistry, not brains, that brought them together. That's why her mom was so determined to give Sara the chance she lost. But was this what her mother had in mind? Did she really belong in Matt's world?

They strolled back toward their box, and this time Matt put his arm around her shoulders as he pointed out track landmarks. By the time they got back, Sara had heard a lot about Derby traditions. It was a dream world, and she was in it. Then she heard a voice that jolted her back to reality.

"Well, where did you two go for so long?" asked Bitsy. "I went to cash my ticket, and when I got back, you two were gone and it looked like you weren't interested in us anymore. This is a Derby group, you know. I thought we were staying together."

"I took Sara to see the paddock," replied Matt. "I thought she'd enjoy seeing the horses saddled."

"And it was so . . . majestic," said Sara. "I got goose bumps."

"I would've enjoyed going, too," said Bitsy. "I wish you'd waited." Her lips turned down in a pout that would have made a two year old proud.

"Oh, Bits, you've been to the Downs lots of times," said Matt. "And the Oaks and the Derby. Don't tell me you've never seen the paddock before."

"Of course I've been to the paddock and the Derby since I was little. But we don't usually come on Friday for the Oaks. We save our energy for the Derby."

"I'll take you over, Bits," said Hal. "We could leave right after this race, or we could go now to be sure we get a really good spot."

Bitsy sat down, but not in the chair next to Hal. "Oh, that's all right. I'd rather stay here for a while and watch the races. That is, if other people are staying."

Since Bitsy wasn't sitting next to Hal, there weren't two seats together for Matt and Sara, but before Matt could say anything, Grace solved the problem. "Hal, I need some betting advice. Why don't you give me the benefit of your wisdom?" She got up and sat by him, which left room for Sara and Matt. Matt put his arm around Sara again, and Bitsy's look was a thundercloud in the otherwise sunny afternoon.

Before the next race, Grace got up and stretched. "Well, thanks to Hal's advice, I think I'm ready to try a bet. And it looks like those mint juleps have finally gotten to me, so I better make a visit to the little girl's room. Anybody else want to go?"

"Sounds good to me," said Sara.

Bitsy smiled, but it looked pasted on, not genuine. "Oh, no thanks. I made my visit when I cashed my ticket. You two go ahead."

Matt squeezed Sara's hand as she left. "Don't get lost."

She squeezed his hand in return and smiled at him as she left with Grace.

As soon as they were out of earshot, Grace said, "See. What did I tell you? He's more than a little interested in you."

"Maybe you're right. I've been afraid to get my hopes up. We've only been dating a few months and that's been pretty casual."

"*Casual* is not the way he looks at you."

"Well, the paddock was nice. It was crowded, so we had to get *very* close to talk to each other."

"Aha, more evidence! And he doesn't care that your family doesn't own a box at the Derby, you twit. And somebody else who *does* own a box is of no interest to him at all."

"But when she looks at me, I feel like a poor relation. Thank goodness Matt doesn't seem to be paying any attention to her."

"And believe me, he won't. She's so obviously making a play for him. And poor Hal. She treats him like dirt."

"I was happy she didn't come with us, so we could talk," said Sara.

"Oh, I knew it was safe to ask her. She wouldn't pass up the chance to be alone with the three guys."

Sara and Grace arrived at the rest room, which they found easily because of the queue stretching into the courtyard. "This line better move fast," said Grace, "or I'm going to wish I was a horse."

The line did move reasonably fast, and soon the two friends were walking back to the box. "That was nice of you to talk to Hal," said Sara. "I'm a little worried about him. I wonder if he always drinks that much or it's just because Bitsy is ignoring him."

"Hard to tell. And I think he's losing a lot of money. I said something to David about it, but he says Hal has the money to lose."

"I guess it's difficult for me to get used to people our age spending this much."

"Well, it is a special occasion. And thanks to Matt, the box is free, so they can spend their money on bets instead. Risking that much isn't my idea of fun, but I guess it's all in what you're used to."

"And I'm not used to it," said Sara. "I *am* having fun, but I still don't think I fit in this crowd."

"Sure you do. You look as good as anyone here. You're smarter than most of this group—your grades prove that. Bitsy is the only one who cares how much money you have, and that's because she's looking for an edge with Matt. But he's not interested in her, no matter how much money her family has."

Sara and Grace arrived at the box to find Bitsy sitting next to Matt and smiling at whatever he was saying. But when he saw Sara, he stopped midsentence and stood up. "Hey, glad you two got back. The next race is about to start."

Everyone stood to cheer for their horses, and there was a lot of shouting as the horses crossed the finish line.

"Did anyone win?" Matt asked.

Hal tore up four tickets. "All losers here. Losers all day long."

"Cheer up," said Matt. "Your luck is bound to change. Sara and I split a show ticket and won."

"You've got to start wagering some serious money," said Hal. "How about some $20 win tickets? I've got a sure thing in the next race."

"Better slow down there, friend," said Matt. "If I bet $20 tickets every race, I'd have to ask Sara for the dough to pay for our dinner. Not a very good impression."

"That's only if you lose," said Hal.

"But you have to be prepared to lose," said David, joining the conversation. "And believe me, my allowance doesn't stretch that far."

"You two are pessimists," said Bitsy. "Why come to the races if you can't afford to lose a few hundred. What's the fun in paltry little bets? 'Bet big, win big,' I always say."

Sara knew the comment was a dig at her, and she wondered if she was keeping Matt from spending the kind of money he usually would at the races. She thought of the twenty dollars she was spending in careful two-dollar increments so that she'd have a bet in every race and could be part of the gang. At the minimum-wage salary she earned from her part-time job, twenty dollars represented a lot of money. And she'd had to spend some on her clothes, even if they were secondhand.

"The point of the races," said Matt, "is to have fun with people you enjoy. You don't have to wager big bucks to do that. Now, if I was here with my stuffy investment club from school, then I'd have to spend more money just to get through the day, but not with the present company."

Sara smiled her gratitude at Matt. She felt like he was telling her he was happy with what they were doing. And he managed to say that without insulting anyone else. Since he was going to be such a good sport, she'd join in. "Well, I'm going to get reckless and try a place bet instead of a show bet," she said. "But I'll need some expert advice."

"Come right into my betting parlor, Miss Gullible," said Matt. "I'll teach you all my trackside secrets." They laughed and he opened up the racing program and started explaining all the numbers and information printed for each horse in the race.

"I see," said Sara, "but I don't understand why they give the name of the horse's mother and father and grandfather. Why is that important?"

"It's the bloodlines," replied Hal. "Good horses come from good bloodlines. If you follow the races closely, you'll know the sires, or fathers, of the horses. Like in the Oaks and Derby, most of the sires will be really good horses who ran in the Derby or other important races. You can't get a champion horse without good bloodlines."

"Yeah," agreed Matt. "A horse without a strong pedigree doesn't stand a chance in an important race."

"That's not always true," said Grace. "I remember my dad talking about some long shots that won the Derby. Wasn't there a South American horse no one had ever even heard of with owners from Argentina or someplace?"

"Yeah," said Hal, "but that was a total fluke. I bet the owners didn't even know how to act in the winner's circle. Somebody probably had to tell them everything to do."

"Okay," said Sara, "so the father is important. Now just tell me which horse in this race has the best father."

With Matt's help, she picked a horse and made a place bet in the next race, but the horse came in last. She got some teasing, but she didn't mind. Nobody else won anything either.

"It's a good thing we're having fun," said Grace. "We certainly aren't making any money today."

"Yes," said Bitsy. "I'm going to have to take out my serious money. I've already run through my fun money."

She manipulated the clasp on her silk triangular purse, unzipped a small compartment, and pulled out a wad of cash. Sara could see denominations of fifties and hundreds, and she gasped.

"Bitsy, you shouldn't flash a roll of dough like that around here," said David. "Anybody could see it and you'd be a target for pickpockets."

"I never go anywhere without a sufficient cash backup. It's something my father always insists on. And not to worry. This purse is its own little vault.

There's a secret to the clasp that would make it impossible for anyone to open quickly."

"Secret or not," said Matt, "you better keep a close eye on it."

"Oh, I intend to, out there in the crowd. But as you said, Matt, here we're among friends and we can just relax." She closed the purse and hung the strap over the back of her chair.

Sara found herself staring at the pocketbook. There must have been close to a thousand dollars in it. But she forgot about the purse when she and Matt got busy discussing the next race. Then they walked around the track some more, and Sara kept her eye out for celebrities but didn't see any.

"I shouldn't have worn these high heels," she told Grace, who sat alone when they returned to the box. "I didn't realize we'd do so much walking."

"But they make your legs look great," whispered Grace. "And that's the most important thing."

"It's not *your* feet that are hurting," said Sara. "But I appreciate the compliment. What's been going on here while we've been gone?"

"Same old stuff. The guys go out for beer or to bet. Sometimes Bitsy goes with them, sometimes not. David and I did some walking around, too, but I haven't seen Bitsy and Hal do anything together. He drinks and bets, and she mostly doesn't talk to him."

"Is anybody winning?"

"Not that I can tell," said Grace as Hal, David, and Bitsy came back.

"Okay, guys," said Hal. "We've got to start getting serious about our Oaks bets."

"I like Misty Maiden," said David. "She's won her last three races."

"Yeah, but that's at cheaper tracks and against lousy competition," said Matt. "And her bloodlines are nothing special. She's coming up too far in class. She doesn't belong in a race like the Oaks."

"I agree," said Hal. "She's just done well in cheap races. The Oaks is out of her league."

"I've got an idea," said Bitsy. "Why don't we all pool our money and bet a lot of combinations in the Oaks. That way we have a chance to win big, and we can treat ourselves to a nice dinner with the winnings."

"Sure," said Sara. "I'll put in two dollars."

Bitsy laughed. "I was thinking of a little more money than that. How about thirty dollars each? That will give us plenty of money for combination bets."

"You've been winning more money than I have, Bits," said David. "I don't have thirty dollars for this race. I haven't cashed a ticket all day."

"Oh, I'll loan you the money," said Bitsy. "I know you're good for it. And you, too, Sara, of course."

Sara tried not to gasp. There was no way she wanted to borrow thirty dollars, and especially not from Bitsy.

"Maybe we'd each be better off making our own big bets," said Matt. "The guys and I haven't agreed on horses today. But I'm willing to put in two dollars on a joint bet just like Sara said. We can pull a number out of a hat. That can't be any riskier than what we've been doing."

Sara felt proud that Matt was backing her. "Fine with me," she said.

But Bitsy wouldn't give up. "We've got to do better than that on the Oaks." She opened her purse and started to unzip her money pocket. "I'll just put up the money for those who can't afford it, and we can all decide on some combinations together. If we win I'll treat us to a steak dinner."

Hal touched her shoulder. "That's nice, Bits, but—"

"My money! My money is gone," wailed Bitsy as she searched frantically in her bag.

"Are you sure?" asked Matt. "Maybe it just fell down in your pocketbook somewhere."

She continued looking, taking each item out of her purse. "See, it's not here." She turned her empty pocketbook upside down, but no money fluttered out. "There should be over four hundred dollars."

"Some pickpocket probably got it," said Hal.

She shook her head in a jerk. "No, that's impossible. My clasp would be too hard to open."

"Bits," said David, "I think you seriously underestimate the skills of the average pickpocket. I bet a professional can get into any pocketbook, secret clasp or not."

"When was the last time you opened it?" asked Hal.

"That time I needed some money, after the fifth race. I took out a hundred and put it in my jacket pocket so I wouldn't have to keep going in for it. I listened to what you said, Matt. I decided not to flash it around in a crowd."

"That was a long time ago," said Grace. "Anything could've happened to it."

"I think somebody here took it," said Bitsy, looking at Sara.

"Bitsy, that's a terrible thing to say," said David. "Nobody here wants your money."

She pointed to Sara and said, "She does. I saw the way she watched while I opened it and then she gasped when she saw all my money. She's the only one here who doesn't have any money. She doesn't belong here."

Sara tried not to cry. "I didn't take your money." She looked over at Matt. "I didn't. I wouldn't do that."

He took her hand. "Of course you wouldn't. Now, Bitsy, I want you to apologize to Sara."

Bitsy put her things back in her purse. "Not happening. Not unless she opens her pocketbook to prove she doesn't have my money."

"She doesn't have to do that," said Hal. "That's insulting. Sara, don't you dare open your pocketbook."

"I think you forget, Bitsy, that you're my guest today," Matt interjected, "and it's not up to you to say what happens. You shouldn't bring so much money to the track. And you keep telling us you can afford to lose it, so what does it matter?"

"It matters if she took it. Even if I can afford it, I don't want her to have it."

"I didn't take your money, Bitsy. I was shocked by how much money you had, you were right about that. But I would never take it. I don't mind showing you."

"No, Sara," said Matt.

But before he could stop her, she opened her pocketbook and started taking things out and laying them on her lap. Bitsy grabbed up the billfold and rifled through the sections, pulling out the four one-dollar bills that Sara had left.

"See, I told you," said Sara.

"That's enough, Bitsy." Matt sounded really angry.

But she snatched the purse from Sara's hands and dumped the remaining items onto the concrete floor. There was no money.

"Apologize, Bitsy," said Matt as he stooped to pick up the items on the floor and hand them back to Sara.

"She spent it," said Bitsy. "Probably on losing tickets. None of you can see what a gold digger she is."

Placing a comforting hand on Sara's shoulder, Matt straightened up and faced Bitsy. "I think you should go out to the gate and call a cab, Bitsy. You've overstayed your welcome."

"So you'd rather be with her than your own kind. But you'll have to put up with me anyway. Thanks to her, I don't have any money for a cab. And they don't take credit." She sat back down and glared at everyone.

"Well, isn't it fortunate that I did cash a winning ticket," said Matt. He pulled a hundred-dollar bill out of his wallet. "Here, this should be enough to cover your ride, even with the higher prices during Derby."

Bitsy took the proffered Benjamin and stood up. "If I'm not wanted, I have better places to be, then. Come on, Hal."

"Matt didn't say I had to leave," he said. "And I want to see the Oaks. You obviously can take care of yourself."

Bitsy almost pushed Hal down as she hurried out of the box. She left muttering awful things that made Sara's stomach turn inside out.

Matt sat down by Sara and put his arm around her. "I'm sorry, honey. She can be pretty snobbish, but I didn't know she'd be so nasty to you, or I never would have invited her."

"I can't believe she thought I'd steal from her," said Sara.

"Don't even think about it," said Hal. "She's not worth it. She thinks her money excuses everything. But, Matt, she's *my* date, *my* responsibility. Let me pay you back the money you gave her for the cab." He pulled two fifties out of his wallet and offered the cash to Matt.

"No, no you don't have to do that. See, that's the irony of this. I was so mad about her treating Sara like dirt and flashing around her money, that when I got a little down on cash, I took a couple of bills from her purse when she wasn't looking. That's *her* money I gave her."

Hal laughed. "Hey, how about that. I was pissed at the way she's been treating me all day, so I took some money from her, too. These fifties are hers."

David asked, "But how did you both get around the secret clasp on the pocketbook?"

"Oh, it is a little tricky," said Matt, "but my mother has a pocketbook just like that she got in Europe last summer."

"It's the in thing to have," said Hal. "My sister got one for the Derby ball. Once you understand how it works, it's no problem to open. Bitsy deserved what she got. Maybe that will teach her not to be so mean."

"Perfect," said Matt. "Now let's go make our Oaks bets. With her gone, we can relax and enjoy the rest of the day. Want me to make a bet on the favorite for you, Sara?"

She shook her head and gave Matt two ones. "No, I'd like you to put this on Misty Maiden, that horse David liked. The one you said doesn't belong in the race. And make it a win bet."

"Are you sure?" asked Matt. "You're probably just throwing away your money."

"It's Sara's money," said Grace. "And you can make a bet on the same horse for me. I've got five dollars left. I'm willing to bet she's the class of the race."

"Your loss," said Matt.

Sara's horse didn't win, but she did come in third. Misty Maiden was close, but like Sara, she didn't belong after all.

Anita and the Maddens

by Sarah E. Glenn

Louisville is not the only city that celebrates the Kentucky Derby. Lexington, located in the Bluegrass Region of the state, also has a long tradition of celebration, specializing in "The Derby Party." One of the area's most famous mavens is Anita Madden. Her charity Derby parties, which benefited the Bluegrass Boys' Ranch, regularly attracted famous figures from all over the country.

The Maddens (most notably patriarch John E. Madden) are a long-established horse family who bred several Derby winners, stretching all the way from Plaudit in 1898 to Alysheba in 1987. Anita, who married John's grandson Preston in 1955, earned her own reputation, serving some time both as a Kentucky State Racing Commissioner and as a Fayette County Planning and Zoning Commissioner.

She is best known for her outrageous Derby celebrations, however. With themes like "Rapture of the Deep," with its giant octopus figure hidden inside swirls of dry-ice fog, and "The Ultimate Odyssey," which reenacted the Trojan War with costumed youths under a sixteen-foot statue of Zeus and his neon thunderbolt, partygoers knew they could always expect something special.

The Lexington television stations and newspapers regularly covered Anita's parties, taking pictures of the platinum-blonde socialite with guests like Kato Kaelin (1995 and 2001), Larry Hagman (1988), and Dennis Cole (a regular). Other attendees have included several Kentucky governors along with sports figures like Rick Pitino and Tubby Smith.

Anita Madden no longer throws Derby parties, but her legend endures. In 2001, John Rice of Thoroughbred Daylilies named one of his creations after her. The bloom is pale yellow with a peach blush, and Rice's wife says it "sparkles in the sunlight, like champagne." Today, large portions of the Madden Farm at Hamburg Place have been converted to shopping malls and subdivisions, but the names of the Madden horses live on in street names like Pink Pigeon Way, Plaudit Place, Star Shoot, and Sir Barton Way, named for the first Triple Crown winner in 1919.

PARTY TO A FALL

by Sarah E. Glenn

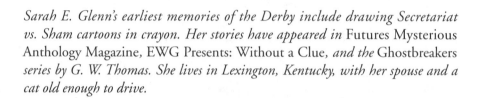

Sarah E. Glenn's earliest memories of the Derby include drawing Secretariat vs. Sham cartoons in crayon. Her stories have appeared in Futures Mysterious Anthology Magazine, EWG Presents: Without a Clue, *and the* Ghostbreakers *series by G. W. Thomas. She lives in Lexington, Kentucky, with her spouse and a cat old enough to drive.*

As soon as I saw the body under the tarp, I dropped the corner and pulled it back over the truck bed. Thank God the thumping music from the pavilion covered up my gasp. I'd thought P. J. might be hiding in the truck, perhaps huddled with that slut Audra, but I hadn't expected to find him dead.

She must have done it, but I knew who was going to be blamed. No one was going to think it was Audra Childers he was dumping. Her mother was hosting the party, her family's horse farm pulsing at the moment as the band played a cover of an Alan Jackson song. P. J. had no good reason to dump someone who could do so much for him, unlike me. I was just the one carrying his baby.

Earlier that evening, during the second playing of "Run for the Roses," I'd pressed close to him during the dance and whispered the news to him. He didn't appear overjoyed, but there it was.

"You have to tell her it's over," I said in his ear. "Or do you want me to tell her you're gonna be paying child support if she keeps you?"

"You did this on purpose, Jenny. It must've been that night—"

"It was *not* on purpose!" I said too loud, making people glance our way. I lowered my voice again. "No one put a gun to your head, as I recall. But you tell her it's over—tonight."

"They won't let me in the house," he said. "That's the private party."

"Then that shows you where you stand with her family. Do you think my news will improve things?"

He grumbled and left the dancing area. I headed for one of the buffet tables at the back of the tent and got some wings and a soda. Then I chose a seat upwind of the cigarette smoke and watched him approach the house. The servant at the door gave him a little grief, but he got in when Audra appeared.

People around me were talking about the party inside the house instead of the one they were attending. The real guests for the Childers bash weren't the ones under the tent; we were just lesser business acquaintances, employees (like me), and unimportant friends from church. We got the tribute band and the finger food; inside, as Audra had been happy to inform me, there was a *real* band and *good* food. There was even a bona fide celebrity: Kimothy Moulton, who had played second banana in several action films. In his honor, the theme of the party was famous adventurers. People in capes had been entering the house all night.

Mrs. Childers had ambitions of becoming the next Derby doyen of the Bluegrass, even if she only lived in little Frogtown. Certainly she wasn't going to have a guy like P. J. in there unless he married Audra, and I swore to myself that it wasn't going to happen.

Two security guards—a man and a woman—passed in front of me. "This is nothing, compared to one I worked in Lexington," the middle-aged man said to his partner. "The theme that year was . . . well, something to do with the jungle. The whole place was done up with plastic leaves and stuffed birds. If you think the costumes inside are bad tonight, you should see a banker in a loincloth. The hostess made her appearance in a bodysuit and swung down from the staircase on a vine—"

They stopped in their tracks, and the woman pointed and said, "Hey, you! What do you think you're doing?"

I turned in my seat and saw a couple of guys loading folding chairs into the back of a pickup truck. They weren't staff.

"Just moving these chairs, ma'am," one of the men said, swaying slightly as he stopped. Both wore sweatshirts with Greek lettering and UK caps. "They're in the way."

"Bull," the male guard snapped. "Take 'em out of the truck now and pile 'em over there. Then you're going to leave. Be glad Mrs. Childers doesn't want any arrests, or you'd be wearing cuffs."

The woman took an imposing stance and rested her hand on her gun. Most security guards the farm hired didn't have guns; these two must have been off-duty cops making some extra money.

The guys got the idea and began unloading the chairs. The male guard stood over them while the woman, hair pulled back into a bun too severe for her age, lifted the camera hanging around her neck and photographed the truck and the would-be thieves. "Folding chairs," she said. "A little unimaginative, fellas."

"Good chairs are hard to find," one of the young men said before the male guard shoved him into the cab of the truck. Then he started the motor.

"Idiots," the woman said as they watched the pickup bumble its way to the farm gates. "What are we going to do with all this stuff?"

"Pile it up, let the people here deal with it tomorrow when the party's over." They began stacking the chairs, and he said, "Lookee here, there's some trophies. Chamber of Commerce Award, Best New Breeder. . . ."

"Bet that would have looked good on the mantel next to the beer beacon," the woman snickered, camera flash highlighting bronze horse heads and loving cups. "We'd best go tell Mrs. Childers some of her stuff wandered out of the house. She's not going to like hearing that two of her special guests took special liberties."

The guards took off, and I watched their figures amble up to the front door. P. J. should be back soon.

My wait was in vain. Instead, Drew Childers, Audra's father, came out with the security guards. He had a good-natured smile on his face, and he wore a costume of true Indiana Jones regalia: scruffy fedora, leather jacket, a heavy gun at his hip, and a bullwhip wound four times around his left shoulder. The getup really didn't go with the thinning blond hair or the small paunch, and the whip kept slipping down. I had a purse like that once, and I got rid of it. The lady guard explained about the chairs, then she showed Mr. Childers the pictures.

Guests screamed as Kimothy came out the front door, followed by a posse of oversized Wonder Women and pudgy Batmen. He sauntered our way, broad-shouldered with blond wavy hair and handsome in a generic fashion. His outfit was almost identical to Mr. Childers's, but on him it looked good.

"What's going on?" he asked. "I hear we had a theft."

Mr. Childers updated his vaunted celebrity on the crime, having to shout periodically to be heard over the squeals of women hoping to draw the star's attention. Then he indicated the male guard, and Kimothy shook his hand and said, "You saved the holy relics, man. Your own little rescue mission."

The three posed together for a picture in front of the stack of purloined goods. One flash later, the woman handed the photo to her partner. She didn't look particularly pleased at being left out of the kudos.

Mr. Childers took off his whip and flicked it around, scattering the impromptu audience.

Kimothy pulled his own whip from his shoulder and said, "Here, let me show you how to use that, Drew. This is the stock, this is the whip proper, and this strap on the end is the fall."

I didn't realize there was a science to this stuff, but I suppose a man had to know his business.

He continued, "That's where they attach the crackers, the part that makes the noise." Soon the pair were side-by-side, swinging their whips to the flashes of several more cameras.

My father appeared at my side. "Are you all right? What happened?"

"Nothing, really. Some guys tried to make off with some chairs, and security stopped them. Then Mr. Childers and his movie star came out and started putting on a show." I indicated the party tent. "Would you like to come sit with me for a bit? I'm waiting for P. J."

We got some pop and chose a table near my former seat. Dad spoke about the get-together planned for the crew the next day, asking if we had enough chips, should we buy more burgers, things like that. I replied with noncommittal uh-huhs, my eyes trained on the house.

The multicolored fanlight above the double doors to the Childers manor glowed in the distance, lit from within. The doors finally opened, by the hands of a servant, and a couple spilled out onto the steps. The woman wore a mask, over her eyes, but I'd know that wavy brown hair and flattened face anywhere—Audra. P. J. was with her. Stars sparked in the sequins of her catsuit as she pulled him close for a kiss. He scuttled away, and she ducked back inside. I couldn't believe it. How could she still want him after learning about the baby? Why would he still kiss her . . . unless he was keeping her and dumping me? I slapped my empty cup down on the table.

My father swallowed the rest of his drink too quickly and rose. "I'm sorry, honey. I really should go see about clearing up that pile of junk the thieves left."

Surely a farm manager could delegate that to someone else, I thought, but perhaps he didn't know what to say about P. J. He was probably embarrassed. I know I was.

I left the festivities and walked down the hill to our house. Its emptiness matched my own hollowness inside. I didn't know which felt worse: being betrayed by P. J. or by Audra. She and I had grown up together, played together, gone to the same schools, taken presents to each other's birthday parties. We were friends when we were young, especially when the farm was still struggling. But that was before boys, before P. J.

The fridge was filled with longnecks for the big Derby viewing we were hosting for the crew the next day. I knew it wasn't good for the baby, but I took one out and twisted the top off. P. J. was supposed to be one of the guests. I'd hoped it would be as my fiancé, but he had apparently made another choice.

Tears burned my eyelids; what if he said nothing to me, not knowing we had seen him with Audra, and came anyway? What would my father do?

If I thought he wouldn't say anything to me, why did I think he would say anything to Audra? Maybe he was stringing both of us along, waiting to see where his bread was buttered. Maybe I'd better speak to Audra directly. But first, I'd confront P. J.

I returned to the party tent. No one seemed to even notice. The band started "Run for the Roses" again, and the sweaty commoners groaned and moved close for another dance. The crowd had thinned a little, and I looked around for P. J. but didn't see him anywhere. That was when I had the brilliant idea of checking his truck, parked near the barn closest to the house. Which is where I found him, dead. Horribly dead. His eyes bulged, wide and staring, the thin bands around his throat made redder in spots by oozing blood.

As I carefully arranged the tarp over his body again, my thoughts whirled without an anchor. P. J. was gone. The baby wasn't going to have a dad, whether he married Audra or me. But the police wouldn't see it that way, and I would sure get blamed for it if they found me with him. I had to get away before someone saw me next to the truck.

A door closed nearby, not loud, but enough to make me jump. It had to be Billy. He roomed in the barn, supposedly in case the horses needed him. I thought it was more likely charity on the part of the Childers family, since he drank his dinner most nights. His presence probably discouraged intruders, though. Drunk or not, if he saw me with the body, he'd get the wrong idea for sure.

I dropped to the ground and scooted into the shadows under the truck. P. J.'s duffel bag, near the tailgate, gave me extra cover. Boots whispered in the freshly cut grass, stopping not five feet from me. I stared at them, hypnotized by the reflection of the party lights. Just about the time I thought I couldn't hold my breath any longer, they moved on, rustling up the hill.

The sound of clinking dishes and hissing pots met me when I slipped into the house through the kitchen entrance. My mother, pulling a tray of stuffed mushrooms out of the oven, greeted me. "Sweetie, why are you back here? I thought you were just attending the party." Her face glowed with perspiration. "Give me that spatula."

I handed it to her, then took an apron. I noticed grass stains on my best dress. Great.

"I'll take this tray here to the guests," I said. "I'd like a closer look at that Kimothy Moulton." I hoisted the hors d'oeuvres—finger food by a fancier name—and left her chuckling.

The room was packed with costumed partygoers. Capes swirled and masks gleamed everywhere. Mrs. Childers, a ridiculously round Princess Leia, held court in the center of the room. I made sure to stay out of her line of vision, not difficult in a room full of important people. Servants were invisible in a party setting. Audra seemed to be invisible as well; nowhere did I see a girl in a catsuit.

I kept a smile pasted on my face, nodding till the guests emptied my tray, then set it on a folding table near the kitchen. If Audra wasn't downstairs, perhaps she had gone to her room. Maybe she'd been hurt fighting P. J. or had gotten blood on her costume. I dodged a Green Hornet of small stature, dancing with a middle-aged Lara Croft, and headed up the back stairs.

In the coolness of the second floor, I became aware of the dress clinging to my sweaty back. Audra's room was the first one on the right. She wasn't there, but two suitcases lay open on the bed, half-filled with clothing and some pictures from her dresser. Peeky-boo, a stuffed bear she'd had since childhood, perched on top of a jewelry box tucked in one corner. She was running away!

Forget keeping quiet; I stomped down the hall, jerking each door open as I came to it. I finally found her in the study with her father and Miz Eulalia. They were assembled as if waiting for something, but from the looks on their faces, I wasn't it.

Audra bore a strong resemblance to her grandmother, but it looked like God had pressed a thumb to the girl's face so He could tell them apart. Audra was teary, probably trying to convince them she'd had to strangle P. J. because he was having a baby with me.

I had intended to just talk with Audra when I entered the house, but she had gone too far. I grabbed her by the front of her catsuit and slapped her face. She shrieked and swatted back at me; I responded by kicking her knee. She fell howling to the floor, and heavy hands grabbed my shoulders, pulling me away before I could step on that hideous flattish face of hers.

"Jenny! Have you gone insane?" Mr. Childers shook me.

Glaring at the whimpering slut trying to stand, I said, "She killed P. J. He's dead."

"Nonsense, girl," Miz Eulalia said. "Audra has been with me for the past hour or so. I wasn't of a mind to join the brawl downstairs." Unlike the rest of the party guests, she wore no costume, only a simple blue gown. A string of pearls circled her withered throat.

"P. J.'s dead?" Audra cried, then burst into tears and threw herself into one of the stuffed chairs. She almost sounded surprised.

Mr. Childers straightened the triple loop of the whip on his shoulder, then took me by the arms and steered me to the door. "Get out of my house. You're fired. And don't think I won't be looking hard at your parents, too."

I held in my own sob as I reached for the door, but it opened on its own. The two security guards I'd seen outside entered the room.

"Mr. Childers," the male said, "I'm very sorry to inform you that one of your employees has died. A foreman, Paul Jameson."

"No!" Audra choked, face buried in the arm of her chair. "Not P. J."

"How interesting," Mr. Childers said. "Jenny was just telling us about it." He glanced at me, then arched a knowing eyebrow at the security guard. My face grew hot.

"I'm not surprised, sir," the guard said. "We're holding her father, Colton Hadlock, downstairs as a suspect."

The rest of me grew hot as well, and I put a hand on Audra's chair. "Why?"

"We broke up a fight between him and the victim earlier. They'd volunteered to move some stolen stuff back into the house, but we think Hadlock volunteered Jameson because he wanted to talk to him about something. I think we have an idea about what."

Had Dad guessed the truth? I thought maybe Mom had figured it out, but I'd hoped to keep it from him until I had things worked out with P. J. I knew he'd do something stupid like this. Could . . . could he have killed P. J.? He was stronger than Audra.

I suddenly felt very bad; the lights were too dim in the room, and the hot shadows crowded me.

The male officer gently took my elbow. "Sit down, miss. Here."

I gripped the overstuffed arm of the seat, regaining my bearings. It wobbled slightly, which didn't help. I guess a good chair really is hard to find. I giggled while voices buzzed around me. The lady guard was Officer Howard; the man was Officer Davis. Yes, my father had specifically asked that P. J. help him. Mr. Childers didn't know why, hadn't thought much about it at the time. All those important guests, you know.

Miz Eulalia, from the innocence of her wheelchair, said Audra had been upstairs with her for the last hour or so and hadn't gone anywhere.

"Suitcases," I gasped over the nausea. "Suitcases in her room. She was packing."

Audra's father said that they were going to Louisville to see the race the next day, though, so no one paid attention to me after that. I just slumped there, staring at Mr. Childers's boots.

When I recovered, the officers sent me downstairs to tend to my mother, who was stunned by my father's arrest. The guests continued to mingle in the central rooms, oblivious to the death outside.

As I walked her back to the house—the house we were bound to lose—thoughts shot through my mind like fireflies, sparking bright but then disappearing into darkness. Audra had seemed so shocked by the news. If she was the killer, she was a really good actress. I'd known her my entire life, and I was convinced. The suitcases on the bed, though—if she had been going to Churchill Downs, she'd have told everyone so they could envy her. She had to be running away, so she must've killed him.

But she was a lousy fighter. If I could take her, then how could she have killed P. J., who was taller and stronger than us both? But if she wasn't the killer, why had Miz Eulalia been so specific about how long Audra had been with her? Why was she protecting her, if her granddaughter was innocent? What was she protecting her from? Why were two suitcases on the bed? There were family pictures packed in those cases, there was Peeky-Boo. That was no day trip she was planning. Why had she stopped?

Mom wanted me to stay home with her, get some rest before morning when we would go down to the jail, but I couldn't sit still. I changed into jeans and headed back to Audra's house. Police lights flashed everywhere, and guests were being questioned. Mrs. Childers had wanted her parties to be talked about, but I didn't think this was what she'd had in mind. Men in jumpsuits were rooting through the Dumpsters. Probably looking for the murder weapon. It had to be a strap or something like that—something that would go around the neck. Maybe leather. A leather strap. Boots. A duffel bag. The firefly thoughts returned, joined together this time, and I saw the events of the evening differently.

I found the people I needed examining the area at P. J.'s truck. He had been taken away, along with the tarp, which was a relief, I'm ashamed to say.

"Now, isn't this better than staying home on a Friday night?" the male officer was saying to his partner as I walked up.

"I could be mixing faux mint juleps right now—minus the mint, of course," she grumbled, taking pictures of the truck bed. Then both noticed me.

"Officer Davis," I said, "The lady here took a picture of you with Mr. Moulton and Mr. Childers. Can I see it?"

He shrugged and pulled it from his pocket.

I studied it, then showed it to both officers. It quivered in my hand. "See? His whip had four loops. Now it has three."

"Maybe he adjusted it to make it more comfortable. It was pretty bulky."

The woman shook her head. "Then it would have been banging his leg all night. He would have had to shorten it."

"If he did, it's nowhere to be found," Davis grunted. "I.D.'s been all over the place."

"Unless," I told him, "it was a straw hidden in a bale of hay."

* * *

Audra, her grandmother, and her parents were drinking leftover punch in the great room when I returned to the house. They looked surprised when I came in behind the two officers.

"How goes the search, officers?" Mr. Childers asked in an overly casual voice. I glanced at his boots one last time to be sure. Yes, they were the ones I had seen. Most of the crew wore Red Wings, and his were something more expensive.

"We've had a breakthrough, sir," Officer Davis said. "We believe we've found the weapon."

The lord of the manor nodded. "Very good. So you'll be clearing out soon? We've had much more excitement tonight than I'd planned."

"We'll be leaving, yes. But we'd like for you to come with us."

Avoiding Mr. Childers's glare, I turned to his mother. "You said Audra wasn't going anywhere. But she was planning to, wasn't she? P. J. was going to leave with her tonight. You heard her packing."

The old woman raised a near-invisible eyebrow. "People think because I'm old that I don't hear well. Sometimes it pays not to correct them."

"You told your son."

"Of course I did," she snorted. "Paul Jameson was an opportunist, a gold digger. I saw how he thought to better himself by seducing you, his boss's daughter. Once he had you in the hand, though, it wasn't enough. He set his sights higher, on Audra. He thought if she eloped with him, he'd get a share of the farm. So I sent Drew down to deal with him."

"Down by the yearling barn," Officer Howard said. "He knew that the night man wouldn't be awake, or at least not very alert. A little privacy, especially in case Jameson wouldn't be dealt with easily. And he wasn't ready to give up his claim on Audra."

The flat-faced girl sniffled and rubbed her eyes. "He wouldn't leave me; I was having his baby."

Miz Eulalia frowned at her granddaughter. "Shame on you, child. I thought we raised you better than that."

Audra looked away and broke into fresh sobs. I decided it was best not to tell anyone about me, although they would find out soon enough.

Officer Howard continued the narrative. "Perhaps he turned down the offers you made, Mr. Childers. Although I think it's more likely that he told you *why* Audra needed to marry him. It would explain where your strength came from, to wrap your whip around the neck of a much younger man and strangle him outright. Perhaps you had the weapon out to intimidate him at first—the archetypal outraged father—and things got out of hand."

Mr. Childers chuckled—more of a *whuff* sound—and tapped the coils at his shoulder. "My whip is right here, ma'am. Do you really think I'd still be wearing it if I'd participated in your little scenario?"

"Not all of it, no." Officer Howard shook her head. "But it's not as long as it was before. You had your picture taken before the murder with Kimothy Moulton and my partner. Here, look." She held out the Polaroid. "Your whip looped four times around your shoulder. Now it only loops three times."

"It was uncomfortable, so I loosened it. Irregularities aren't necessarily clues, young lady."

"It is if it connects with what we found in the tack room," Officer Davis said. "We found a leather strap, just long enough to be the fall of a whip, in a stack with some other pieces of leather, where someone hoped it wouldn't be noticed during a police search. It has some blond hairs caught in the edges, along with what could be blood from Jameson's neck. I figure the lab can sort out whether it's human or not, and whether it belongs to the victim. May I inspect your whip, sir? I'd like to see if the end is still intact."

Mr. Childers hesitated, and his mother laid her hand on his arm. "Of course you can, Officer Davis. And then you will excuse me if I call our attorneys. Obviously there has been some misunderstanding about what happened between my son and the young man."

"Of course, ma'am. But, in the meantime, I think he should come downtown with us. I think there's a fellow there who'd love to swap places with him."

The Clarks and the First Kentucky Derby

by Sandra Cerow Leonard

The family name *Clark* resonates through early Kentucky history. George Rogers Clark, well known for his Revolutionary War campaigns, was one of the founders of the city of Louisville. His sister Lucy married surveyor William Croghan, and in 1790, near the family home of twelfth president Zachary Taylor, they built their home, Locust Grove. It became a center of hospitality in the area and had many famous visitors like Presidents James Monroe and Andrew Jackson. In 1803 at the request of President Thomas Jefferson, younger brother William Clark began the exploration of the Northwest Territory with Meriwether Lewis.

William Clark's grandson Meriwether Lewis Clark, Jr. created the Kentucky Derby. The young man's mother had died when he was six, and his father divided the children to live with various relatives, sending M. Lewis Clark to two uncles, John and Henry Churchill, who owned land south of the city limits. Though M. Lewis Clark's family ties to horse racing went back several generations, he went into banking and tobacco after graduating from St. Joseph's College in Bardstown, Kentucky. So he had no real knowledge of horse racing when he was approached by a group of breeders who wanted his help in reviving the flagging sport.

Horse racing had been a rich part of Kentucky's history for decades. The first racetrack was laid out in Lexington in 1789, but safety concerns about racing on increasingly congested city streets and the bankruptcy of a major local racecourse in 1870 caused talk among the racing industry of abandoning the sport.

In 1872 and 1873, M. Lewis Clark, then twenty-six years old, traveled to England and France to study European racing operations. He was particularly impressed with the English stakes races, especially the Epsom Derby. A meeting with the breeders was held on his return in which he outlined a plan for founding the Louisville Jockey Club and establishing a track with permanent stakes races, the most prestigious to be called the Kentucky Derby.

The track was built on Churchill land south of Louisville, and the first Kentucky Derby was run in 1875 at what would later be called Churchill Downs. The winner, Aristides, ridden by young black jockey Oliver Lewis, thundered to the finish line in front of ten thousand racing fans, and a racing tradition was born.

Murder on the Fourth Furlong

by Tamera Huber

Tamera Huber, a freelance journalist, completed her first mystery novel, Void of Course, *and is working on her second book with the same protagonist. In 2000 her screenplay,* A Killing Moon, *won honorary mention in a* Writer's Digest *competition. "A Dish Served Cold," a short crime story, won first-place honors and appeared in* Snitch *in October 2002.* Derby Rotten Scoundrels *includes two of her short stories. In 2005 she won first place, Metro Division—Enterprise Reporting, at the Society of Professional Journalists Awards (Louisville chapter).*

This will be your last mount, Carerra.

Steam poured from a chipped but sturdy ceramic mug filled with coffee black enough for Stephen Hawking to debate its origin. Private detective Mike Gardner closed his eyes and leaned into the vapor. After inhaling deeply, the java addict smiled and grasped the cup with his left hand while holding the threatening note in his right.

His shoulders relaxed a bit more with each savored caffeinated sip, and he filtered out the noisy over-capacity crowd pressing in on his booth island. His rump sank farther into the vinyl-covered seat in one of several booths situated in front of large picture windows overlooking the fast, well-groomed track. Posing as the detective's temporary office, the backside kitchen actually served as a cafeteria for racetrack workers. The locale presented a highly prized location from which to view races during Kentucky's Derby Day.

Mint juleps and beer flowed throughout the racetrack's grounds, nowhere more freely than the track kitchen. A record crowd, as reported by all four local television stations, filled the stands, infield, and backside as more bodies poured into the already packed venue. Bus passengers and pedestrians who had hoofed it from a mile or more away—and paid handsomely for the privilege—seemed like ants converging on the same picnic. Seasoned horsemen and women rubbed shoulders with amateur wagerers.

Only one pane of glass separated kitchen spectators from the pedigreed horses thundering past them. Equine athletes in the first race galloped between the half- and three-quarter-mile poles on their way to the third turn, kicking up dirt as they sped toward the finish line. The horses ran on the outside, farther away from the infield and closer to grandstands, a mere fifteen to twenty feet from the plate glass. Screams, groans, and curses erupted forty-five seconds later as the Thoroughbreds crossed the wire.

The groom in the booth behind Gardner pulled both hands on top of his dusty cap and bellowed, "Sparks is a bum trainer. What was I thinking?"

The woman sitting next to him, a twenty-something pony rider whose weathered skin looked ten years older, squealed with delight and poked him in the side with her elbow. "Too bad, Harris. Tell you what . . . I'll have a party with my winnings, and I'll let you sniff the food."

Her shrieking laughter pierced the air throughout the kitchen, but Gardner's focus stayed on the note: *Your last mount.* He held the message at arm's length as his eyes squinted at the text. The detective scanned the room, then reached into his vintage houndstooth jacket and pulled out a pair of drugstore reading glasses he had reluctantly purchased due to his inability to grow longer arms. He pushed a swatch of gray-tinged brown hair away from his forehead before he placed the glasses on the tip of his nose. Pulling the note to a normal reading position, he reexamined the message. Neither the nondescript paper nor the pseudo bifocals shed any light on the threat's origin.

Ruggedly handsome with a football player's physique, Gardner sighed as he quickly shed the spectacles, depositing them inside his jacket. Nearly everyone working the backside—over a hundred people, by the seasoned detective's estimation—could have touched the paper. He consulted his Timex. Eleven-thirty. The note had been found nearly an hour earlier, tacked to the community bulletin board in the jockeys' locker room.

No need for gloves, the detective thought as his eyes narrowed.

The individual letters, cut at random angles from weatherworn newsprint, appeared much like a ransom note. Gardner smiled. *Drama major?* Although the threatening communication in his calloused hand revealed little about its author, it left no doubt about the target.

Raymond Carerra.

Gardner jumped at the mention of Carerra's name from somewhere other than his own thoughts.

Backside workers, crammed shoulder-to-shoulder in the small diner, watched local coverage on a seventeen-inch color television mounted near the ceiling in the far corner of the kitchen.

"Raymond Carerra," another reporter said, "is the jockey to beat in this year's Derby. Gulf War hero and retired four-star general Mason Randolph says his Thoroughbred Sunny Valley and Carerra can't lose. And Green Day, his horse in the second, looks mighty fine. Apparently the oddsmakers agree the Triple Crown might be within his reach."

Gardner smirked. "Yeah," he said under his breath. "If he can stay alive."

The first phone call from Mason Randolph, Gardner's current and only client, had come at 5:00 a.m. two weeks earlier.

"What?" Gardner had mumbled into the phone, still groggy from a late-night Peeping Tom divorce case.

"Heard from Lieutenant Colonel Franks you're a good man in a tight situation," Randolph said.

"How do you know the commander?" Gardner sat up in bed at the mention of his former boss.

"He's the best man on the Louisville Metro Police force, and I make it my business to only deal with the best."

"And you are?"

"General Mason Randolph." The veteran of four wars paused a moment before adding, "Retired."

Smart, stern, and honest. Gardner could think of no greater compliment for a battlefield leader who had presided over the lives of thousands of young men. "Honored," he responded without embarrassment.

"I own Thoroughbreds," Randolph said matter-of-factly.

"Yes, I've seen your profile in *The Blood-Horse.*" The Thoroughbred Owners and Breeders Association published the prestigious magazine.

Randolph cleared his throat. "Um, you read that?" the horseman asked.

Choosing to interpret the surprise in Randolph's voice as respect rather than condescension, Gardner said nothing.

"Of course," the older gent continued. "I'm sure in your field you must keep up on any number of subjects."

"What can I do for you?" Gardner asked.

"I hired Ray Carerra to mount my Derby contender."

The dead air that passed between the two men was almost audible. After the long silence, Gardner said, "Surely you know his reputation, sir."

"The drugs, the women? I don't put much stock in whispers, son."

"I know for a fact the rumors are true, sir."

"Don't ask, don't tell. I couldn't care less, as long as he's focused on the big day." Randolph coughed so loudly, Gardner's ear rang.

"You okay, sir?"

"Never should have taken up cigars." He wheezed more than laughed. "Or maybe it's those damned Iraqi oil fires."

The headlines in the previous week's local newspaper had made it obvious this Derby signaled the horseman's last. Lung cancer had reached an inoperable stage, a fact the general, who had fought thousands of battles, refused to concede.

The old man cleared his throat and continued. "There have been three attempts on Carerra's life in the past week. Narrow misses . . . could have been fatal."

Gardner rolled his eyes, well aware Randolph could not see the gesture. "Well, maybe the little man's just accident prone."

A burst of controlled anger traveled over the phone line and into Gardner's ear. "Murder attempts, not accidents," Randolph said.

"What makes you think—"

"Green Day's not bad, but the combination of my colt Sunny Valley and Carerra is unbeatable. Everyone knows that. We're riding to the Triple Crown, and no one's stopping us, but someone could make a fortune by bumping Carerra out of the way."

"Or by harming Sunny Valley," Gardner said.

"I have a man on it."

"Who?"

"Jim Cantrell," Randolph replied.

Color rose in Gardner's cheeks. *Watching a horse and a stoner jockey is just about his speed*, he thought. Though Cantrell remained tight in the Kentucky horse circle, the former-cop-turned-detective couldn't reason his way out of a paper bag. "You've got your man—and I use that term loosely. So why call me?" He didn't attempt to disguise his growing irritation.

"I need someone smart. Someone who can work the little gray cells."

Gardner smiled at the reference to one of the greatest fictional detectives of all time.

"I realized Cantrell wasn't exactly the best man for intellectual deduction, but I hear he's the man to call when it comes to keeping his eyes open."

"Yeah. I've seen him in action. On the force." After an awkward pause, Gardner continued. "It cost me my badge."

"I hope your unfortunate past association with Mr. Cantrell won't influence your decision," Randolph said with a questioning tone. Almost as an after-thought he added, "You may need to work together at some point."

The old man's words echoed in Gardner's ears. In one fluid motion, the detective hung up the phone and threw it against the wall of his sparsely fur-nished basement apartment.

The following day, Gardner awoke in a pool of tequila. He peeled his body off the kitchen floor where he had fallen earlier. The toaster's chrome caught his reflection, and he rubbed his indented face, pockmarked to match the fleur-de-lis pattern in the linoleum.

A civil defense siren would have been quieter than the ringing doorbell that morning. Covering his ears, he cursed and wished the sound, and its maker, would die a slow, painful death. His door wouldn't oblige, so he bounded toward the entryway, wincing at each heavy, head-throbbing step.

Ready to rip the throat out of the visitor, he forced the sun-bleached front door open with gusto. Louisville's second-highest-ranking police official, Lieutenant Colonel Robert Franks, stood in Gardner's doorway.

"You need to do this." The commander spoke with quiet authority. "As a favor."

"But Cantrell!" The sound of his own raised voice made Gardner cringe.

"I know. I vouched for him with Randolph."

Gardner clenched his fist and jaw. His only answer—to stare in disbelief.

"Hear me out," the commander continued, stepping inside. "Cantrell is just the right person to watch a stupid horse and an even stupider jockey. But this is not about the horse. It's about Carerra. Sources say someone's out for blood. Nothing to do with the Derby. It's personal."

"Says who?"

Franks smiled. "Reliable sources."

The private eye nodded. He knew better than to question the veracity of the commander's unique informant network.

"Randolph assured me he would keep Cantrell away from you. I know you don't believe this, but he got a raw deal, too."

Gardner slammed his fist onto an already beat-up coffee table. He winced, rubbing his aching knuckles.

Franks remained calm and seemed to ignore the outburst. "He's in a stall watching the horse. Carerra's promised to stay in the barn within eyeshot of Cantrell. You'll do the investigative work, not running the day care."

"Why isn't the department on this?"

"We are, but Randolph needs someone on this full time. You know we don't have the resources during Derby week to baby-sit a civilian."

"You're still working on reinstatement?" Gardner, desperate, looked it.

"Absolutely," Franks replied without flinching.

"For me?"

"Of course," Franks said but then looked away.

"Cantrell, too?"

The commander nodded slowly.

Gardner sank into a dilapidated easy chair and remained quiet for several minutes. Without looking at his former boss, he said, "I'll do it."

"Yay!" screamed the small, hunched-over cafeteria worker with gray-streaked hair when the first race replayed. Sporting a hairnet, she craned her neck toward the television screen and shouted, "I love you, baby!"

Spectators who attempted to occupy the booth seat facing Gardner met with a flash of his badge—the fake one he had bought at a novelty store. Whenever the booth crasher sat down anyway, Gardner flashed a peek at metal of a different kind. The kind with bullets.

Judging from the lack of recent squatters, he figured word had circulated about him: armed and, if not dangerous, at least in no mood for company. The detective appeared an island in a sea of people pushing in from all sides whenever horseflesh came around. The second stakes race, sponsored and named after a credit card company, was about to run, and the masses thronged toward the windows. The booth in which he sat functioned as a large rock in a stream—everything flowed around it while leaving it untouched.

He looked at his watch. Almost noon. While everyone else in the diner jockeyed for position at either the windows or the television, he sat alone in his booth, uninterested in the mayhem surrounding him.

Carerra is most definitely in danger. Gardner, tilting his head to see over the frames on the tip of his nose, scanned the room. *A circus.* For a better purview, he stood on the booth bench with his back to the windows. The entire kitchen, the size of a medium-sized diner, lay before him.

"Down up front!" a male voice yelled.

The detective flashed his tin badge and bored a hole into the small-framed man, who flinched and pushed his way to the opposite end of the row of window-framed booths.

The kitchen vibrated—literally—with hot walkers, trainers, and a couple of B-string jockeys, all there on the first Saturday in May to participate in the nation's most prestigious race day. Each voice, each sound, each movement echoed against the concrete walls.

Gardner had done his homework on the backside workers. Many had been around long enough and could have managed to leave a note in the jockeys' locker room, even with tightened security. Plenty of folks with credentials. A crapshoot. It could be anyone.

He looked up when a Midwestern beauty with long legs and a killer smile entered through the heavy steel door leading from the dusty backside to the hyperactive kitchen. Heads—both male and female—turned as Laura Miles, lavender-clad with a spectacular feathered hat over her straight, shoulder-length tresses, strode the ten steps to Gardner's trackside booth. No need to push the crowd out of the way; they parted like the Red Sea.

"I'm desperate for a caffeine fix," Miles said as she gulped several giant-sized portions from Gardner's mug.

He glanced at the remnants of her bright red lipstick on the edge of his cup. The thirty-something Channel 7 reporter sank into the booth seat across from him, somehow avoiding the squishy Naugahyde sound most patrons made when doing the same. Once seated, her Salvatore Ferragamo pump rubbed against Gardner's sockless ankle before traveling upward underneath his khaki pant leg.

His blood raced. "Shouldn't you be reporting on something?"

"I am," she said with a full grin. "Word is that someone's threatening to kill Carerra."

"Really?" Gardner downed the rest of the liquid adrenalin. "Are you here working that angle?"

"I assumed *you* were here working that angle."

In the next booth, a scruffy, dust-covered man wearing a cap leaned his head back to hear more of the conversation.

Gardner lowered his voice. "Confidentiality prevents me from—"

"Bull!" She glanced around the kitchen, now packed even tighter than when she entered it. The newswoman guarded her Rebecca-of-Sunnybrook-Farm public persona vigilantly. As Gardner leaned in, Miles lowered her tone and continued. "You know you can't resist my charms." She fluttered her caked-on lashes. "Besides, that idiot Cantrell told me as much. Come on, give me an exclusive."

She placed her silky hand on top of his. He shook his head and she quickly retracted her hand.

"How'd Randolph get Carerra anyway?" she asked. "I heard the cokehead hated military men."

"Gladiator."

"Excuse me?" she asked. "Oh, I get it." Miles removed her ornate hat and fluffed her hair. A beam of light streamed through the window and caught the highlights in her honey blonde locks. "The guy's Gulf War strategies remain legend. Required reading at military academies everywhere. I'm sure his tactical skill proved an advantage during the negotiations."

"Not to mention his money. Millionaires. All of them, these owners."

"Not all," she said. "I would have given anything to watch the monetary hand-to-hand combat needed to secure Carerra."

"Anything?" Gardner leaned forward with a sly glance. Her reciprocating smile melted him. Before he could stop himself, he said, "The general definitely has skills. He even got me on the cheap."

"So, you are working for Randolph."

Gardner swallowed hard but remained silent.

"Fine." Miles stood abruptly and straightened her form-fitting Versace jacket and skirt. "Feel free not to call me next time you need information." She pivoted gracefully on one heel while grabbing her hat. Debris from the oversized ostrich feather rained down into Gardner's empty coffee mug. Halfway to the door, about four feet away, she paused.

He stood on the bench and called after her, "We still on for dinner at Z's?"

With a slight glance over her shoulder, she said, "Eight. And be on time for once."

Gardner read her lips more than heard her. He shuddered, trying to purge the impure thoughts rambling through his brain. His attention quickly returned to the case at hand.

The eavesdropper in the next booth stepped into the aisleway, and Gardner moved quickly to intercept him. The detective pegged him as a groom or a hot walker, and he wondered why he had been so interested in his conversation with Laura Miles.

"Excuse me," Gardner said as he bumped against the dirty little man, checking for weapons. A glance at his security badge revealed a familiar name: Emilio Rodriguez. "I know you," Gardner said with enthusiasm and a hint of surprise.

Moving aside, Rodriguez didn't look up. "Don't think so."

Gardner matched his sidestep. "Sure I do. You're Emilio Rodriguez."

"Impressive. You can read." He stepped to the other side.

Gardner blocked him again. "I followed your career when you were a jockey. Looked like the triple for you until Belmont last year. Still have the bum knee?" he asked, although the brace on Rodriguez's right leg revealed the answer. "How'd it happen?"

"A bump. On the final stretch. Fell and didn't get out of the way quick enough."

"Yeah, I saw that on television. Come on, pal. I need the juicy details."

Rodriguez took another side step with his good leg, trying to maneuver around Gardner. "Just bad luck."

The detective stepped in front of him again. "No kiddin'. Awful luck. Especially after you kicked your habit. What was it? Cocaine or—"

"I'm clean now, that's all that matters."

"Of course. Of course." Gardner studied the ex-jockey. Lowering his tone and his eyes, he said, "Sorry to hear about your daughter, too. Cancer, wasn't it?" The pain in Rodriguez's face tugged at the detective, but he pushed his empathy aside and continued. "By the way, who bumped you?"

"Doesn't matter."

"So, what are you doing these days?"

"Groom. It's all I could get. After."

Gardner understood and acknowledged with a nod.

"If I don't get back to the barn soon, they'll can me," Rodriguez said.

The detective stepped aside, allowing the jockey-turned-groom to go around him. He glared at Rodriguez and followed his every step with his eyes. The little man pushed through the crowd and headed for the door that led to the barns. After a few steps, he changed directions and started back toward Gardner. The detective sat down and waited.

Two feet before reaching Gardner's booth, Rodriguez turned down a small hallway adjacent to the windows and entered the men's room.

The track announcer read the second-race entries as the horses took the track and trotted toward the starting gate. Thunderous applause rose from the grandstands, the infield, and the kitchen. Fans expended the enthusiasm usually reserved for the big race later in the day on the second for the win-ningest jockey of the year, Raymond Carerra. Squatters who had lingered in the booths next to the kitchen windows since early morning pressed up against the glass.

Squeals, prayers, and curses wafted past Gardner, who sank back into his booth, watching the men's room with one eye while keeping the other on the track. Ponies led ten Thoroughbreds to the starting gate. Energy and anticipa-tion filled the room, mingling with the smell of bourbon and beer.

As track workers shoved and cajoled each horse into the gate, the news-caster rambled to fill time before the race. "Green Day, Carerra's mount, drew an excellent post position, fifth. Carerra has won every start of his career from that spot. The jockey generally stays back on the outside, a couple of horses off the lead, until he reaches the second turn. Then he picks off the competition one by one. If his strategy holds, Jim, it'll be a preview of the big race. I'm not a betting man, but I'll go out on a limb . . . if he wins this one, I wouldn't bet against him and Sunny Valley in the Derby."

"And they're off!" the track announcer's voice, familiar to those on the back-side, blared from the sound system and from the television in the kitchen. The horses lurched forward and gained speed quickly. As usual, Carerra kept just slightly off the pace, waiting for his opportunity in the final half of the mile-and-a-quarter race.

Bodies pressed against the glass, and necks craned in the kitchen as the Thoroughbreds approached the windows overlooking the third turn. Gardner turned toward the track, abandoning his men's room surveillance. Right where Carerra riding Green Day should be. The nine-to-five favorite wouldn't return much on his hundred-dollar bet, but it would be enough to pay for dinner afterward with Laura Miles. Easy money.

As the horses ran the stretch between the second and third turns, shouts erupted in the kitchen.

"Get the lead out, you stupid nag!" screamed a dusty groom.

"Come on, Big Jim!" called another spectator.

Gardner stood on the bench.

Carerra leaned forward in the saddle, ready to break away from the pack of four horses converging near the rail just ahead. Unexpectedly, he sat back in the saddle.

Go on, make your move already.

Not only did Carerra fail to make his trademark move at the expected time, but he and Green Day began to drop off the pace, toward the pack bringing up the rear.

Flying Halo's jockey fought fiercely to avoid the inevitable collision, but the third-to-last place horse bumped Green Day's right flank. Carerra's mount slowed abruptly, sending him facedown into the dirt.

Spectators drew a collective and horrified gasp as the last two horses in the field trampled the fallen jockey's head and torso underneath their hooves.

Gardner spun around to face the short hallway leading to the men's rest room. Rodriguez emerged, pale and shaken, holding his stomach. The detective ran to him, pushed him against a cinder-block wall, and patted him down.

"Hey! What's with you, man?"

Satisfied Rodriguez hadn't carried a weapon, Gardner released him. "Why in there so long?"

"Not that it's any of your business, but I've had a stomach flu for two days. I—" Rodriguez stopped as his eyes moved to the throng silently pressed against the windows. "What happened?"

"Carerra was bumped. That's him on the track."

Rodriguez shook his head. He removed his cap and bowed his head. "May God be a fair judge."

Medics from the ambulance that trails the field in every race sprinted onto the track. Gardner held his breath, along with over 140,000 spectators in the stands. Some thirty or forty feet from the kitchen windows, the track doctor joined the ambulance attendants. He hovered over Carerra for a few moments, checking his vital signs. Track workers constructed an impromptu tent around the pair to keep media lenses away from the jockey whose formerly white silk pants resembled a candy cane with ribbons of red streaking down his leg.

Within a minute, the doctor walked out of the tent, looked down, and shook his head. A dull mumble hung in the air. The medics retrieved a stretcher and a blanket from the ambulance. After a few moments, they carried Carerra's body from the tent, covered from head to toe with the blanket.

Gardner swept through the kitchen, but Rodriguez had vanished.

The detective pushed through the crowd and arrived at the ambulance, only a hundred yards or so from the kitchen, and found Mason Randolph talking to the track doctor. A contingent of Louisville's finest kept the media at a respectful distance.

After catching Gardner in his peripheral vision, Randolph turned to him and said, "He thinks it's either an accident or a heart attack. But thank God Green Day's not hurt. He's Sunny Valley's stable mate. My three-year-old would be lost without him."

Ignoring his employer, Gardner pushed past the older man and confronted the doctor. "Look again. For a bullet hole."

"What?" questioned the doctor. "A horse trampled this man."

"Yes," Gardner said, "but a horse didn't cause his death. Look again."

"Do it, Doc," Randolph said with an authority few ever questioned.

The doctor reluctantly bent over Carerra's blood-soaked body. Half-heartedly checking the jockey's head and chest for trauma other than what he expected, he found it. "Well, paint me red and call me Susan. Looks like he's got a bullet wound in his chest." The doctor turned to Gardner. "How'd you know?"

But the detective was already sprinting toward the kitchen. He shouted over his shoulder to Randolph. "Have the gates locked down. Be on the lookout for Emilio Rodriguez. Hold him for questioning."

"The jockey?" Randolph questioned, but the detective had already rounded the corner.

Gardner pushed on the men's room door. Locked. He pounded repeatedly.

"Keep your pants on!" came the echoed reply from the lavatory's occupant. The man emerged, still zipping his fly. "All yours," he said.

Cantrell stood before him.

"Why aren't you watching Sunny Valley?" Gardner demanded.

"You kiddin'? Randolph just fired me. Said he felt like the danger had passed." He smirked. "Can't do much about a heart attack, but you still lost your man. I guess we'll be standing in the unemployment line together."

Gardner grabbed Cantrell by his Armani lapels and pulled him off the ground. "He didn't have a heart attack, you idiot!"

Cantrell looked around. "Witnesses."

"If I had time. . . ." Gardner threw the man hard against the wall then rushed past him and into the men's room. Cantrell scampered away. A groom tried an end run around Gardner, but a forearm to the chest kept him out of the rest room.

After locking the door from the inside, Gardner sifted through the garbage, searched the supply cabinet, looked in the commode tank, and pried open the towel dispenser. Nothing. He pushed down the toilet seat lid and sat down, throwing his head back in frustration.

As he looked upward, his eyes settled on the light fixture overhead. The far light didn't work. He stood on the toilet and reached his hand over the lip of the heavy plastic housing. A misaligned fluorescent tube. He pulled his hands through his hair. A fine white powder clung to his fingertips.

Drywall dust?

In the corner to the right of the light, a square panel had been cut in the ceiling. He grabbed a broom and poked on the panel. Stepping on top of a small wooden cabinet just underneath the attic access, he pushed the panel up and to the side. Lifting himself through the opening, Gardner climbed into the attic.

A Beretta with a detachable stock lay across two of the rafters. The silencer remained attached to the rifle's muzzle. Gardner leaned down and sniffed. Recently fired. A makeshift hole had been drilled into the wall facing the track—just enough to allow for the barrel and the gun sight.

A crowd formed around Rodriguez, who spat Spanish epithets at two security guards and Randolph, as Gardner approached Gate 5. Lieutenant Colonel Franks and a police sergeant followed closely behind Gardner. The uniformed officer wore plastic evidence gloves and carried the rifle, which had been hidden in the kitchen attic. Rodriguez stopped his tirade.

"Recognize this?" Gardner motioned toward the weapon.

The crowd gasped and backed up a step.

Rodriguez's shoulders slumped and he stared at the dirt.

Randolph's jaw twitched. "Why?" he asked the former jockey.

"Bad luck," Gardner replied, and Rodriguez nodded slowly. "Carerra ended Emilio's career. That bump at Belmont. Insiders suspected a fix." He turned to Rodriguez. "You knew the truth, didn't you?"

The former jockey looked absently up to the sky. "Carerra was my supplier until I came clean. I talked to him, tried to get him to do the same. He thought I'd expose him, so he ruined me." Clouds formed in his eyes. "Then *mi niña*, my Angelina, got sick. I couldn't work, and the doctors wanted so much money. She died in my arms."

"Tough luck," said Randolph without a shred of pity. "Why didn't he fire you when he discovered you working the backside?"

"He didn't know. I've been drifting from one track to another. Signed on here a few days ago and kept low. God will be his judge now."

"I think you already took that job," said Gardner.

"Can't you see?" With outstretched hands, Rodriguez took a step toward Gardner, but the police sergeant pushed him back. "I couldn't let him win. Not after my Angelina."

Gardner nodded. He understood the pain of defeat, harboring murderous thoughts toward another human being who had ruined his livelihood and his dreams. A fine line between thought and deed.

It was a line Gardner hoped, but couldn't promise, he would never cross.

Derby Punch

by Gwen Mayo

Derby Rotten Scoundrels Punch is a renamed, and slightly revised, version of an old family recipe. My great-grandmother Dovie Davis first ran a popular restaurant, and later, an old-fashioned boarding house in Grayson, Kentucky.

I am not sure how old the recipe for her Derby Punch is or if it originated with her or some other long-ago relative.

She made her punch by soaking fresh cherries in bourbon overnight, then draining the juice and baking the bourbon-soaked cherries into a wonderful cherry chocolate brownie pie.

It is a method my schedule rarely allows time to duplicate. I have found concentrated cherry juice to be an acceptable substitute, though I do occasionally mourn the absence of her brownie pie.

Derby Rotten Scoundrels Punch

1 quart iced tea
3 T. brown sugar
½ cup concentrated cherry juice
3 T. Rose's lime juice
1 pint bourbon
1½ quarts ginger ale
ice
thin slices of lime (optional)

Steep your favorite tea in hot water. Sweeten the tea with the brown sugar, chill for an hour, and then add cherry and lime juices and mix. Pour the mixture into a punch bowl, add the bourbon and ginger ale, and stir. Add ice and garnish with lime slices just before serving.

THE DERBY WEEK PUNCH

by Elizabeth L. Kutak

Elizabeth L. Kutak was born and bred in Louisville, Kentucky, with a family heritage in the Bluegrass Region beginning in 1800. During her childhood, her mother, Rosemary Kutak, published Darkness of Slumber *and* I Am the Cat. *A graduate of Columbia University, Elizabeth practiced social work in New York City for a while before boarding the Queen Elizabeth for a new life in London. There she worked in a teaching hospital, was editor of the London Symphony Orchestra Bulletin, and later tutored at Bedford College, University of London. Now retired, she has returned to Louisville and is taking up writing.*

Derby Punch
Start with a tornado,
stir in a search for a corporate CEO,
add a generous amount of three-year-old Thoroughbreds,
top it off with a pinch of human behavior.

Friday, April 26th, 1974, dawned sunny and a cool 50 degrees in New York City. Dr. Marc Castleman left his office on Long Island at 10:00 a.m., eagerly anticipating his visit to Louisville to attend the 100th running of the Kentucky Derby. His hosts would be Sallie and Henry Hart, a couple he had befriended when he and Henry's father served on the staff of Oaklawn Psychiatric Hospital in Louisville.

As his plane ascended over Long Island and circled the glistening harbor, Marc thought that the New York skyline was one of the man-made wonders of the world. He could never get enough of the view: the Statue of Liberty rising above the sea, the bridges over the East River, and the skyscrapers reaching toward heaven in the commercial capital of the world.

As the plane turned west, Marc noticed the middle-aged brunette sitting next to him. A worried expression creased her attractive face.

"Is something wrong?" he asked.

"I'm worried." She gave him a tight smile. "I'm on my way to visit my daughter and grandchildren in Louisville. A tornado came through their neighborhood on April 3rd and left their house in ruins. My name's Jenny Smith, by the way."

"Marc Castleman. Some friends have invited me for Derby. The tornado didn't damage their house, but the old trees around it are unstable. The tornado was a shock for everyone."

She nodded. "Especially the children. My grandchildren are three and five, and they just can't understand what happened."

"Some of my most serious cases have been treating people following traumatic loss."

"Are you a therapist?"

"Psychiatrist."

They chatted about his background in private practice and as a staff psychiatrist stationed at an Army Air Force Hospital on Long Island after the war. By the time they had moved on to his interest in horse racing, the plane had come out of the clouds and the Ohio River was coming into view.

Turning his attention back to the window, Marc noticed the trees were more full of leaves this far south. Downtown Louisville looked about the same as it had ten years earlier on his last visit. The plane touched down, and as it taxied to the gate, the stewardess announced the day was sunny and 75 degrees.

Marc entered the baggage claim area and saw his dear friend Sallie eagerly looking for him. She wore an attractive navy blue pantsuit that complemented her glowing blonde hair. Her face looked strained, but when she noticed him, her eyes lit up and she pushed through the crowd.

After they were settled in Sallie's blue Buick, she offered her condolences on the death of his wife, Mary, in January.

Marc squeezed her hand. "I'm grateful for your invitation. I needed to get away, and this gave me something to look forward to—an exciting race plus your famous grits, country ham, and biscuits. It's been a long time since I've had bourbon balls."

Sallie started to nod, then surprised Marc by bursting into tears.

He held her in his arms until she cried herself out. Finally, he whispered, "What's wrong?"

"The next ten days will be the most important days in Henry's career—and his life. When you still lived in Louisville, you must have met Henry's boss, Ed Everett."

"Yes, I remember him. The founder and CEO of Dixie Filter."

"Well, Ed is retiring, and Henry wants his job."

Marc nodded. "Henry waxes lyrical about only two passions—you and Dixie Filter."

Sallie's face clouded over. "Henry's passion for Dixie Filter left his love for me behind a long time ago."

"Sallie, I'm sure Henry loves you."

She shook her head firmly. "Ever since I had that miscarriage and learned I couldn't have children, things have gone from bad to worse. Henry refuses to support me in adopting a baby. He's convinced that only his flesh and blood should be his children."

"Perhaps you two should consider some marital counseling."

"Henry would never agree, especially now that this promotion has come up. He's changed from being the sweet and sensitive man I married to an overly ambitious, self-centered corporate climber who refuses to even listen."

Marc shook his head, remembering happier times. "I'm so sorry, Sallie."

She dabbed her eyes with a handkerchief and started the car. As they merged into the traffic on the Watterson Expressway, she said, "At least you're here. Your presence will help me get through this week. Tonight we're giving a dinner party for the executive board of Dixie Filter and some other important guests. After I ordered our menu from Burgers last week, Henry overruled me and arranged for the Pendennis Club to cater our dinner. He wants to make the best possible impression."

They reached Brownsboro Road, and Marc was shocked by the destruction still evident three weeks after the tornado. Trees were down, roofs torn off, and houses blown from their foundations. Even Zachary Taylor National Cemetery had huge, century-old trees lying on the ground with their roots exposed.

Sallie turned north and they soon arrived at the Hart home. The 19th-century red brick house still stood proudly, but some of its trees were down, too. One big old oak leaned precariously toward the side of the house.

"The tree removal people came shortly after the tornado struck to clean up the worse of the mess," Sallie explained to Marc as they walked up the sidewalk. "They have an appointment to come back at the end of May and take out the oak tree. I'll hate to see it go. I feel like everything is falling apart."

Marc smiled as he entered the familiar central hall with a curved staircase going up the left side and doors opening on the right into the living room. Sallie's soft pale green walls gave elegance to the gold curtains in the living room. French doors opened into the dining room at the back of the house, which was full of activity. Elsie from the Pendennis Club was preparing the dinner, and Mike, the bartender and waiter, helped her. Sallie showed Marc to his room in the carriage house, and he tried to relax until it was time for tea.

At precisely four o'clock, Sallie served tea in the spacious screened porch at the back of the house. Red and yellow tulips were coming into bloom, and dogwoods were still in flower. Marc hoped he would get to see the lilacs bloom during his visit. The balmy stir of the wind was in stark contrast to the cold north wind that prevailed in New York City, and the household seemed more peaceful than Sallie had described. He hoped things were not as bad as she feared.

But when Henry came home that evening, Marc was startled to observe how much his friend had aged since his last visit. Henry's receding pale brown hairline had expanded, and his forehead contained many worry lines.

Henry shook Marc's hand and said, "Welcome back to Kentucky, old man. You've come at an auspicious time. I'm aiming to be appointed CEO of Dixie Filter, and tonight's dinner party kicks off my campaign."

The entrance of the first dinner guests made further conversation impossible. Charlie and Missy Ball arrived a little early so they could visit with Marc and the Harts. The Balls were well suited to each other. Charlie, with his sparkling brown eyes, was good-natured but impatient. Missy was a redhead with just enough temper to keep her husband's exuberance under control.

Charlie and Henry were the best of friends and the worst of enemies. They competed against each other in golf and tennis, and now they wanted the same job. Like Henry, Charlie was also a mechanical engineer. He worked at a competing company but had Dixie Filter in his line of sight.

Greeting Marc with an affectionate slap on the back, Charlie said, "You lucky New Yorker, you got to attend the Belmont Stakes last June when Secretariat won by thirty-one lengths in world-record time."

"One of the privileges of living in the East," Marc replied.

Missy said, "We gave a TV party last May to watch the Preakness in Baltimore. It was thrilling to have a Triple Crown winner after twenty-five years."

The next guests to arrive were the chairman of the board of Dixie Filter, Andrew Chism, and his wife, Helen. They brought an out-of-town applicant for the CEO position with them, Jerry Glass.

Mike took drink orders from the guests as Elsie passed a tray of canapés. Henry welcomed Jerry and asked about his background and interest in Dixie Filter.

"I'm a graduate of City College of New York," answered the tall young man with bright blue eyes and a commanding presence. "And I have an MBA from Harvard. My goal is to run a large company away from the Eastern seaboard."

"What engineering experience do you have?" Henry asked.

"I'm a business manager in a wholesale company in Manhattan, and, with my MBA, I have the skills to manage any business. One of my professors at Harvard used to say, 'You don't have to be a physician to run a hospital.'"

Knowing Henry's philosophy of business management, Marc wasn't surprised to see his friend's cheeks turning red.

Henry said, "A company as complex as Dixie Filter requires an engineering graduate at the helm."

"That's one of those old-fashioned ideas I mean to change," Jerry shot back.

Trying to defuse some of the tension, Marc asked, "What draws you to Louisville, Jerry?"

"From what I've read about Dixie Filter, it has the potential to become much larger. Perhaps even a Fortune 500 company."

"You'll find that Louisville has a good business climate," Helen added. She sparkled in her emerald green silk dress with gold earrings that complemented her upswept black hair and dancing blue eyes. "We have an active Chamber of Commerce and national Fortune 500 companies such as General Electric, Philip Morris, and Seagram's."

Her husband nodded his silver-haired head judiciously, watching all three candidates with keen eyes.

With Marc's help, Sallie managed to turn the conversation to horse racing. Jerry admitted he had never been to a horse race, adding this was his first visit to Kentucky.

"Since this is Derby Week," Marc said, "you'll have plenty of opportunity to become acquainted with the sport during your visit. You might like to take a drive over toward Lexington—beautiful horse farms over in the Bluegrass. That's where I was born and bred."

Charlie laughed and said, "Unlike people, horses are 'bred and born' in the Bluegrass."

"I go to the meets at both Belmont and Aqueduct when time allows," Marc continued, "and I'm really looking forward to opening day at Churchill Downs tomorrow. I'll be glad to give you some tips on betting, Jerry."

The waiter appeared with a bourbon old-fashioned for Helen and a bourbon on the rocks for her husband.

Jerry seemed glad to get his martini. He turned to Andrew and asked, "What's your line of business?"

"I'm senior partner in the law firm of Brown, Boone and Bray."

His wife added, "It's one of the oldest law firms in Louisville—goes all the way back to 1866, just after the War Between the States. We're proud of our history here in Kentucky."

Jerry answered with a smirk, and Marc imagined how quickly this young Turk would root out what he considered backward ideas if he managed to get control of Dixie Filter.

The final dinner guests arrived, and an increasingly distraught Sallie introduced Walter Lindsay, president of a local bank and secretary-treasurer of Dixie Filter's Board, and his wife, Susan. Then she left to attend to some last-minute details of serving the dinner.

Marc found an excuse to follow Sallie and caught up with her in the hall. "How are you holding up, old friend?"

She was pale above her elegant, long, royal blue hostess skirt with a flowered blouse and dangling earrings. Her attire gave prominence to the stunning string of pearls around her neck, Henry's gift to her on their first anniversary. "Henry's about to blow up at Jerry. I can read the signs. I just can't stand this tension. Why can't he be happy with what we have instead of wanting more?"

Marc patted her hand and returned to the group, wondering what he could do to help the couple he'd always been so fond of. Soon, Sallie returned to settle everyone around the cherry table in the dining room.

Henry sat at the head of the table, while Sallie sat at the opposite end. Over the centerpiece of silver mint julep cups filled with red rose buds and white baby's breath, Henry and Sallie threw chilly glances at each other. The guests applying themselves to their first course of Kentucky limestone Bibb lettuce and shrimp cocktails didn't seem to notice.

As he munched on a shrimp, Marc cast around for a safe topic of conversation. "I'm shocked to see such destruction from the tornado. Did any of you have damage to your property?"

Everyone had a story to tell about where they were when it struck. Walter said, "My neighbor's ordeal had a happy ending for their ten-year-old daughter. Her pony was in the barn, which was blown down. The horse disappeared but came home four days later."

Missy said, "The Episcopal Bishop of Kentucky and his wife were out of town at the time. When they came home, their house was in ruins with the front door ajar and a book lying open on the threshold. Can anyone guess what book?"

"The Bible?" Marc suggested.

"Nope." Missy chuckled. "Nature outwitted mere humans. The book was *Gone With the Wind*!"

The main course arrived: baked country ham, corn pudding, fresh asparagus with hollandaise sauce, browned potatoes, and beaten biscuits.

"What wonderful ham, Sallie," Susan said. "Last Derby, my sister attended a party in Lexington. Before the guests arrived, the cook placed a newly baked country ham on the porch to cool. She returned to the kitchen to retrieve a second ham from the oven, and when she looked back at the porch, the ham had disappeared and she saw the dog tearing into it at the end of the porch!"

Marc glanced at his hostess and was relieved to see that she seemed to be relaxing.

"My parents gave a dinner party back when I was a child," Sallie said. "While everyone was having drinks in the living room, my father went to the bar to mix more martinis. When he came back, our large dog preceded him with the entire roast beef in his mouth!"

Changing the subject, Susan said, "Have you heard who's coming to the Derby this year? Princess Margaret and Lord Snowden. They're arriving the day before Derby and staying in Lexington with C V and Marylou Whitney."

"Oh, yes," Sallie said. "I heard the Whitneys are even bringing their New York chef down."

Missy said, "The Whitneys' menu couldn't taste any better than what we're eating tonight, Sallie. You've done a beautiful job."

Sallie started to thank her, but Henry interrupted. "Don't give Sallie the credit. The Pendennis Club cooked this meal. They cater the best food in Louisville."

To cover Sallie's crestfallen look, Marc quickly asked the table, "Who's the favorite to win the Derby?"

"I follow spring racing closely," Charlie responded, "and this year the field of three-year-olds is especially promising. Cannonade won the Kentucky Jockey Club Stakes at Churchill Downs last November as a two-year-old."

Henry, seeming blissfully unaware that his wife was near tears, added, "Few winners of the Kentucky Jockey Club Stakes go on to win the Derby, but Kentucky-bred Cannonade is in the running."

"I was at Keeneland yesterday," Andrew put in. "Had a talk with my old friend Seth Hancock. His horse, Judger, won the Blue Grass Stakes and will be running in the Derby. Woody Stephens from Midway, Kentucky, trains both horses. This Derby will really be something."

Everyone discussed a favorite horse while Mike cleared the table of the main course and brought in a fabulous looking chocolate bread pudding with warm bourbon sauce. After dessert, Sallie announced that coffee would be served in the living room.

As the group straggled through the hallway, Marc pressed a hand to Sallie's elbow. "Doing okay?" he whispered.

She turned toward him with a calm smile. "Yes, I'm better now."

In the living room, Mike offered brandy after serving coffee, then quickly left. The ladies took chairs around the window and continued to talk. The men settled in leather armchairs around the fireplace, eager to talk about Dixie Filter and its future.

"The business has come a long way since its founding," Andrew said. He gestured toward his host and added, "Over the last twenty years, Henry has set up plants in four Southern cities. In fact, we've grown so much, we had to move our headquarters from the suburbs to downtown Louisville."

Henry beamed and Jerry Glass glared at his rival.

"With the expansion of foreign markets," Walter added, "the future looks great for air filtration."

Andrew elaborated on that topic and ending by saying, "I have my eye on Dixie Filter opening a plant somewhere overseas."

"I'm your man for that," Henry said quickly. "I have firsthand experience running businesses in several countries."

Not to be outdone, Jerry said, "When I graduated from Harvard, I worked for a firm in Canada. Plenty of opportunity up there."

Henry glowered but remained silent. The ladies joined the group, and the conversation turned back to Derby activities.

After a few stories of past Derbys and great horses, Andrew responded to his wife's nod, and they stood up to thank their hosts for a special evening. "Since tomorrow is opening day of the spring meet at Churchill Downs," he said, "Helen and I want to have an early night so we can take in the first race."

The remaining guests soon left, and Henry suggested a nightcap in the library. Sallie pleaded a headache and went off to bed. Left alone with Henry, Marc hoped to have a frank talk about the state of his friends' marriage. But as Marc sipped his bourbon and Henry ranted at length about Jerry Glass's modern ideas, Marc realized that any such discussion would have to wait until Henry had calmed down.

Marc told his friend good-night and walked down to the carriage house. The wind murmured in the trees, and the leafy branches of the oak tree swayed gently over the west side of the house. He shared Sallie's concern about the safety of the tree and house.

Saturday dawned clear with the temperature in the low fifties. Marc, Henry and Sallie enjoyed a breakfast of grilled country ham, eggs, grits, and coffee before leaving. The men looked dapper in sport coats and trousers, while Sallie wore a smart jacket dress and flowered straw hat.

Henry drove his party to Churchill Downs in his big maroon Volvo. As the Twin Spires came into view, Marc's heart leapt in anticipation. After finally finding a place to park, the trio headed for the track, where they took the elevator to the 6th floor Clubhouse Skye Terrace.

They located their reserved Dixie Filter table by the finish line and accepted mint juleps from the waitress's tray. Andrew and Helen Chism looked elegant as usual; Missy and Charlie Ball were deciding which horses to bet on; and Jerry Glass was standing at the window admiring the track, field, and the backside barns as the first horses made their way to the paddock.

Marc tried to enjoy the racing, but the constant sniping of the three CEO candidates cast a pall over the entire day. Even at the luncheon buffet between races, Jerry seemed determined to make his mark. He bragged about winning a good return on a two-dollar bet and made sure that everyone knew this was an omen for him to be appointed CEO of Dixie Filter.

Henry muttered under his breath that if Jerry got the job he would kill him. Marc heard him and looked around quickly. As far as he could tell, no one else had picked up on the threat. Sallie sat at the other end of the table, picking at her food. She had a serene, detached air about her that Marc didn't like. He had seen that look in some of his patients.

The three friends returned home after the next-to-last race, and Sallie fixed Marc's favorite Kentucky food for supper. After a companionable meal, she said, "I know it's just past eight, but I'm exhausted after two days of entertaining. I'm going to leave you two to your nightcaps." As she left the room, she paused to brush Marc's shoulder with her hand. "I'm so glad you came down from New York. It's wonderful seeing you again. I hope you don't mind that I'm turning in early."

"We still have plenty of time to catch up. I'll see you in the morning."

Henry filled their glasses and reflected on the events of the previous two days and his future with Dixie Filter. "You know, Marc, my first and only boss is retiring, and my lifelong goal has been to take his place. I used to think I would be a shoo-in, but now I'm not so sure."

"Sounds like this is a real turning point for you."

Henry nodded. "It means everything to me. If I don't get the job, I'll have nothing to live for."

Swirling the bourbon in his glass, Marc replied, "Strong words, old man. What about Sallie?"

Henry shook his head. "My work is my life. She doesn't understand."

"From where I sit, it looks like she's helped you in every way a wife could."

Henry thought a long moment. "You're right. Sallie was a sweet kid who has grown into a sweet woman. She doesn't deserve what I've been dishing out."

"Will you talk to her? Try to work things out?"

Henry nodded. "I will. Tomorrow." He raised a weak smile. "You always did have a good effect on us, Marc."

"Glad to be of service," Marc replied lightly. He added more seriously, "And I don't want to hear any more talk about not wanting to live."

Henry chuckled and said, "Don't worry, you won't find me digging up any hemlock."

Marc returned his chuckle. "Don't suppose there's any of that around here."

"Actually, Sallie told me some hemlock is invading the asparagus garden. We can't even eat our own vegetables for fear of getting sick."

Marc frowned. "I'd get that rooted out right away."

Henry nodded. "I'll do it tomorrow. Right after I apologize to Sallie. If you'll excuse me, I think I'll go on up to bed now."

"Of course. Good-night, Henry."

Marc slept well and retrieved the Sunday morning *Courier-Journal* from the mailbox. The bold headline on the first page of the sports section read, Happy Trainer Stephens: 1-2 Derby Punch. A story on the Stepping Stone, one of the races they'd witnessed the previous day, followed.

Using his guest key to open the front door, Marc was greeted by utter silence. The kitchen was empty. He called the names of his hosts but got no reply. He hurried to the master bedroom. After receiving no answer to his frantic knocks, he opened the door only to find Sallie peacefully asleep.

He looked a little closer and noticed her lips were blue, her face translucent and relaxed. He sprang to the bedside to take her pulse. Nothing. As he sank to his knees, he noticed the empty bottle of Seconal on the bedside table. The box with her pearl necklace sat beside it and held down a handwritten note.

In shock, Marc read Sallie's last words: Henry—you have mistreated me for ten long years. I have nothing left to live for. I have waited until the right moment to wound you as much as I could—not by gunshot, but by ending your vainglorious career with the scandal of a wife's suicide.

Marc stared at Sallie's lifeless face in disbelief. "How could you?" he whispered. Then, with a wave of anger, he said, "Why couldn't I see what you were planning?"

Finally he realized that he must tell Henry. Where was he anyway? Marc stood and noticed a man's legs on the floor on the opposite side of the king-sized bed. Heart pounding, he ran to the body.

It was Henry, as still and lifeless as his wife.

Knowing it was useless, Marc knelt and pressed his fingers to Henry's wrist. Marc was no cardiologist, but he recognized massive heart failure when he saw it.

The Kentucky Oaks

by Tessue Herring Fields

The Kentucky Oaks, an important race for three-year-old female horses (fillies) run on the Friday before the Derby attracts an outstanding field. Many of the trainers and owners who have horses in the Derby also run horses in the Oaks. However, there is no rule to prohibit fillies from running in the Derby, and some try their luck "against the boys." Three fillies have won the Derby, most recently Winning Colors in 1988.

Oaks Day has traditionally been known as "Louisville's Day at the Races." With many out-of-town guests arriving later on Friday, area families with young children fill the infield, instead of the raucous college students who occupy it for Derby. The pricey box seats are a Friday-Saturday package, and sometimes their owners sell the Oaks tickets (under the table, since direct selling is frowned on by the Derby) or pass them to friends or family. So the Oaks becomes a hometown party, albeit one with over 100,000 guests each year.

Area public and private schools now dismiss for Oaks Day, a bow to the inevitable. So many teachers previously called in sick or took personal days that it became impossible to find enough substitutes.

In Louisville, it doesn't pay to go up against Derby weekend.

More Than Bourbon and Kentucky Fried Chicken

by Sandra Cerow Leonard

Sandra Cerow Leonard grew up in New England and lived in Southern California for almost thirty years before moving to Kentucky. Her first published short story, "River Bluff," appears in Derby Rotten Scoundrels. *Before retiring, she was an attorney and a public administrator. She now lives near Louisville with her husband, son, granddaughter Megan, a dog, three cats, and a feline marmalade, Guy, who knows he's really human.*

Click, tap. As her sleek Italian shoes crossed the black and white marble tiles of the Glendenning Club's entrance hall, Delia Winterbourne flashed a smile as bright as the sparkle from crystal chandeliers crowning the third-floor ballroom. She hugged the woman who bustled through the massive mahogany door as they air-kissed each other's rouged and wrinkled cheeks. The security system buzzed as the door locked again.

"Lissie, I'm glad you got back from New York," she said in her light, Southern lilt.

"I'm always ready to help my best friend, specially when it involves royalty," Lissie Strather said in her gentle trill.

Delia grinned and pushed the button to call the elevator. "Do you realize we've been having lunch here since our debutante days, about fifty years ago?"

"True, and I swear I've gained twenty pounds since Chef Catalanio started managing the kitchens." Lissie patted her ample hips.

The Glendenning Club, a purely social organization founded in the late 1800s, was a haven for the genteel in Louisville. The Strather and Winterbourne families were founding members, and Delia and Lissie had been introduced to Society at an annual Bachelor's Ball, amid white ties, tails, and yards of organdy and lace.

The hostess seated them at their usual table near the white marble fireplace in the soft light from the Palladian windows swathed in gold velvet. After placing their orders—a Hot Brown sandwich for Lissie and snow crab croquettes for Delia—they got down to planning the Kentucky Oaks brunch to introduce visiting English royalty to the Winterbournes' closest friends.

"Lissie, I want the brunch to shine as an example of Kentucky food and hospitality. The brunch'll be where our friends first meet the Barton-Smedleys. I've booked the private room nearest to the kitchen. Things have to move along because the chartered limos will be here promptly to get us to the first race."

Lissie nodded her flaming red curls in approval. The room Delia had selected was magnificent. Murals on the walls, painted by a famous French artist more than seventy years earlier, depicted Revolutionary War engagements. A crystal chandelier glowed over lovingly polished wood in the backs and arms of Biedermeier chairs. Tables would be set with Limoges china rimmed in a gold laurel pattern echoing the sterling silver service. Neither Delia nor Lissie saw any irony in the subject matter of the murals and their English guests of honor.

Delicately cutting into turkey and bacon covered by a cheese-pimiento-and-heavy-cream sauce, Lissie sighed. "Chef Catalanio says he only makes these sandwiches because they were created in 1926 at Louisville's Brown Hotel, but his sauce is so light, I ignore people calling them 'cholesterol in a dish.'" She glanced at Delia. "Are you going to serve Hot Browns at the brunch?"

"I'm thinking about it, maybe appetizer sized. I'm probably starting with mint juleps made with Kentucky bourbon and fresh mint, served iced in the Club's sterling julep cups. If I can get the chef to cooperate, I'd like Benedictine canapés, country ham, stew greens, Kentucky fried chicken, fried green tomatoes, cheddar cheese grits, bourbon and fresh mint sorbets, and Derby-Pie. What do you think?"

Lissie sighed again, more audibly. "That's my idea of a meal! But I see why you need my help. You want me to tackle Catalanio because Arthur is president of the Club this year. Right?"

"Well, Catalanio and his three sous chefs take themselves very seriously and are notoriously difficult. They've all graduated from Johnson & Wales within the last six years, and, as they've said before, Kentucky cookin' is definitely not their idea of haute cuisine."

Lissie pulled out the steno pad and pen she always carried in her purse and wrote down the menu. "Okay, I'll talk to the chef, but you've got to handle the pastry chef, Mignon. I can't stand her. When Catalanio brought all three with him from that fancy New York restaurant, he gave each one a big raise. But I'm told she's trying to get rid of him and take over the managing position.

"She calls herself an artist, but I can't see what's wrong with a peach cobbler topped with a large scoop of Graeter's ice cream. Everything she does is a foot tall, brittle, and impossible for me to eat without getting pieces all over my bosom." Lissie gestured toward the ample area of concern. "I always seem to be wearing a white silk blouse when she does something in chocolate."

"She's also supposed to be a man hunter." Delia chuckled.

The old friends were having a late lunch, so the room was almost empty when they finished the last of their sweetened ice tea. Folding her linen napkin and placing it beside her plate, Lissie visibly girded her loins as she headed through the swinging double doors to the main kitchen. Delia made for the much smaller pastry kitchen to the right.

"You want me to what?" Chef Catalanio exploded. "Serve Kentucky country food to royalty?" His courtly but often overblown manners gone, he slammed his twelve-inch knife into a cutting board on the table next to Lissie.

She jumped, her knees shook. She knew he had lost control. No professionally trained chef would treat his knives that brutally. Was something else agitating him, she wondered. The knife dropped to the floor.

"Who are the English?" he asked.

"Barton-Smedley," Lissie said, furious with herself because her voice quivered. But she drew herself up to her full five feet and, in clear command, said, "If you've forgotten, my husband is president of the Club this year. You won't get the convection oven you put in your next budget if I make a formal complaint to the board. I'd have to tell them that you're not cooperating with one of our oldest Club families, the Winterbournes."

He wrote out the selected menu with bad grace and then meekly promised to buy all of the ingredients in Kentucky. Lissie didn't think it wise to rub salt in his wounds by complimenting him on the Hot Brown sandwich.

Stirring a smooth brown concoction in the top of a double boiler, Mignon bent over to sniff. The smell of warm chocolate scented the room.

Delia's bosom wasn't as large as Lissie's, so she didn't have trouble eating Mignon's creations. She remembered last Easter when Mignon made exquisite lacy individual chocolate baskets and piled them with luscious French-vanilla-cream-filled chocolate eggs.

"Mignon, I want to talk to you about a brunch I'm planning."

The pastry chef looked up, her handsome features framed in a perpetual sneer. She was a good-looking woman, Delia thought, maybe thirty-five.

Delia laid out her brunch plans concluding with, "I'd like you to make Derby-Pie."

"No way. The name and recipe of that chocolate-and-walnut pie are trademarks of Kern's Kitchen. I don't want to get in any trouble."

"What do you suggest for a Southern dessert?" Delia asked diplomatically.

Mignon agreed to create a confection she quickly named "Tart avec la Tour de Chocolat." It was to be a bourbon, walnut, chocolate pie topped with a superstructure of lacy semi-sweet chocolate. It would probably be a foot tall and brittle, and Delia would need to warn Lissie not to wear a white silk blouse.

After a short weekend in New York City, Henry and Hilda Barton-Smedley arrived, ready for Kentucky hospitality. They both were reputed to be relatives of Queen Elizabeth, although no one was sure of the lineage. George Winterbourne had mistaken Henry, who was always clad in a Savile Row tailored suit and tie, for an usher at the Victoria and Albert Museum on his latest trip to London. Despite this inauspicious beginning, the two had become friends, resulting in the invitation to visit for the Derby festivities.

Thunder Over Louisville, the largest display of fireworks and music in the United States, was loud, colorful, and glorious. All of the other events leading up to the Derby went according to plans. They had breakfast on a Lexington Thoroughbred horse farm, went to a fancy dress gala under florally decorated tents packed with entertainment and political superstars, saw the steamboat race from the bank of the Ohio River, and spent several days at Churchill Downs for the opening week of spring racing season. The Barton-Smedleys were ready for a smaller, quieter social activity, and both looked forward to the brunch and Oaks Day at the races. Henry and Hilda had won a fair number of United States dollars so far with lucky bets.

Friday dawned dark and stormy. Regularly scheduled television programing was suspended. Broadcasts from local channels consisted of weather people pointing to spinning yellow spirals on maps as they issued dire warnings to the Kentuckiana viewing area.

"Where is Bullitt County?" Henry asked, hurrying into the kitchen. "Hilda and I've been watching the telly. Someone named Jay keeps saying the weather is spawning tornados. We don't have them, you know, in our part of England," he said wistfully.

"Bullitt County is south of Louisville," Delia replied. "The storms are going east, so we're probably all right, but we need to keep checking the warnings."

Telephone calls came into the Winterbournes' home from Lexington, Versailles, Frankfort, and Indianapolis. Friends said regretfully, "We're sorry to miss brunch, but it isn't safe to travel." No question about it, for some of them, it wasn't! Brunch was down to eighteen.

With a sense of impending doom, Delia called the Glendenning Club kitchen. "Chef Catalanio," she said, "because of the tornados, we've had cancellations for today's brunch."

"What tournedos? We're not having beef tournedos today," he boomed. "I'm trying to make a delicate sauce, and you're bothering me."

Good heavens, Delia thought, *how typical of the perfectionist that he has no idea the weather outside his kitchen is killing people.* She managed to make him understand the situation.

Like shafts of light shining through nimbus clouds created by Baroque religious painters, the sun came out in blazing, innocent glory. The brunch would be held as scheduled, just with fewer guests.

As the invited arrived, the beautiful Georgian building was resplendent in gleaming rain drops that gave a radiant burnish to the old stone-and-red-brick structure. Delia and George greeted guests and introduced them to the Barton-Smedleys. Hilda looked particularly smart with a modest peach hat on her head. Mint juleps in frosted silver cups flowed freely.

The Sedgwicks—two elderly unmarried sisters, a brother leaning on his cane, and a married sister with her even older husband—hadn't missed an Oaks in more than fifty years. Like most native Louisvillians, they preferred the day to the Derby, which attracts hoi polloi from all over the world.

"I hope you enjoy the Oaks today," said Lissie.

"Oh, I will," the gentleman with the cane said. "The Derby can be so tatty."

"Why, last year there was even someone from Hollywood," the married sister lisped through her false teeth in a horrified tone to Lissie. "She bared her enormous plastic breasts at a charity ball!" she added before hobbling with her siblings toward the bourbon.

Lissie looked down at her capacious shelf, prudently clad in brown silk, and cringed.

Hal Grantham had his political ambitions, and he and his wife worked the room, making sure they spoke to everyone. Lissie had told Delia cattily when the couple wed six years earlier, "Hal married Emma for her money. He wants to make sure he'll always have funds for his political campaigns."

But whatever the initial reason for the marriage, Emma and Hal had become an effective team. They traveled a lot; his international law practice required it, and she loved the jet-set life. For convenience, they maintained a pied-à-terre in New York City.

They knew being seen at a Club function hosted by Delia would enhance Hal's chances of getting his party's nomination for an East End Metro Council seat in the upcoming election. Since Amanda Plumly, one of Delia's best friends, had been a social columnist for decades, a feature article and pictures were bound to be in the newspaper.

The Blooms and the Wrights arrived together.

"Delia, how brave of you to have brunch after the awful weather," said Elgin Bloom. "Louisville seems okay, but our poor neighbors will be cleaning up for months."

The others nodded soberly.

The door slammed open and an apparition in pink bustled in. Amanda Plumly had arrived. Her lips were slashes of hastily applied shocking pink that matched her enormous hat, more askew than fashion dictated. She was always late but never missed a good party.

"Amanda, I'm so glad you're here." Delia led her to the table bearing Amanda's place card. "I'm just going to ask them to serve."

The columnist plumped her purse under her chair and headed for the mint julep table.

Delia made her way through the swinging doors to check with the chef before the entrée was served. Silence filled the usually tumultuous kitchen as Catalanio arranged plates aesthetically, while two of the sous chefs were working near the bread and salad cutting boards. All stood with rigid backs.

The sous chef serving salads slammed his serving spoon against the side of the stainless steel bowl harder than seemed necessary. *Trying to keep this brunch on track is one disaster after another*, Delia thought. *If everyone doesn't start working as a team, we'll never finish in time to get the guests to the limos.*

"Chef Catalanio, thank you and your sous chefs for everything you've prepared for my guests," she said in a Southern accent only slightly more musical than usual. "The Benedictine was wonderful, and I know the rest of the meal will make me proud. Please, let me introduce all of you to my guests? The royal couple particularly want to meet you."

Three backs released tension but remained straight, now with pride.

"Most hosts don't know the work we do to make their parties successful," said the chef in his Tuscan accent as he pushed his toque blanche back into position on his head.

The others agreed.

Mignon entered carrying some of her pastry tools. Delia told her about the introductions and led the four of them down the hall to the Mural Room.

The guests, seated in anticipation of the entrée, looked up as Delia made pretty speeches thanking each chef, the longest for Catalanio. She used the word *team* four times and it seemed to work. The chefs went back to the kitchen with their usual teasing comradery.

Brunch *was* wonderful. The service was prompt and smooth. Crystal, silver and conversation sparkled. Delia spoke to everyone at each table and returned to her own seat. Hilda and Lissie, seated at her table, were regaling their husbands and George with tales of Derby hat shopping. Delia joined in the laughter, and stories swirled around as she relaxed.

Serenity did not last long. *Dessert should have been served by now,* Delia thought as she excused herself and, once again, made her way to the pastry kitchen. It was empty. On the work table, the desserts were works of art, each a gossamer chocolate rose blooming from a leaf-shaped pastry filled with a puddle of gleaming walnut, chocolate, and bourbon. The sensuous odor of bourbon and semi-sweet chocolate enveloped the room.

As she moved to the back of the table to admire them from another angle, something snagged her foot. She grabbed the sink to keep from falling. Mignon lay face up on the floor, a tiny red stain spreading slowly around the twelve-inch knife protruding from her left side. Ignoring everything she learned from the mystery novels she loved to read, Delia reached down. Mignon's neck was warm, but there was no pulse. Delia tried her wrist. No pulse. Mignon was dead!

Catalanio entered the room. Self-absorbed as usual, he saw the desserts on the table and said, "I'll have Edmund serve those immediately," then abruptly turned back into the main kitchen.

Delia groaned. Her party was doomed! She felt guilty for the selfish thoughts. But surely Mignon's death had nothing to do with her guests. If she could get the desserts served, she could get the guests into the limos and off to the races. But those same mystery novels told her that her first duty was to notify the police. She couldn't make up her mind; hospitality warred with responsibility.

Edmund, the salad chef with the attitude problem, looked at Delia once, rather furtively she thought, as he loaded desserts on a serving cart. In less than five minutes, he left the room and never went behind the table where Delia remained standing.

She came out of her stupor and returned to her seat in the Mural Room. George gave her an inquisitive look.

"Can't tell you now," she whispered as she reached down to take her cell phone out of her purse. She walked into the hall and dialed 911.

A few minutes later, two police officers arrived. The Club manager, Charles, and his administrative assistant, Alice, happened to be in the entrance hall checking a notice board.

"One of your guests called 911," an officer said. "Would you please show us the body in the kitchen?"

"A body?" Charles asked in obvious confusion. Such things did not happen at the Glendenning Club. Not since 1943 when old Byron Frobisher died of a heart attack while entertaining Candy LaTrice, an exotic dancer, in one of the private dining rooms.

Delia, not thinking clearly, had returned to her guests after making the 911 call, so the employees had no idea what had happened. Charles took the officers to the pastry kitchen, where they secured the crime scene, called head-quarters, and explained the situation to the Homicide Unit.

"What do you mean, Mignon's dead?" said Catalanio with only slightly less volume than his normal bellow. "She hasn't finished cleaning up yet."

The officers asked the chef, Edmund, and the other sous chef to remain in the main kitchen.

"No, Mr. Sedgwick," said an officer in answer to a question asked through a large cloud of bourbon fumes, "you may not go downstairs to board the limousines."

The investigation began in earnest when Lieutenant Patrick O'Brien arrived with a policewoman named Megan Blackwell, who turned out to be his second in command, and the crime-scene technicians. After a few preliminary questions by the professionals, it became apparent that Delia was in the pastry kitchen when the murder was committed or just afterwards.

"Are there a couple of rooms in the Club we can use for interviews?" asked O'Brien.

Charles showed the lieutenant to the Persian Room, a much smaller room close to the Mural Room, and the same one Byron Frobisher had made infamous years earlier. Megan Blackwell was shown to another room across the hall.

For what seemed like hours, O'Brien carefully took Delia through her personal contacts with Mignon, plans for the brunch, her guests, and the events of the day. They could hear the door to the room across the hall open and close as people came and went. Because her interview was so long and detailed, Delia became afraid she was the primary suspect.

"Did you know your husband, George, was instrumental in getting Catalanio and the sous chefs hired by the Club?" Without waiting for an answer, O'Brien went on, "I've been told Catalanio refused to move to Louisville without his three helpers." He finally cut to what he thought was the heart of the matter. "Mignon was a good-looking woman. I'm told she liked men. All men."

Two can play this game, Delia thought. "Last year, George and I ate at the New York restaurant where they worked. We were impressed with their skills. In fact, I recommended the four of them to the hiring committee, too."

Both became weary. Delia had clearly had an opportunity to kill Mignon. A preliminary examination at the scene of the crime indicated the murder occurred at or close to the time Delia entered the pastry room. Since it was to the side of the main kitchen with a separate door to the hall, unless someone was coming or going from the main room, it could be entered unseen.

"I don't remember seeing anyone in the hall," Delia said. "But I wasn't paying attention. I just wanted to see what was holding the desserts up."

Someone could easily pick up a sharp knife. During food preparation knives were all over both kitchens on cutting boards, tables, even serving stations in the hallway. After being cleaned they were stored on magnetic holders on the kitchen walls.

Motive was the problem. There wasn't any reason for her to kill Mignon. In fact, as Delia pointed out more than once, the murder had ruined a party she had worked hard to make special and was a dreadful example of Southern hospitality for her royal guests. If she was going to kill Mignon, she'd have done it after the guests were safely in the limos on their way to the races.

O'Brien finally let her go back to the Mural Room. George, at the buffet pouring coffee, gave her a sad smile. He was acting like a gracious host to the Barton-Smedleys on either side of him. Coffee and several open bourbon bottles sat on another table. No mint juleps; this was unadulterated stuff.

Lissie ran up and gave her a hug. Despite the disaster, she'd obviously enjoyed dessert. The evidence was clear. Her brown blouse was not as dark as the semi-sweet chocolate. "How're you doing, honey? You were with the lieutenant for a long time."

"I'm tired, Lissie."

"When you throw a party, you throw a party. Some of the guests thought this was some kind of mystery game you'd arranged for us. It took a while for the truth to penetrate." Lissie moved closer. "Most of us have been interviewed by the police. But, at the rate they're going, it looks like it'll be another hour before they finish. The policewoman talked to me first. I went over our brunch planning, what happened earlier today, and why I didn't like Mignon."

"How'd they know that?" asked Delia.

"I don't know. Maybe someone overheard me the other day at lunch. That she was egotistical, aggressive, and a pain in the tush didn't seem enough for them." She leaned in even closer. "The police told us not to talk to anyone, and most of us were pretty good. But Amanda went behind that screen in front of the housekeeping table a while ago and whipped out her cell phone. I just know she was calling her newspaper!"

Delia moaned as they walked to the far corner of the room and sat down. She took off her Italian pumps and wiggled her toes. "Lissie, at first I thought a guest couldn't be the murderer but, now I just don't know. It has to be someone who was in the Club. The front door locks automatically and is only opened from the outside by the parking attendant, who has a special button in his little building."

Lissie frowned, and Delia went on. "Not many people were here this morning—only Charles and Alice, the three servers who helped us earlier, and the chefs. The lunch crowd hadn't really come in yet."

"But, Delia, the servers had been sent three floors down to the basement rathskeller just after our entree. Remember? They were supposed to get ready for a special afternoon party. The chefs were to serve the dessert."

"You're right, Lissie. I'm afraid it has to be one of our guests or chefs. It could have been Charles or Alice, but their surprise at the police showing up seemed genuine. Or so they seem to have convinced the lieutenant. His questions to me sounded like he was excluding them."

"What do you think we should do, Delia?" Her eyes were bright as her red curls, and her pert nose quivered. She looked like a chubby terrier happily about to rout a mole out of a flower bed.

"I think we need to figure out who killed Mignon."

Just what Lissie wanted to hear as she took the steno pad and pen from her purse. Watson was ready for the wisdom of Sherlock. "I'll start by listing all of the guests and the three remaining chefs. Excluding you and me, there are nineteen suspects. Catalanio and the two sous chefs, the five Sedgwicks, Emma and Hal Grantham, the Blooms, the Wrights, Amanda Plumly, Henry and Hilda Barton-Smedley, George, and Arthur." She bit the end of her pen.

"How long have you been married, Lissie?"

"Forty-three years. What's that got to do with this?"

"We have an advantage over the police because we know the suspects. Could Arthur have murdered Mignon?"

"I see your point. Arthur is one of the sweetest people I know. More important, he was next to me the entire brunch, including when you came back from the kitchen looking like a ghost was on your tail."

"Cross off Arthur and George," Delia said.

"You're right, Delia. George was with Arthur and me. Down to seventeen. You know, the Barton-Smedleys were part of our group all the time, too. Fifteen! People were moving around talking, but it was too early for the group to go to the rest rooms. They'd have gone just before getting on the limos. Our table, like one or two others, stayed put. But anyone who was moving around could probably have gone to the pastry kitchen unnoticed."

Delia thought out loud. "Mignon was killed by the murderer plunging a twelve-inch knife into her chest, which takes a certain amount of strength. I think we can eliminate the Sedgwicks, Lissie. They are all old and very frail. If she'd been beaten a few times with a cane, maybe, but not stabbed to death in the chest with that knife."

Lissie drew a line through five names. "Down to ten."

"I wonder if this has anything to do with New York?" Delia mused. "She knew the other chefs in culinary school and New York City, but I wonder if she met any of today's guests up there."

"Why'd you say that, Delia?"

"Because nothing seems to have happened since the four of them came to Louisville. They're hard to deal with, even arrogant, but they have done their jobs superbly. If anything had been going on here, Arthur or George would have heard about it and they'd have told us."

"That makes sense. What do we know about the rest?"

"We know the Granthams have an apartment there."

Conversation in the room stopped as Lieutenant O'Brien entered. "We're sorry to keep you, but it's necessary. You should be able to leave in about half an hour. Thanks for your cooperation." He turned and quickly left before they could pelt him with questions or complaints.

"Delia, we don't have much time. What about the Wrights and the Blooms?"

"I don't know anything incriminating about them. They don't do much traveling anymore. Let's ask them when they last went to New York. We know Mignon was in New York less than six years. And, Lissie, let's try to be subtle!"

"Delia, I'm always subtle. It's my Southern charm!"

They went to the coffee pot and poured steaming cups. Lissie used three lumps of sugar and enough cream to make a latte. Delia left hers black. The Barton-Smedleys stood near the buffet drinking tea George had gotten for them. They looked exhausted. Delia was sure they were thinking that New York would be restful after Kentucky. She knew that like her, Hilda was an Agatha Christie fan and had read all of Christie's eighty-some books. But, as Hilda had whispered to her earlier, this was their first real murder and they were not Miss Marple or Hercule Poirot.

Delia and Lissie approached the Wrights and Blooms together near the door. Both couples looked poised to run as soon as they were released by the police. Lissie got right to the point with all subtlety of a sledgehammer. "The pastry chef was from New York. Do y'all ever go up there?"

"We haven't been anywhere near the Northeast in the last ten years," Elgin Bloom said. "Too hectic and congested!" The others nodded in agreement.

As Lissie was wielding her verbal cudgel, Delia was down to six suspects. She thought about them and rejected Amanda Plumly, a woman she'd known for years. Amanda could barely dress herself and was never on time, but could she write! It was her one overwhelming skill. She was invited to every party in town and rarely left Louisville. She just did not make sense as the murderer. That left five.

Delia entered the Persian Room, Lissie by her side with pad and pen. The lieutenant listened politely as they went through their deductions. He was a native Louisvillian, and rudeness was as foreign to him as it was common to people raised in some other parts of the country.

When they finished he said, "The three chefs were together all the time. Catalanio saw Edmund trying to sneak out for a smoke, grabbed his coat, and dragged him back into the kitchen. Since that was the second time today Edmund'd tried to sneak out, Catalanio was furious. He doesn't allow smoking near his kitchens. Says you can smell it in the food."

Lissie scratched wide lines through the chefs' names. Two names remained. The Granthams.

The Lieutenant questioned Emma Grantham. Blackwell interrogated Hal. Hal, a coward, knew he hadn't committed the murder, and he had an alibi because he had never left the Mural Room, so with little prompting he blurted out he was having an affair with Mignon. He was terrified the police would find out if they questioned his landlady in New York.

The policewoman went to the Persian Room and motioned O'Brien out. "Hal Grantham says he had an affair with Mignon and used the Grantham New York apartment."

"You don't say. Let's see what his wife knew."

When Emma was confronted with Hal's confession of the affair, she became enraged and then broke down. "That sniveling weasel. I've dedicated my life to getting that stupid man an important political position. He can't keep his stupid mouth shut."

Then the lieutenant listened to the old, old story: the defeat of common sense at the hands of blind ambition.

"Mignon knew I had the money," Emma said, "so she's been blackmailing me. This morning she telephoned and demanded a huge payment because some restaurant she wanted to buy came on the market. If I didn't pay by Saturday, she'd leak the affair to the press. It would never end."

Kentucky, unlike other parts of the United States, likes its politicians without certain moral deficiencies. In Kentucky, you can lie to the populace and the law, and you can cheat and steal from the taxpayers, but you should never get caught with your pants down, being unfaithful to your wife. The downfall of a Kentucky governor was fresh in everyone's mind.

To make up for Friday's storms, Derby day was brilliantly clear. White and pink dogwoods were in full bloom, and violets made lush, fragrant carpets as the Winterbournes drove the Barton-Smedleys to Churchill Downs. Dew nestled like glowing spangles on red tulip petals in the circular entry to the track. Hilda's hat with forget-me-nots and blue satin ribbons was in the height of Derby fashion, and she seemed to enjoy wearing something so different from her reserved attire.

Hilda and Henry analyzed the field for the tenth race. "Henry, bet this long shot to win," Hilda commanded, pointing to the name of a chestnut filly. He did, and, to the thundering roar of the crowd, Filet Mignon won by a nose, triggering the largest winning payout in Kentucky Derby history.

At the airport the next day, Henry leaned over and, with total lack of British reserve, kissed Delia. "You certainly gave us a time we'll always remember." With a twinkle in his eye, he added, "There's more to Southern hospitality than bourbon and Kentucky fried chicken!"

Benedictine —Kentucky's Green Sandwich Spread
by Sandra Cerow Leonard

A few phenomena become traditions; most fade after a short time. Who would predict that Kentucky Derby goers would be eating a mild, green cream cheese spread more than a hundred years after it was first created?

Jennie Carter Benedict, a woman before her time, began the first of her careers by studying at the Boston School of Cooking with the renowned Fannie Farmer. In 1893, when she returned to Louisville, a small kitchen was built in her parents' backyard near Harrods Creek and she started catering parties for her wealthy friends. The Benedictine tea sandwich was one of her popular offerings.

The next year she became editor of the Household Department of the Louisville *Courier-Journal,* and in 1900 she opened Benedict's, a restaurant and tearoom. The first edition of *The Blue Ribbon Cookbook* hit bookstore shelves in 1902.

Miss Benedict also founded or was active in the Louisville Board of Trade, the Louisville Businesswoman's Club, the Training School for Nurses, the King's Daughters' Home for Incurables, and the Woman's Club of Louisville. But she is remembered today for a pale green concoction we put on crackers or bread.

Benedictine

8 oz. cream cheese
1 T. finely grated onion
1/4 cup cucumber juice, about 1/2 to 3/4 of a cucumber
1/4 tsp. salt
1/8 tsp. cayenne pepper

Bring the cream cheese to room temperature. Grate the onion on the small side of a hand grater. If you dice the onion by hand, do it until the pieces are almost pureed. Add the onion to the cream cheese.

Peel the cucumber, cut the pulp into thin strips, and press with your fingers through a strainer until 1/4 cup of juice is collected. Add juice to the cream cheese mixture. Add salt and cayenne pepper and beat the mixture well. Add more cucumber juice, if necessary, to reach spreading consistency for crackers. A thinner mixture makes a great dip for vegetables or chips.

Makes about one cup.

This recipe, courtesy of Yvonne Schenk, has been slightly revised for today's palates and available products.

CITY FOR A DAY
by Jeffrey Marks

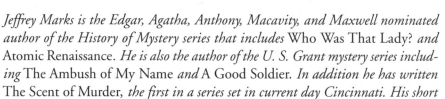

Jeffrey Marks is the Edgar, Agatha, Anthony, Macavity, and Maxwell nominated author of the History of Mystery series that includes Who Was That Lady? *and* Atomic Renaissance. *He is also the author of the U. S. Grant mystery series including* The Ambush of My Name *and* A Good Soldier. *In addition he has written* The Scent of Murder, *the first in a series set in current day Cincinnati. His short fiction has appeared in a number of anthologies. He lives in Cincinnati, where he teaches middle school.*

They call it the third largest city in Kentucky, even though the immense party crowd on the infield of Churchill Downs exists for only one day a year. A booze-soaked Brigadoon. This twenty-four hour settlement of more than 100,000 people has no organization and no social structure, unless you count the pokey that's set up for revelers who cross some mythical line of disorderly conduct. Still, it's bigger than Frankfort or Bowling Green or Paducah.

I stood on the outskirts of the Kentucky Derby infield, feeling every minute of my thirty-five years. This party was for college kids, frat boys, and those in search of a good time. I was working.

I'd been asked by his parents to follow Rich Garner. I'm not a big proponent of families hiring private detectives to resolve issues, but they had told me that their only son and heir to the family construction company had been acting oddly in the past two months. They'd tried the usual ways to connect with him, but nothing had worked. Rich had been sullen and secretive. While nothing was said, I could tell they suspected drugs. They made sure to tell me that he wasn't dating anyone, so he should be free of the tumults that go with young love. Well-off, intelligent. I figured he'd just gotten in over his head, starting his graduation celebration a few months early.

The Derby infield was the ideal place to abuse a few substances. Even though alcohol is restricted, there was enough booze saturating the infield to transform the Ohio River into one big shot of bourbon and water. Rich was twenty-one, old enough to drink. But he'd come to Louisville with another guy and two girls, and the girls looked like they weren't even old enough to vote.

I'd followed the group down I-71 from Cincinnati, and I'd somehow managed to keep them in sight while trying to maneuver through the crowds near Churchill Downs, but I'd lost them in the tunnel. I'd spent the past half-hour wandering around the infield, searching for Rich. At least at a horse race, no one cared if you had out your binoculars.

There's no way to describe the mob that rules the infield during the Kentucky Derby. With the ruckus, the crowds, and the general insanity, it's hard to know that one of the premier races of the country is taking place a few hundred yards from where you stand.

I realized I would likely lose Rich and his friends in the throng, but it was the first weekend since the Garners had hired me. I knew they expected quick results. I brought the glasses up to my eyes again and scanned the crowd. At least Rich had unwittingly shown me the courtesy to wear a bright gold shirt to the event. I would have no problem spotting him unless he took it off in the unseasonably hot weather. The woman next to me lifted her shirt above her head and wiped her brow with it. She wasn't wearing anything underneath it.

I sighed again and moved on. Someone bumped a watermelon against my knee as I walked by. I suspected that the watermelon was as lit as most of the Derby Day infielders, plugged full of rum or vodka. I limped a little as I made my way between the tents.

I thought I caught a glimpse of a yellow shirt in the distance, but when I focused my glasses, it turned out to be a sunburnt girl in a yellow tank top. I gave better odds to her leaving without the top than to the favorite in the race.

The crowd seemed to blend into one as I wandered around the infield. The whole area was something over twenty-five acres, so the traditional roses would have wilted before I could have run a lap. Still, I owed it to the Garners to roam around and look for Rich, even if I didn't think I'd find him.

I did manage to pick up some cash from the first race. The long shot, Forelock Holmes, had come in at 60-1, and I'd bet two dollars on him to win. I had considered the payoff professional bonus, but now I had the money for the electric bill and a nice dinner. The announcers tried to make a big deal of the odds, but I wasn't feeling too lucky, considering that I'd lost my subject.

I'd given up and had bought a mint julep to get into the spirit of things when I finally saw him. He was standing with his friends no more than fifty yards from me. I took a hit from the eight-dollar drink I planned to write off on my expense account. Lifting my binoculars, I studied Rich. I couldn't see any traces of sullenness in his face. He was smiling and happy, one arm around his friend and another around the shorter girl.

He looked like the all-American kid, not the withdrawn son his parents had described. I watched him, not sure what I expected. Even with the freewheeling atmosphere, I doubted that he would hold up a sign to tell the crowd or me what was going on in his head.

I had my answer in less than two minutes. Rich was laughing one minute, smiling at the short blonde girl who was all sunburn and tank top, the next he was kissing his male friend. I dropped the julep and held the binoculars with both hands. He hadn't planted a friendly peck on the boy's cheek; it was affection, pure and simple. To the credit of the revelers, no one was fazed by the kiss.

The two pulled apart and smiled at each other. I was torn between moving in closer and keeping a distance to see what would happen next. I was spared a choice when Rich walked toward the line of porta-potties. The friend said something to the girls, and one of them went with him in the opposite direction.

I decided to keep an eye on the remaining girl, thinking that everyone would come back to her eventually. I was wrong.

The next time anyone saw Rich Garner, he was lying behind one of the potties with a belt wrapped around his neck.

It actually took longer to get the half-dressed drunk girl off the potty roof than it did for Louisville Metro Homicide to show up. The on-site security force had radioed for help as soon as they saw that Rich wasn't going to watch any more races. The police arrived in a few minutes, wading through the crowd. I picked them out immediately. They were overdressed in shirts and ties in an infield full of shorts and wet T-shirts.

Just as I had lost Rich in the crowds earlier, apparently now so had his friends, because I didn't see any signs of the trio. I'd wandered around the infield as the big race was run, hoping to catch a glimpse of them, but my luck had run out professionally.

I opted to head home. I couldn't add anything for the detectives. I hadn't witnessed the murder. I didn't have any clues to what had happened. Louisville Metro wasn't likely to share anything with me, even though I was an ex-cop. Outside of Ohio, my PI license was worth less than the abandoned betting slips that littered the area. I wanted some time by myself to make sense of the tragedy. He'd only been a kid; he hadn't deserved death. His last gesture, kissing that boy, had seemed defiant and full of life, yet now that life was snuffed out.

With a pall cast over the day, I made the long walk back to my car and got in. The ninety-minute drive back to Cincinnati seemed eternal under the circumstances. I thought I saw the car that Rich had come down in at one point, but when I pulled beside it, my mistake made me realize how much Rich had enjoyed life that morning on the way down. I wanted to catch the person who had killed him. No matter what had been going on in his life, it wasn't bad enough to die for. His needless death was worth avenging.

My first task was to contact the Garners. Officially my case was over. I didn't want to charge them for a report on what Rich had been up to. Grieving parents wouldn't want to hear any dirt that I could dig up now on their son. They wanted to remember him as a good boy, the innocent child he had once been. Besides, the cynic in me wanted to verify their whereabouts. If they'd been at the Derby, they couldn't have made it home before my call.

I had just crossed the river into Ohio when I picked up the cell phone to call them. I wanted to tell them in person. I could be a coward, but no one should hear that kind of news on the phone. As soon as Mrs. Garner answered, I knew that she'd already heard the news. Her voice was raw and shaking, a kaleidoscope of emotions.

"Mrs. Garner, this is John Rittenhouse. I wanted to stop by to talk to you."

She started to sob, then gasped as if to catch her breath. "He's dead. Did you know that? He's dead. Someone killed him at the Kentucky Derby today."

"Yes, ma'am. I was there too, but I lost him and his friends early on. I saw the aftermath and wanted to pass on the news and convey my sympathies."

"Who did this? *Who did this?*"

Her voice rose to a screech that made me pull the phone away from my ear. Even though my knees were shot, there was nothing wrong with my hearing.

"I don't know," I replied.

"Then find out."

The phone went dead, and I took it that I was still on the job. I had to play it safe. It was an open police matter, and I knew from experience how annoyed the police could get with a PI trying to solve a case. Still, it wouldn't hurt to ask around and see what I could find out. I'd hand anything I learned over to Metro Homicide and make a report to the Garners.

I drove past Rich's apartment in Clifton, but the lights were off. There was no sign of the car that had taken him to Louisville. I made my way home and went to bed, knowing there was nothing else I could do at the time for Rich. It was days like this when I wished I'd just taken my pension and bought a boat instead of trying to run a private investigation firm.

The next morning was a different matter, though. I was surprised to see that the murder had received only a paragraph in the Metro section of the paper. I would have thought that the Garners' importance in Cincinnati would warrant a bigger mention, but maybe Mr. Garner wanted it that way.

I figured that everyone who knew Rich would be talking about the murder. I wanted to hear their words the first time, not after they'd had time to rehearse a good story. Louisville Metro Homicide would not be far behind me in trying to track down Rich's companions.

Taking a chance, I swung by his place, one of those rundown houses near the university that had been converted into multiple apartments. I was hoping to get names on Rich's three companions who were only in my notes as Male #1, Female #1, and Female #2.

I knocked on the door and waited.

Someone scrambled from inside; the door opened to reveal a nose, a chin, and little else. "Yeah?"

"Is this Rich Garner's residence?" I opted for the stoic, business-like demeanor. I wanted to sound official in some manner: law, insurance, the like.

The door opened wider. "Are you the press?"

"Do I look like a reporter? No tape recorder, no cameras." I slouched a little to make sure I didn't look too nice.

The ploy worked. The door opened more, and the young man from the day before stepped onto the porch. I caught my breath but tried not to let on like I knew anything.

He looked older in the morning sun. Crow's-feet ran from the corners of his eyes. The bags under his eyes helped to mask their redness, unless you were looking close. His blond hair was tousled from what I assumed was a bad night's sleep. He wore a pair of sleep pants and an oversized T-shirt. "So if you're not the press, what exactly is this about? What do you want?"

"I'm John Rittenhouse. Rich's parents asked me to look into his death." I held out a hand to him, trying to lure him a bit farther from the door and from any quick end to my questions.

"Jeremy Knight." He didn't offer his hand and I didn't force the issue. Answers would suffice for me.

"You were with him yesterday. What exactly happened?"

He eyed me with suspicion and stepped back inside the door. "How did you know that?"

"The reports said another man was with Rich yesterday. I just assumed that he'd be a good friend, maybe a roommate."

He nodded as if that made sense. "We went down together, but I wasn't with him when . . . it happened. I wish I had been. I might have saved him." He sniffled and ran his arm under his nose. Not exactly upper-crust behavior.

"I doubt that would be the case. It doesn't help to replay the what-ifs in your mind."

Even in the warm morning, he shivered slightly. "So what do you need to know?"

"The reports said that two women were with you. I'd like to talk to them as well."

"Yeah. Megan and Adriana. They went down with us."

He gave me addresses and phone numbers for each of them, and I scribbled them down quickly. He seemed anxious to help, to get me to leave. I was sure he wanted to be alone with his grief. It wasn't like he could share his suffering with the Garners. Maybe someday, but not now.

I put my pad back in my pocket. "Did you notice either of them missing a belt when you came home? Rich was strangled with one."

"No. Adriana was still wearing a belt when we came home. She was wearing those low-rider jeans, and I would have noticed if the belt was missing. Megan wasn't wearing one."

I cleared my throat. "I don't want to pry, but you left him there. Did you know he was dead, or was he just missing?"

He shook his head and looked down at his feet. His voice cracked when he spoke again. The veneer was breaking down, and the interview was about at its end. "No, the girls saw the police. I knew it was Rich immediately. The shirt, the hair, you know. The face didn't look like him at all. It was blue and kinda bloated. Anyway, the girls wanted to leave. 'No reason to get involved in another state's crimes,' they said. I had to leave or get stuck there with no way home."

He deflated slightly with the speech, and I knew I wouldn't get anything else out of him. A few of his mannerisms set off my gaydar. I'd thought about trying to make him come out, mostly to toughen him up for the police, but decided against it. Enough people would be happy to tell the police.

I hadn't asked Jeremy about the kiss. It would have alerted him to too many things, most of all that I'd seen them. Even in public situations, people maintain the illusion that no one sees them. It's human nature. If you don't believe me, just watch the man in the car beside you dig one out of his nose.

I decided to pay a visit to Adriana next, only because she was closer. She lived around the corner from Rich in a high-rise apartment complex that catered to students. All the amenities in one place: a gym, a pool, and even a bar. No worries about driving drunk when you can stumble home.

I found her name on the board and hit the buzzer. She answered immediately. I explained who I was and what I wanted. Before I finished my story, she buzzed me up. If I were her parents, I would have been pissed to find that she didn't ask for any identification.

She met me at the door. She was the blonde girl Rich had had his arm around at the track, still wearing the same tank top as the day before, though now she'd changed to sweat pants. I could see signs that she'd been crying: the red nose, the bloodshot eyes. I wondered why grief and alcoholism seemed to have the same physical characteristics.

"Are you really a private eye? Like the movies?" Her sunburned face studied mine as she talked.

"Well, not really. Nothing as glamorous as that. Mostly, we're just ex-cops trying to make a living. It's not a bad life. I just talk to people. It's pretty mundane work, but I like meeting new people and finding out about them."

She tucked one leg under her after she sat down on the sofa. She pointed to an oversized chair for me. "So what can I tell you? I want to see whoever did that to Rich punished."

Enthusiastic witnesses always made me a bit nervous. I was usually involved with matters that no one would cheer for—like divorce and stealing. I cleared my throat as I decided on my approach. "Were you and Rich involved?"

Her eyes grew wide. I could see the red veins just under her lids. "You mean like dating?" She laughed. "No offense, but you're not very good at this. Rich was gay."

"He told you this?"

"He didn't have to. He brought a date. You'll have to let me know what you think about Jeremy. He's not what I would have picked for Rich."

"I met him. That's how I got your name."

"Ah, I see. Jeremy's a few years older than Rich. They met in a physics class. Jeremy was the TA. They started dating in March, after the quarter ended."

"And you and this other girl, Megan?"

Adriana laughed. "No, I like boys, Mr. Rittenhouse. Rich and I dated freshman year. He broke it off and told me why. We stayed friends. He's easy to be around. What's not to like? He's good-looking, rich, and lucky as anything. Oh, I mean *was*." She seemed shocked to realize that the past tense was more appropriate.

She didn't appear to be the type to hold a grudge, but sometimes it's hard to tell. Her story covered what I'd seen at the track, but if she was telling the truth, then I still was missing one killer.

"Did you notice if both Jeremy and Megan were wearing belts when you came home?"

She gasped slightly. "You think . . . you think one of us did this? Mr. Rittenhouse, we're not like that. We couldn't do a thing like that."

I nodded, thinking of all the killers who had said the same thing, as if only a specific type could became a killer. I believe there's a little bit of criminal in all of us. "And the belts?"

"Jeremy had one on. He was wearing baggies, and they'd have been around his ankles if he hadn't worn something. Megan didn't wear a belt. That doesn't mean much, though. I saw at least three or four people take off their clothes at the Derby. Anyone could have swiped a belt, and no one would have been the wiser. Personally, I think Rich was just in the wrong place at the wrong time."

We said our good-byes. I slipped back into my car and headed out for the last interview of the morning. There was always the chance that the murder was a purely random thing, but the Cincinnati *Enquirer* had said Rich's wallet along with $700 had been found on his body. Robbery was the most likely motive for a random killing, and yet his money had not been taken.

Megan's address was more upscale than the others. She lived just north of the university in an area of old mansions and gaslighted streetlamps, a far cry from the overcrowded houses nearer to campus.

If I had been a movie dick, like Adriana suggested, then Megan Palmer would have been the dangerous dame of the flick. She was hips and curves in all the right places, with nearly black curls that fell down to her shoulders. I caught her just as she was returning from a shopping trip; her arms were full of bags and boxes.

"Miss Palmer, do you have a minute to answer a few questions about yesterday and the murder?" I thought I should come directly to the point with her. She didn't look like the type who engaged in small talk.

She looked me over and assented. "Get the door for me, will you?"

I opened the door and followed her into the house. The sunlight played with the colors in the stained glass doors, lighting the entryway. I thought I saw a Rookwood fireplace in the background.

"Can I get you something to drink, or are you on duty?" She smiled at me as she dumped the packages on the sofa.

"No, thanks. So what exactly happened yesterday?" I didn't bother to correct her assumption that I was a cop.

"None of this would have happened if Rich and Jeremy had listened to me. I wanted to get a box and watch the races from there. My daddy said he could get one for me. But Rich and Jeremy insisted on going into the infield."

"I'm sure it wasn't up to your standards," I said, trying to keep a straight face. "Did you win any money there?" I looked around at the labels and bags, wondering if she had gotten a windfall.

"I didn't bet. The others did, but I'd rather buy clothes than waste money on gambling."

She picked up a pair of shoes as if to prove her point. I'm sure another woman could have identified the brand. To me, they were just black.

"For what Rich was betting," she continued, "we would have had all the free juleps we wanted."

"What happened after you all got there? You separated?"

"First, Rich said he had to go to the bathroom, as if those porta-potties could be considered anything more than barbaric. Then Jeremy went to get some beer. Adriana said she'd go too, and I was left, watching people throw up. Not exactly what I had in mind for entertainment."

"I've been before too. It's not exactly the same as the box-seat crowd, is it? So who found Rich?"

"Jeremy did. When Rich didn't come back from the toilets, Jeremy went to look for him. Said that there were police there and everything. I insisted on leaving immediately. I didn't want anything to do with that."

"What did the others say about that?"

"Jeremy was shaken up. I probably could have talked him into driving to Los Angeles about then. Adriana didn't seem to have any problem with leaving either. So we came back."

I left Megan's and swung by Kroger to pick up a few things for dinner. I was feeling flush from the winnings at the Derby the day before, so I splurged on name brands instead of house brands and went home to make dinner.

Three messages were waiting for me when I walked in the door, all of them from Mrs. Garner, wanting to know what I'd found out. Telling a client that you know squat is one of the worst parts of the job.

Even as I thought that, I knew it wasn't true. I had some ideas, so after dinner I hit up an old pal to confirm my suspicions. I'd known McMahon since my days at the Academy. After we spent a few minutes catching up, I made my request. I gave him one name, and then threw in the other two in case my hunch didn't pay off.

He paused for a few seconds before responding. "If you're right, you know that I'll have to report this to Louisville Homicide, too."

"Sure, man. I'm not out to grandstand here. Just want to have something to tell the parents."

McMahon called back in an hour. The perp hadn't even waited to deposit the cash. $6000—a $100 bet at 60-to-1. I had a hunch that this was Rich's lucky streak his friends had mentioned. It hadn't ended lucky at all.

I drove out to the Garners' house and called them as I turned onto their street. They were both home. I parked and had barely made it out of the car when they met me in the drive. The day was nice, and the Garners' yard was bigger than most shopping malls.

"Well?" Mrs. Garner practically ran the distance to my car. I wished I could tell her that I could bring Rich back. I doubted that any consolation I could mutter would make a difference in the long run.

"The Louisville Metro Police are going to be making an arrest as soon as the paperwork goes through. I was able to track down the killer for them, and I shared the information with them about an hour ago."

"Who?" Her voice was a whisper now. Mr. Garner had wrapped his arms around her as if to hold her up.

"Adriana. Rich won a bundle on a horse. She strangled him before he had a chance to collect his winnings, then she took the ticket."

"Adriana? She was always such a nice girl."

"I think that she had much higher hopes about her and Rich's relationship. Ostensibly it was about money, but I wonder if she would have killed him if he hadn't dumped her. The money would have paid for the rest of her education. She was about tapped out on student loans and grants. Rich's friend Jeremy was a grad student and teaching. Megan has family money. Adriana was the likely candidate if it came down to cash."

"Are you sure?"

"The police found her deposit. It matched the amount of Rich's winnings for the day. The girl can't afford a high-priced attorney. She'll snap soon."

Mrs. Garner began to cry. Her husband led her back to the house, and I got in my car. The sky looked a little darker as I pulled out of the driveway and headed toward home.

The 1895 Derby

by Gwen Mayo

The crowd for the 1895 running of the Kentucky Derby saw what could be considered the first modern Derby. Track founder Col. M. Lewis Clark had never been able to translate the success of the Kentucky Derby into success for the track. As a result, on November 24, 1894, the New Louisville Jockey Club was incorporated, and William F. Schulte was appointed president. Schulte began an aggressive renovation of the facility.

One of his first decisions was to abandon the clubhouse, which had members facing the afternoon sun to watch races. Under Schulte's direction, a new grandstand was constructed on the opposite side of the track. The now legendary twin spires crowning the club's $100,000 grandstand were a new sight for many at the twenty-first running of the Kentucky Derby.

Schulte knew that the building alone was not enough to change the fortunes of the track. He needed a fresh, festive image for the track's most popular event. For the 1895 Derby, he spent several thousand dollars of the New Louisville Jockey Club's money on transportation, hotel rooms, entertainment, food, and drink for major sports writers covering the race. His efforts generated publicity for the race and laid the foundation for the Derby festival.

Leaders of the New Louisville Jockey Club also listened to owners' complaints that the 1½ mile race was too long for three-year-olds so early in the racing season. At one of its first meetings, the club voted to shorten the spring race to 1¼ miles in order to attract a better field of horses.

Schulte and his club had come up with a winning combination for the race. The Derby and the city of Louisville received a great number of positive reviews from the crowd, the press, and horse owners, all of which help to make the Derby the international event it is today.

FOOL'S GOLD

by Gwen Mayo

Gwen Mayo spent most of her life in the hills of Eastern Kentucky raising her daughter and working as a locomotive engineer. Her published poems have been read aloud at the dedication of the Vietnam Memorial, and assigned as university course work. Her interest in writing expanded after she spent the summer of 1994 experiencing the music and stories of the Caribbean at the University of the West Indies, Trinidad. Currently, she writes poetry, short stories, and micro fiction, and is plotting her first novel.

Noise of a scuffle excited the horses. Otto, Galon d' Or's trainer, leapt for the reins as the startled Thoroughbred reared. "What kind of fool would be fighting in the barns?" he hissed between clenched teeth. The only answer, a loud crack of splintering wood, echoed through the barn.

"I'll be right back," I shouted over the general chaos that erupted. "Stay with the horse."

The big German nodded. His attention was fixed on calming Galon d' Or before the pony rider arrived. One wrong move, and the three-year-old's racing career would be finished. Causing one of the Thoroughbreds to be injured would also end Otto's career, and that of whoever was stupid enough to start a fight in the backfield on a race day.

The new owners of the Louisville Jockey Club's track were trying desperately to make the Derby profitable for the first time in its twenty-one-year history. They had spent a fortune building the gleaming white grandstand that now greeted guests. There was even talk that they had hired a special train to bring sports reporters from every major newspaper on the East Coast to cover the race. Having a horse injured through carelessness was not the sort of publicity they wanted to generate. Injuries were bad for business.

An injury to this particular horse was also bad for my business. As a former employee of Allan Pinkerton, I had been able to build a lucrative business.

My agency attracted an assortment of cases from all over the Ohio River Valley. Usually, those jobs did not entail being a bodyguard to a horse, but this was not my first case to involve a racehorse. Kentucky Thoroughbreds were sort of four-legged royalty. I wouldn't place Galon d' Or among the bluest of the Bluegrass bloodlines. Halma, the favorite for a Derby win, was the only horse in the race rated above common plate class. But I wasn't about to argue the necessity of my services with a man who was willing to pay me ten dollars a day plus expenses to stand around watching his horse run circles around a dirt track.

I couldn't blame him for not risking the loss of another horse. His stable had suffered badly after the thefts in Sarasota a few months earlier. Larkin was a small-time operator. He had purchased most of his horses in claiming races as two- or three-year-olds. He couldn't afford to lose even one horse without taking a loss on the season. Someone had stolen three horses—nearly half his stable—in one night. Rumor had it that he had borrowed heavily to stay afloat until the spring meets. If that was true, it was probably not a wise business decision. Without a major purse win for the season, he might lose the remaining horses to his lenders.

It occurred to me, as I raced toward the south end of the barn, that leaving the stall might not have been the best business decision I had ever made. Larkin had hired me to guard Galon d' Or. Whoever was causing the trouble was at least eight stalls away. Larkin might not believe that a fight that far away from his horse required my attention. Maybe it wasn't my job to check it out, but the way the hair stood up on the back of my neck when that wood snapped led me to believe otherwise. Besides, I was certain the Thoroughbred was in better hands than mine. Otto clearly loved the big golden bay. There wasn't much danger anyone would get near enough to harm Galon d' Or with his trainer at his side.

The crowd gathering near the end of the barn told me I was right to be concerned. Thoroughbreds are skittish animals. Everyone working in the backfield should have been busy getting the half-ton animals under control after that fright. Instead, about a dozen people were milling around by the stall gate. I quickly made my way through the crowd to the open stall, stepped inside, and closed the gate before anyone thought to follow.

It took a few moments for my eyes to adjust to the dim light inside the stall. Not that it took much light to identify the murder weapon. A small man with weather-beaten features lay on the floor with a broken barley fork sticking out of his belly. One by one, the faces of the other occupants of the stall came into focus. A thin young man with a watchman's uniform bent over the dead man. Behind him, two grooms tried hard not to look scared.

"Did you know him?" a voice behind me asked.

I picked up a horse blanket and slowly draped it over the dead man's face, giving me an excuse to get close enough to examine the body without appearing ghoulish. The broken tine of the barley fork lay several inches from his right hand. Three of the oak tines had ripped through his midsection, and blood soaked the front of his shirt and pooled in the straw under his body. My stomach knotted at the sight. Four long weary years with the Army of the Potomac had not hardened me enough to witness a death without feeling sick. I blinked once or twice to stop the stinging in my eyes.

Real men don't cry, I reminded myself for about the ten-thousandth time. You might think the pretense of being a man would become easier with time, but it never did. I had been posing as my brother Ness for nearly thirty years, and I still had to work at appearing to be one of the boys.

Ness and I had been among the best of Mr. Pinkerton's teams of agents. When my twin was murdered near the end of the war, I had taken his identity in order to follow the trail of his killer. That trail had grown cold some months later when the last known link to Ness's murder led me to a Kentucky horse farm. Although the killer's trail was lost, my detective agency had solved several other prominent cases. Along the way, I discovered that being Ness was much more lucrative than any job a woman could get, so I left Nessa Donnelly dead in the shallow grave where I'd buried my brother. After all this time, I doubted that anybody outside the small circle of friends who knew my secret would believe the truth without irrefutable proof. But I knew, and was painfully aware of the dangers I faced living and working as a man. I drew in one last breath to calm my voice and turned to see who was talking.

I was surprised to see another watchman leaning over the top of the stall door. I had attended eleven of the twenty runnings of the Derby and had never seen backfield security leave the gatehouses. Apparently, the track's new ownership was still concerned about the thefts in Florida a year earlier. The newly arrived watchman made no effort to enter the stall, but the way the younger man looked at him made it obvious which officer was in charge. I made a mental note to discuss any information I uncovered with this man.

"I can't say that I know him," I said, choking back the bile that rose in the back of my throat, "not more than a speaking acquaintance anyway. His name is Jay Redding. He works for Crosswell Farms." I studied the watchman's face carefully as I spoke. "Do you know who was fighting with him?"

"Just got here myself," he said. He glanced in the direction of the two grooms, daring them to disagree with him. Surprisingly, he contradicted himself immediately. "These two swear they don't know nothin', but the big one there in the corner was bending over the body when I came in." He pointed to the broken tine of the barley fork lying a few inches from the body. "It's a clean fresh break. Had to be a powerful blow to snap it like that."

I could tell from the tone of his voice that he wouldn't be looking much further if he could blame the young groom. He was waiting for me to agree. The silence was oppressive as I glanced from him to the two young Negroes nervously watching us, then to the face of his partner. There was a look of anticipation on the younger watchman's face that made my skin crawl. Louisville hadn't been a Southern town during the war, but in the years that followed, it had certainly become one. Thirty years had only deepened the divide between black and white, I thought, as I picked up one of the grooms' forks.

At five foot six, I was a little taller than most women, but rail thin. No stretch of the imagination would lead anyone to consider me a "powerful man." I carefully pondered the risk of what I was about to do. If I was wrong about what had happened, if the fork didn't break, the two youngsters would probably end up dangling from the end of a rope. If I did nothing, they would probably hang anyway.

Without saying a word, I swung around and thrust the fork violently into the canvas hay bag in the corner of the stall. I had calculated the blow to land only three tines in the bag. Just as I suspected, the tines that landed in the hay were cushioned enough to remain intact, but the fourth snapped with a loud crack when it hit the wall. I picked up the broken tine and wordlessly handed it to the senior watchman.

"They were bending over the body when I came in," the young watchman protested, as his eyes traveled from his partner's face to mine.

"You were bending over the body when I came in," I calmly countered. "Gentlemen, look at those two!" I demanded, pointing to the two grooms. "There was a fight going on here before Mr. Redding was killed. I could hear it eight stalls away. Do you see any scraped knuckles, torn clothing, or other indications that those boys have been in a fight?"

"Maybe it was all one-sided," the young watchman grumbled. "The little feller here wouldn't have been much trouble to those two. Heck, he's older than you."

I chafed at the comment about my age. Even though I was past fifty and dressed like a man, I had enough female vanity to resent being called old. Fortunately for the two grooms in the corner, I was not so vain that I was going to let it cloud my thinking. "I doubt that they could have made the ruckus I heard without leaving some evidence of being in a fight," I said. "Besides, no Negro in his right mind would attack a white man in a public place." There was no need to remind either of the watchmen of what would happen after the fight. "Don't you think you should look for someone who shows some signs of being in a fistfight?" I said quietly. "Maybe you should question some of the people who knew Mr. Redding."

"An excellent idea, Mr. Donnelly," a distinctively female voice said. "You should be doing just that."

I turned abruptly and found myself facing an enormous white hat. Long black feathers draped over either side of the wide brim, brushing the top of her shoulders. The effect nearly hid her face. All I could see was the end of a long aristocratic nose, thin lips, and a rather pointed chin. For a moment I just stood gaping at her. I wasn't sure which had startled me more, a woman's voice in the backfield or the assumption that I would be handling the investigation. "Excuse me?"

"Now, now, Mr. Donnelly, there is no need for you to protest," she said, pushing the watchman aside and opening the stall door. "Time is of the essence, don't you agree?"

I did. But she didn't bother waiting for me to say so.

"I have persuaded your employer that your services are needed to find my night man's killer." She pulled open the stall door and was about to enter, but I recovered myself enough to block her path.

"That's no place for a lady," I said, feeling like the world's biggest hypocrite. "Suppose we step outside and you can tell me a little more about your night man."

She sighed and tilted her head up enough for me to get a good look at her face. I realized that beneath the silk suit with its rather foolish looking leg-o'-mutton sleeves was a woman of substance. The fire flashing in her storm gray eyes said she was not accustomed to being refused anything. I could tell she was considering putting me in my place, but the firm resolve in my face must have changed her mind.

She stepped aside with a graceful sweep of her flaring skirts and allowed me to lead her to the shade of a nearby tree.

"You said Mr. Redding was your night man," I prompted her.

Mrs. Crosswell seemed to ponder the question for a long while. "Well, when I first met Jay—Mr. Redding, that is—he was the lead apprentice at my husband's farm. Of course, the late Mr. Crosswell and I were only courting at the time." She smiled at the memory. "That was back in the old days, when his stable was golden. It seemed like nothing stood between Crosswell Farms and its being the most prominent stable in the state, except time and another champion."

Her gaze drifted toward the newly constructed twin spires. I could tell from the wistful tone of her voice that she was thinking about how far down she had come to be entering one of her three-year-olds in the Derby. She was not calling the Derby "a race of dogs" the way some of the papers had, but big stables were not bothering with bringing their best horses to regional tracks. The limestone deposits that made Kentucky's bluegrass excellent for grazing horses kept the Louisville Jockey Club's track firm and fast in all sorts of weather. In New York a similar track would have drawn the best horses for a major stakes race, but now there were only five horses slated to compete. The previous year—the twentieth running of the Derby—had been even worse.

I realized she had stopped talking and prompted her again. "You were saying he used to be a jockey?"

"Oh, my, yes! In his prime, Jay was one of the most sought-after jockeys in the country." Mrs. Crosswell paused again, the wistful look returning. "It was a golden time for all of us, Mr. Donnelly. You wouldn't know it by the way he looks now, but that's the only way to describe Jay back then. Golden brown from winters spent riding in the Florida sun. His hair sunburned to the bright gold of fresh wheat straw. All those trashy young girls who love white jockeys would hang all over him when he raced."

She suddenly recalled her social position, and her back grew rigid as her features hardened into a mask of disapproval. "Shameless, if you ask me, but the war has changed things considerably. Modern girls have no sense of propriety. Not like when the late Mr. Crosswell first came calling on me."

Inwardly, I cringed at her remarks. In the fifty-two years I had lived, I had not noticed all that great a difference in how young women behaved. It was too early to know where Mrs. Crosswell was leading the conversation, so I bit back my tongue. You never knew what people would let slip when they were allowed to talk freely. I leaned against the railing and waited while she dabbed at an imaginary tear in her eye.

"Of course, he was fond of spirits even back then," she confided, dropping her voice to a hoarse whisper as her eyes trailed toward the stall where her night man's body lay. Her pale cheeks blushed slightly as though just the mention of whiskey was a mortal sin.

She must have expected me to disapprove, because her whole posture went stiff and she looked me over more carefully, paying special attention to my close-cropped, red-gold curls that were beginning to show ginger streaks now that I was getting older. Over the years I had lost most of my brogue, but the red hair, blue-green eyes, and slight build always pegged me as Irish. There was nothing I could do about that. I took a deep breath and waited for her to continue.

Those stormy eyes of hers looked shrewd. Her steady gaze was beginning to make me nervous. Men always saw what they expected, but now and then a clever woman would see right through my disguise. I shifted uncomfortably, hoping Sarah Crosswell didn't bring my life to an abrupt halt by figuring out I was a woman.

She might have been sharp enough to guess, if she hadn't already been blinded by her image of the Irish. Her chin tilted ever so slightly as she looked down her nose at me. "Mr. Crosswell was deacon at First Baptist for near fourteen years before he passed on. We didn't approve of strong drink, Mr. Donnelly," she said, in her most condescending tone.

I know the reputation we Irish have for drunken brawls on Saturday night and Mass on Sunday morning, but I hadn't been to Mass in years and limited my use of whiskey to the drop I put in the hot toddies I consumed most evenings. Still, the way those words oozed through her lips made my stomach constrict and brought just a wee trace of temper. I hid most of my anger and met her gaze. "Is that a fact, Mrs. Crosswell? Then perhaps you would enlighten me on why you hired Jay Redding?"

She dabbed her eyes again and looked over the infield wall as if some distant memory lay beyond the fence instead of the grass and dirt of a real track. "Ordinarily we wouldn't have taken on a drinking man, but Mr. Redding was an exceptional horseman. Sat flat in the saddle, just waiting on the horse to tell him how to move, then just vanishing into the flow of muscles so he was one with the beast. It was poetry, pure poetry to watch him run for the wire."

She must have noticed the way I was watching her, because she turned to face me. That defensive look returned in force. In an instant, her gray eyes turned the shade of thunderclouds. Her jaw clenched tight, giving her face a harsh line. "Everybody," she said, with an emphasis that meant *everybody who was part of the Kentucky horse royalty*, "thought it was just a matter of time before Jay got a shot at a favorite."

Her hands were on her hips, and she unconsciously planted her feet more firmly on the ground. "If we hadn't taken him, someone else would have snapped him up," she said defensively. "He was born to ride. Over the years, he did ride a lot of winners for us. That's why Mr. Crosswell kept him on, even when his drinking was bad. He worked as a groom for a while, and then moved to the night man's job. He is the best man I have to travel with the horses. Most of the other night men drink, but at least Jay didn't smoke, so he wasn't likely to burn down the barn. Besides, he had such nightmares that there was never any danger he would sleep sound enough to miss a mare in foaling."

"Was he a fighting sort of drunk, Mrs. Crosswell?" I asked before she could lead the conversation any further into the sad tale she was spinning. "Was there anyone who might have hated him enough to want him dead?"

"Now see here, Mr. Donnelly!" she exclaimed. "There is no call to think a troubled life made him a bad person. It's perfectly obvious that he walked into some unfortunate situation. I expect you to find out what happened." She turned abruptly and walked away.

I took a deep breath and tried to order my thoughts. I had noticed the watchmen leading their suspects over to the tack room where they could be locked up. I decided my first stop should be to question the grooms. Belly wounds didn't kill a man instantly. There might be a chance he was still alive when they arrived, but I didn't hold out much hope for a deathbed utterance of the killer's name. There had been no scream accompanying the crack of the barley fork. That told me the killer had already rendered him unconscious before delivering the fatal wound.

The watchmen were not eager to let me talk to the young grooms alone. But I knew I wouldn't get anywhere with those two glaring at the boys while I questioned them. I finally suggested that I could have Mrs. Crosswell get approval from the track manager if they didn't have the authority to allow me to question the Negroes. I didn't know if Mrs. Crosswell had any pull at all with the track manager, but my bluff worked. They reluctantly unlocked the door and let me go into the tack room alone.

The grooms were too young and scared to be of much use. Gabe, the smaller one, couldn't have been more than twelve. He had been mucking out another stall when the fight broke out. "I was mindin' my own business," he said sullenly. "I don't go messin' in the doin's of white folks."

"So Mr. Redding was fighting with another white man?" I asked.

His partner cast him a sharp glance, and Gabe suddenly developed a keen interest in the toes of his boots.

I sighed. "Look, the two of you are going to hang for this murder if you don't start talking."

Their heads shot up and their eyes got wider at the mention of hanging. They took a step backwards, away from my sharp gaze, as if they thought putting some distance between us would change the trouble they were in. "We didn't kill nobody," they said in unison.

"I don't believe you did," I said, "but if I don't find out who did kill Mr. Redding, you are probably going to hang for it."

"He was fightin' over Galon," Gabe said. "That's all we heard. Honest. They was talkin' real low, and then Mr. Redding said something about Galon. After that, the fightin' started. Billy and me reached the stall just before them two outside." He motioned toward the door.

I frowned. "Did you see anyone leaving?"

"No, sir. He never come out the front. We'd've seen him if he did."

I left the pair and returned to the watchmen, who confirmed their story.

They said they had arrived only a moment before me and had not seen anyone enter or leave.

By the time I got back to Galon d' Or's stall, I was feeling stupid. The pony riders were leading horses out for the second race. We were one race away from the Derby, and all I had was a gut feeling that the murder and the race were connected. I was no closer to figuring out who had killed Redding than I was when I began. Over the previous hour I had heard the same story from over a dozen witnesses. It couldn't have been more than a minute between the time Otto and I first heard the fatal blow and the time I reached the stall where Redding was killed. Someone had fought with Redding, knocked him out, and stabbed him with a barley fork while he lay unconscious on the stall floor. Yet, I hadn't been able to find any evidence to point me toward the second person in that fight or explain how he got away without being seen.

I was still brooding when John Burnette, Galon d' Or's jockey, showed up dressed in Larkin Stables racing silks. He was older than most of the jockeys in the day's races. Larkin had brought him up from Florida in the hopes that a more experienced rider would be able to race his three-year-old to victory despite appalling odds. The dark-faced man planted his foot on the bottom of a bucket, hoisted himself up onto the upper board of the stable wall with an easy grace, then started talking to the big Thoroughbred. Seeing him and the horse together, I couldn't help thinking they looked like a winning pair. Then I realized how easy it was for him to perch on top of the wall between the stalls. It would be equally easy for any of the jockeys to swing over the wall dividing one stall from another and drop into the adjoining stall in a matter of seconds. Jockeys were light and lean, but they were all muscle and moved as gracefully as dancers.

The thought burned in the back of my mind. I looked from Burnette to Otto and suddenly knew how all the pieces fit together. "I'll be right back," I yelled to Otto. "I want to check something out."

It took all the willpower I could muster to keep from running as I made my way back to the stall where Jay Redding had been murdered. Once inside I quickly climbed the rough timber wall and looked around for the most likely escape route. There was a loud thud when I jumped down into the stall on the other side. I doubted that anyone would have noticed that sound over the noise the horses were making after the murder. The killer could have easily escaped during the ensuing chaos.

From the backside of the barn, it was only a short walk to the jockeys' room. I tried to walk slow enough not to attract anyone's attention and still made it in less than two minutes. I hesitated outside the door. It was late enough that most of the jockeys had already finished changing for the Derby, but I was not sure what state of dress any of the remaining men would be in. *There's no turning back now,* I silently told myself as I pushed the door open.

Fortunately, most of the jockeys were huddled around the window nearest the track while they waited for the second race to begin. I found Burnette's street clothing stashed in the locker with his spare racing silks. His shirt was torn. It could have happened in a fight, but I could think of half a dozen other ways it could have been damaged around the barns. His shoes were another matter. They had been freshly polished, but the leather soles were stained with blood. I took them and the shirt and left. We were half an hour away from the Derby run, and I had to get from the backfield to the new grandstand and find the track manager before the race started.

I hired one of the pony riders to get me to the grandstand quickly, then raced to the owner's box, praying that someone with the authority to act was actually watching the races. Elbert Rodgers, the assistant manager, recognized me and came over. I explained the facts I could prove about the murder as quietly as I could, showed him the bloodstained shoes, then paused for a moment to let it sink in before launching into speculation. If I was acting on the wrong theory, it would embarrass Mr. Rodgers and the track, and cost me my fee for guarding Galon d' Or. The stakes were much higher for the track, though, and for those two youngsters locked in the tack room.

"I don't believe Mr. Larkin hired me to guard his horse because he was worried that someone would steal Galon d' Or. I think he wants me there to keep anyone not closely associated with him away from the stall. Odds on his three-year-old were twenty-eight to one the last time I looked. At those odds he would stand to make a fortune if he ran a ringer, say the four-year-old Galon de Soleil that was stolen at Saratoga this winter."

Rodgers's face drained of color. "But . . . surely someone would have noticed," he stammered.

"Not without close inspection," I argued. "They are from the same bloodline, alike enough in color and build for one to pass as the other with anyone who was not intimately familiar with both horses."

"Wait here," he said, leaving the box at a run.

He returned just as the announcer called, "Galon d' Or has been scratched from the third race. . . ."

"I have sent the law over to arrest Burnette and the trainer," Rodgers said. "All the windows know to hold anyone wishing to recover large wagers on Galon d' Or. But I still don't understand why Burnette killed the old man."

"They didn't count on their horse being stabled in the same barn as someone who could recognize Galon de Soleil on sight. Jay Redding was an old jockey. I confirmed with Mrs. Crosswell a short time ago that he raced at

Saratoga some years back. He probably visited the track often when he was there. Redding must have recognized the horse while watching the morning exercise and confronted Burnette about it. The two men fought. Burnette is half Redding's age and in top racing condition. It wouldn't have been much of a fight. But knocking Redding out didn't solve his problem. His racing career, maybe even his life, was on the line if his part in the scheme was discovered. He picked up one of the forks the grooms use to muck out the stalls and ran Redding through with it. Burnette was able to duck out the back of the barn during the confusion."

The gates flew open and the four remaining horses ran for the first turn. Just as predicted, Halma took the early lead. Basso and Laureate were running neck and neck for second when one of the track watchmen arrived to tell Mr. Rodgers that Larkin had been caught.

"I hope you got paid in advance, Mr. Donnelly," Rodgers said. "You seem to have just worked yourself out of a job."

"No," I said with a smile as I watched the race. Laureate's saddle had begun to slip and he was dropping back. "But I'm not really worried." Halma crossed the finish line a good five lengths ahead of Basso, who followed four lengths ahead of Laureate. "The odds were so tight on Halma I was obliged to wager a hundred on Basso to place. At nine to two, I believe I will survive the loss of my wages."

Gallopalooza

by Rick McMahan

In 1998, a herd of sculpted and painted cows were the rage in Zurich, Switzerland. The following year, Chicago became the first American city invaded by the artistic animals, which captured the imagination of thousands of people. When Louisville sought a similar project for the Derby City, it was only natural that equines replaced bovines. What became known as Gallopalooza was designed to give the community an artistic outlet as well as a way to raise money for Brightside, an organization dedicated to beautifying the city.

People as far as away as Iowa, Florida, and New York submitted their visions for the life-size fiberglass horses. Along with professional artists, many individuals and community groups applied to decorate a Gallopalooza horse. Once selected, all of the artists worked on their 223 figures side-by-side in a community atmosphere at the Mellwood Arts Center. Some chose to express Derby-related themes, while others used the horse to raise social awareness about illnesses that needed medical cures. A few were more off-beat. Louisville's eclectic Lynn's Paradise Cafe sponsored a toaster horse. And Royal Fine Jewelers' pink-and-white zebra-like horse was adorned with a diamond lariat and diamond tennis bracelets. A wide range of artistic expressions emblazoned the hides of the Gallopalooza creations.

Drawing thousands of interested admirers in April 2004, the colorful herd was displayed at the Kentucky International Convention Center, the only time all 223 were in one place following their completion. A third of the horses took part in the annual Kentucky Derby Pegasus Parade. Then all of them were dispersed throughout the Louisville area, where they still proudly stand for the public to enjoy every day of the year.

THE CASE OF THE
PURLOINED DERBY DOG

by Rick McMahan

In his "day job," Rick McMahan is a special agent with a federal law enforcement agency in the US Department of Justice, and in his spare time he writes mysteries. His writing can be found in several publications, including magazines Over My Dead Body *and* Hardboiled *and anthologies* High Tech Noir *and* Year's Best Horror Anthology. *His stories are slated to appear in* Fedora *as well as Mystery Writers of America's* Relationships Can Be Murder, *an anthology edited by Harlan Coben.*

"Lucas, will you and Marlowe take the case?" she repeated, leaning forward to put her hand on my knee.

We were sitting on a park bench. I find it hard to resist pretty clients free with their touch. As far as taking her case, that was solely my choice. My partner left all the business decisions to me. He was busy at the water fountain flirting with a long-legged female who had just sprinted twice around the park.

"Kristi," I said, "tell me again what happened."

Dr. Kristi Foley let out a sigh, blowing locks of hair away from her face. She tried to put on an exasperated expression but failed. We were friends enough that I could call her Kristi, not Doctor. Young, pretty, and smart, all she lacked was a stethoscope around her neck for her to match the central-casting image of a TV doctor.

"A couple years back," she began, "as part of the Derby celebration, there were a bunch of sculpted horses made and put in the Pegasus parade. They called it Gallopalooza. You can still see the statues around town."

I remembered. The life-like fiberglass horses were adopted by local businesses, and artists painted the statues to a theme. Some of the creations were then put into the pre-Derby Pegasus Parade that went through downtown Louisville—a sign that mint juleps were in the air along with Derby-Pie, pretty hats, and plenty of parties.

At the fountain, my partner got snubbed by the lanky female. Ignoring him, she took a long drink before trotting off. He took a drink of water and turned toward me, giving me a devil-may-care grin.

"You know Roger Keyes?" Kristi asked.

I knew of him, though I had never met the man. The Louisville icon had brokered many back-room business and political deals in his long lifetime. Like many rich people who climb and club their way to the top of the social heap, as he got older he wanted to be remembered for social good deeds. Now retired, he spent his time on his east Jefferson County estate as a gentleman farmer and breeder of champion Irish Setters. And like every other rich person in Kentucky, every year he hosted a lavish Derby party.

"Roger is a supporter of our cause," Kristi said. "He commissioned Leigh Van Meter to sculpt his Derby Dog."

I raised my eyebrows. Leigh Van Meter's work was a staple in Soho galleries. "The statue of an Irish Setter," I said. I have to let clients know that I am a real detective and can think a few steps ahead. Sometimes I'm just guessing.

"That's right. The statue's eyes were emeralds. In addition, he commissioned a diamond choker for its neck." A breeze tugged a lock of hair from behind her ear. Absently, she tucked the black strand back in place. "Christened the Derby Dog, it was to debut at Roger's party. The necklace was going to be auctioned off and the proceeds donated to the Foundation. The Derby Dog was going to be put on display at the Jefferson Animal Hospital."

All of this would have been a great boost for the Hastings Foundation, a nonprofit organization that rescues homeless animals. Working on a shoestring budget, it depends on volunteers and donations to keep running.

"The dog was stolen," I stated.

My partner, having decided he had struck out with the ladies in the park, wandered over and dropped to the grass next to my feet.

Kristi nodded. "We had volunteers standing guard."

"Louisville Metro charged one of your volunteers for the theft," I replied. The *Courier-Journal* had carried an article in the morning paper, and even in print, the volunteer's claim of waking up from a nap to find the statue gone was weak.

Kristi shook her head. "George Ablow didn't do it. Lucas, I'm just asking for you and Marlowe to spend one day looking into the case."

I gave her my best dubious look. The case sounded open-and-shut, and the police hate it when outsiders second-guess their work. Besides, it was unlikely

I'd solve a case in one day. "Kristi, I don't know. . . . "

"Let's ask Marlowe and see what he thinks," she suggested.

My partner perked his ears and cocked his head. I could tell by the way he wagged his tail I'd been outvoted by my partner and his vet.

"What have we gotten ourselves into?" I said.

Marlowe ignored my comment as he watched the other dogs running behind the chain-link fence. We were sitting in my Bronco in the parking lot of the Tom Sawyer Dog Park after escorting Kristi to her car so she could return to work at the Jefferson Animal Hospital. She had been so sure I would take the case, she had already lined up interviews for me in addition to giving me a copy of the Louisville Metro Police arrest citation for George Ablow.

Annoyed, Marlowe barked.

"Okay, okay, I hear you." I turned on the CD player.

Marlowe was on a Days of the New kick. I was just glad he was out of his Conway Twitty phase. As a joke, a friend once slipped a Twitty disc in, and it was three weeks before I could get the Big Guy to let me change the CD. Marlowe's an easy-going partner and doesn't expect much of a salary, but he is demanding when it comes to his music.

He's no purebred. When I stopped a man from tossing the pup off the Second Street Bridge into the Ohio River, Marlowe was a ball of black fur. Now he weighs ten pounds less than my own 140. His dark coat and webbed feet show that he's got black Labrador leading the pack in his genes, but his blocky head and thicker bone structure led Kristi to surmise he may have some bull mastiff as well.

Once the music started playing, Marlowe sat up straight. This was the cue that we were ready to roll.

I wasn't sure if I could solve this case, but I had a place to start.

Finding Officer Danny Neher was easy. His cruiser was backed into a parking spot at a Thornton's gas station. He sat behind the wheel, eating his daily healthy noon meal—hot dogs baked under heated lights. Two dollars for three dogs.

I pulled my Bronco alongside his cruiser and eased my window down.

"Well, if it ain't Ace Ventura," Danny said around a mouthful of loaded hot dog. The meat that peeked out from the weary bun was almost gray in the sunlight.

"Hiya, Danny. I see you're still adhering to sound food groups."

"A well-oiled machine," he replied, patting his thick stomach.

I nodded at his badge and said, "Should I expect the 'Dragnet' theme to start playing?"

He almost sneered at the shield pinned on his chest. "LAPD-style badges. Another brilliant idea from the brain trust downtown."

"Just the facts, ma'am," I deadpanned.

"You slumming?" He worked a toothpick into his lower gums, rooting around.

"The Keyes burglary."

Danny gave me a wry smile. "Another canine caper."

"It sounds like a clean case," I said. "Still, I'd like to speak to the detective handling the investigation, and since you were the responding officer, I thought you could give me an intro."

"There is no detective assigned to the case. With the new administration decentralizing special units, everything is being pushed onto the district dicks, from assaults to car theft. They're swamped. If one of us patrol-monkeys makes an arrest on a call, we do the follow-up investigation ourselves."

"Hard to do follow-up while chasing radio runs during a shift," I observed.

Danny nodded.

"Tell me what happened?"

Settling back in his seat, he told his tale. Two nights earlier, Danny was working a midnight shift, when he was dispatched to the Keyes estate. The 911 call was made by one George Ablow after he was awakened by slamming car doors and noticed the statue was gone. Running to the barn door, he saw a car's taillights speeding down the service road through the fields toward the main road.

"When I got to the barn," Danny said, "Keyes, his operating manager, Billy Richmond, and the other volunteer, Gloria Williamson, were in the barn with Ablow."

"Why does Richmond's name sound familiar?"

"He was a jockey until he took a spill about six years ago," Danny replied.

"It was a Kentucky Derby run," I said as the memory came back. Back then I'd been a police officer, and like most Louisville cops, I worked the Kentucky Derby. That year, I was posted at the gate where the horses and riders entered the track.

"A hell of a ride," Danny said. "He was riding one of the favorites, but his horse tangled with another rider in the second turn, and both horses went down. Richmond was trampled by several other horses. Never raced again."

I nodded and went back to the topic at hand. "Why'd you suspect Ablow?"

"His story didn't add up. The girl—Gloria—said she was wide awake in her car at the end of the service lane and no other vehicle passed her. Anyone leaving the barn would have driven right by her. Then, when I checked outside the barn, I saw drag marks leading right to Ablow's car door. Both he and Gloria consented to searches of their cars."

He paused to listen to radio chatter. Some days, I missed the radio banter and the brotherhood that came from carrying the badge and working the streets. Satisfied that the radio call didn't concern him, Danny picked up his story. "The girl's car was clean. When I searched the trunk of Ablow's car, I found an emerald in the wheel well under a blanket. He denied knowing anything about it, but Keyes identified the jewel as one of the emeralds that made up the dog's eyes."

"So you hooked Ablow up?"

Danny nodded. "Booked him. I tried talking to him on the ride to the jail, but he stuck to his story that he didn't know what happened."

"Where's the Derby Dog?" I asked.

Danny shrugged. "According to Gloria, Ablow went out around midnight. He said he was going out for some cigarettes and to make a call, which doesn't make sense. When I searched him and his car, I didn't find any cigarettes. Plus, there's a phone in the barn. He called 911 from the barn phone, so why did he leave? I figured an accomplice snuck in and helped him steal the statue and hid in the car when George drove out. They transferred the dog to his partner's car, came back to the barn, and concocted his story."

"What did Ablow say?" I asked.

"When I laid it out to him, he lawyered up."

Not good, I thought. "Why did Ablow have to have an accomplice?"

"The Derby Dog was over 400 pounds of wrought-iron metal, so I don't think he could get it loaded into his car by himself. He's not that big. Plus, the statue wasn't in his car."

I nodded. "And the emerald fell out when they put the statue in George's car."

Officer Danny Neher nodded. A solid case.

Roger Keyes's estate sat off the road behind the type of white fence popular with horse farms. A mother and foal watched the road and idly batted flies away with their tails. I pulled into the brick circular drive behind a shiny BMW and a battered truck. Two men stood at the tailgate of the truck. Both were thin and wore polo shirts embroidered with Keyes's kennel emblem, a silhouette of an Irish Setter. One was my height and had the toll of a hard-lived life etched into the lines around his eyes. Racing horses around a track is hard on a man's body—and, some say, his soul—and I guessed he was the ex-jockey Billy Richmond. The man I assumed to be Keyes was taller and wore a leather fedora to protect his skin and bald pate from the sun.

While we made introductions, Marlowe sat at my side and studied the two men. As I shook hands with Richmond, I said, "I was at the Derby the year you had your accident."

He grimaced theatrically. "Hope you didn't bet on me." A wide smile showed white capped teeth.

I just nodded.

Keyes jumped right in with both feet, so to speak. "Kristi said you were once a policeman." His deep baritone voice commanded an audience. "Until, some . . . incident." He said the last word with the implication of a darker meaning.

I nodded back, unblinking. "Now I'm a private operator."

"Kristi thinks the police arrested the wrong man," he said with a doubtful shake of his head.

"She does," I replied.

"The kid's guilty," Billy Richmond said. He had a harsh accent, maybe New York. "The gal at the end of the lane didn't see anything, and he had one of the gems."

I asked the men to tell me about the night of the theft. Keyes's sole involvement had been to identify the jewel from Ablow's trunk. Keyes had left the nuts and bolts of the "volunteer" security to his farm manager. Richmond scheduled volunteers and checked on them during their shifts. The ex-jockey even arranged for coffee and snacks to be in the barn. The only thing that interested me was that of all the volunteers, only Gloria Williamson and George Ablow worked more than one shift. They both attended the University of Louisville, and Gloria worked for the vet who took care of Keyes's animals.

"Unless you have any other questions," Richmond said, "I need to get going. I'm headed to Churchill Downs. Some of my old riding mates are in town."

Since Marlowe couldn't think of anything else to ask, we bid him goodbye. I was surprised when he climbed behind the wheel of the Beemer.

Keyes must have seen the surprise on my face, because he said, "Oh, I let Billy use my cars whenever he wishes."

"If being a farm manager pays that well, I ought to switch careers," I said.

He laughed. "Heavens no, but Billy's been with me a long time. I should have listened to him. He didn't want me to leave the statue in the barn. He wanted me to hire real security instead of the Foundation's volunteers to guard the Derby Dog."

"Professional security probably would have been wise."

"That's not the half of it." Seeing my perplexed look, he explained. "The jewels were not the most valuable thing in the dog." He leaned against the truck. "Are you familiar with Van Meter's work?"

"I've seen her work," I replied.

"Leigh enjoys making puns in her art. She'd painted a bright blue heart in the Derby Dog's chest. A hidden lock in the heart opened a secret compartment inside." From his pocket, Keyes pulled a blue skeleton key. "Inside the Derby Dog's heart were more jewels. A pair of diamonds worth more than the necklace and the jewels in the Dog's eyes. That was my *real* donation to the Foundation. With the diamonds as collateral, the Foundation could do a lot of good for the canines in this community." To emphasize his point, he leaned forward and patted Marlowe on his head. "I fear now that the thieves stole the jewels outside and destroyed the Derby Dog with those diamonds still inside."

"Did anyone else know of the compartment?"

"No one," Keyes replied. "Only Van Meter and I."

I pulled up in front of Gloria Williamson's apartment near the university campus and parked between a classic GTO and a new Dodge Magnum that had an expired U of L parking pass hanging from the mirror. The sound of heavy metal music pounded through the open door to the apartment.

A young man, shirtless and wearing shorts, was waxing the muscle car. Even if he didn't have his team number tattooed on his bulging bicep, I would have recognized Shaun Devon, one of the linebackers for the Louisville Cardinals.

"Is Gloria around?" I asked him.

Devon looked up from his work. "A bill collector?"

Marlowe wandered to the rear tire, and I hoped he didn't decide to mark the GTO as his property.

"No," I said with a smile. "I'm a PI looking into the theft from the Keyes estate."

Marlowe sniffed the tire and then examined his reflection in the gleam of the rear bumper.

"Oh, dude, that was crazy," Devon said. "Didn't the cops arrest the right dude?" His attention was divided between me and my partner. I guess he was afraid Marlowe would leave nose prints on the chrome bumper.

"I'm trying to tie up some loose ends, and I need to talk to Miss Williamson."

The thick football player raised his voice. "Hey, Glory, someone's here for you!"

He had to yell again before the music was turned down and Gloria came out. She was dressed for work in pink scrub pants and top. Her round face wasn't quite pretty. Her blonde hair was gathered high on her head in a ponytail that bounced when she talked. We got the preliminary info out of the way.

She said she was a biology major who'd been supporting herself by working at a veterinarian's office.

"I don't know George that well," she said when I broached the subject of her coworker. "We had a class together, so I thought he was okay. I guess you never really know anyone."

Her boyfriend came up and put his arm around her to give her support.

"What made you suspect George?" I asked.

"Easy," she replied, tossing her head, which made her ponytail swish. "He told the cop that a car came down the access lane. That didn't happen. I was there the whole time, and no car left except for George when he went to the store. He lied."

"Mrs. Van Meter, thank you for meeting with me," I said.

The lady herself had greeted me when I rang the doorbell at her home in the Highlands after Marlowe promised to be on his best behavior. "My pleasure," she said, her voice laced with bourbon. Even though she wore faded jeans and a man's flannel shirt, she had the quality of someone dressed in a dinner gown. She was in her mid-fifties, and she didn't try to hide the gray.

From a news story I had read, I knew the artist did her painting in her welding studio in the carriage house at the rear of the house. She ushered me into her workshop, which smelled of turpentine and paint.

"I understand only you and Mr. Keyes knew about the Derby Dog's secret compartment?" I asked, after taking in the paint-spattered drop cloths amid several works in progress.

Marlowe sat quietly at my side without embarrassing me by scratching or licking himself.

She nodded. "I only showed Roger the compartment after Billy and I unloaded the statue in the barn. Roger confided his plans to me about using the compartment to hide the diamonds. And before you ask, I told no one. I am able to keep a friend's confidences."

The Jefferson County Jail, a modern brick structure that sits on a downtown corner, looks like a business building from the outside, but once you pass the lobby, it's a cacophony of too many men jammed into cells and the echoing of steel doors slamming shut. The visitor rooms are small cubicles with a plastic chair and a stainless-steel ledge in front of a thick plastic window. On the other side of the window is a mirror-image room.

George Ablow wore the jail's stylish orange jumpsuit. Collapsing into the chair, he eyed me like a drowning man who sees a life preserver bobbing in the water—hope mixed with trepidation. "You really a private eye?" he asked suspiciously.

My Levi's and Big Dogs T-shirt did nothing to bolster my image. "I left my trench coat and snap-brim hat at home."

"I don't know if I should talk to you," he said.

"Without your attorney. I know." I waved my hand. "You have a public defender who probably spent five minutes talking while he tried to juggle a foot-high stack of case folders before your arraignment."

George sat up straighter.

"Your case is only one in a hundred your PD has," I said. "I'm your best shot of getting out of here. Besides, for the foreseeable future, your social calendar is free, so why not talk to me? Dr. Foley thinks you're innocent."

"I am. I didn't steal the dog," he said emphatically.

"Your story to the police was lousy. You look guilty."

"But it's the truth!"

"The part about buying cigarettes was a lie," I countered.

He dropped his gaze to his lap. "That's the only lie I told."

"Well, one lie coupled with the emerald in your trunk will send you to prison." I blew out a deep breath. "Tell me how you got involved with the Derby Dog."

"I'm pre-vet," he said. "Several of my professors volunteer for the Foundation and asked for people to baby-sit the statue. I signed up for three nights, figuring there wouldn't be much to do. The other two nights were boring, and I had time to study and even watch TV. Can you believe there's cable in the barn?"

I wondered if the horses watched "SportsCenter."

"How well do you know Gloria?" I asked.

He shrugged. "Okay, I guess. We're both science majors, but I've not seen her around campus lately. I think she's taking this semester off."

"Tell me about that night."

George gave me his version of what happened: He and Gloria reported for duty that night at nine and were to be relieved at seven the next morning. Billy Richmond checked in from time to time, but mainly they were alone. One person was to stay in the barn with the statue, and the other would sit at the end of the service lane leading to the barn. George drove a ten-year-old Honda with no working radio or AC, whereas Gloria's car had a television with a DVD player in the dash, so she took the road duty.

Those new cars with surround sound, DVDs, and refrigerated glove boxes have always reminded me of rolling movie theaters.

Around midnight, he asked Gloria to cover for him while he went out for an hour. When he got back, they had a cup of coffee and chatted before returning to their posts. George fell asleep studying for his chemistry finals. And just like he'd told the cops, he woke when he heard a car speed away after its door slammed shut. He called 911.

"Did you see the driver of the car?" I asked.

"No. I mostly heard it. It was loud and had a thick rumble."

"George, why did you lie to the cops?" I shifted in my seat. They put the most uncomfortable chairs in visiting rooms to discourage long conversations.

"I'm in debt," he mumbled.

"Everyone in college is in debt," I replied.

"No, I owe some people ten thousand dollars," he said.

The way he said the phrase made me think these weren't FDIC loans. "Loan sharks or bookies?"

"Both," he replied. "I took a beating on the Final Four. Then I couldn't get ahead. The guy wouldn't take my word anymore until I paid off what I owed him, so. . . ."

"You went to a loan shark to pay off your bookie?" I asked, dismayed. Talk about the ultimate robbing Peter to pay Paul.

"If I could just get ahead, I could pay off the loan shark and almost even out with my bookie." He caught my expression and said, "Hey, it's just like the stock market. It's a gamble too, and people borrow money from banks to dabble in the stock market."

"If you get behind on a loan from the bank," I commented, "they don't send guys with baseball bats to deliver their late notices."

He shrugged. "I have a system. I can make it work."

How stupid can you be? I thought. "So what does this have to do with the lie you told the cops?"

"I did go out that night like I said. I just didn't go to the store. I met my bookie."

"Why didn't you just call him and place a bet?" I asked.

"He won't give me any credit until I'm caught up. Cash only."

I nodded, both in understanding and for him to continue with his story.

"I've been trying my luck with the horses. Once I found out Billy Richmond was a jockey, I've been getting some tips from him. He has a lot of friends at the track, and he gets inside scoops. He'd given me a tip on some of the Oaks races. I just left to make my bet and returned. When the cop asked me where I went, I panicked. I didn't want to admit I'd been placing bets."

"You thought the cop would arrest you for gambling?" I asked incredulously.

He nodded. I didn't know which was worse, that he had lied about going to the convenience store or that he had lied to make a bet. Even a daft attorney could weave a good tale of a desperate man in debt who steals valuable stones to cover gambling debts.

Sherlock Holmes or Miss Marple, one of those super-sleuths, once said something about dogs that don't bark as being a clue. After leaving George, I was convinced he should go to prison for being stupid, even though I was sure he hadn't taken the Derby Dog. Proving his innocence was going to be tricky.

I'd never actually done one of those scenes where you put everyone in a room so the brilliant detective—that would be me, in case you've not been following along—could solve the case. In books and movies, it's done all the time, but this was a first for me.

I asked everyone to gather around the empty pedestal in Roger Keyes's barn. He and Billy Richmond were both there, a little amused and annoyed. Dr. Kristi Foley was there. Gloria Williamson and Shaun Devon needed a little finessing, but I had persuaded them to show up. The only one missing was George Ablow.

George was right; a television mounted in a corner of the barn picked up every channel known to man.

"I appreciate you all coming back to the scene of the crime." I looked down at Marlowe, sitting at my feet, his tongue lolling out of his mouth. "George Ablow didn't steal the Derby Dog."

"That's crazy," Keyes said. "I saw the emerald in his car trunk."

"It was planted," I replied.

"But George lied," Gloria said.

"No, Gloria," I replied. "George told the truth. You lied. You three stole the Derby Dog." My finger danced between her, the former jockey, and the hulking linebacker.

Devon clenched his fists. "This is bull, and I ain't gonna take it." He pushed himself out of the folding chair with a clatter and started toward me.

Marlowe stood. Gone was the lolling tongue. A low growl started in the back of his throat.

"Shaun, sit down," I encouraged in a conversational voice, just a hint of an edge underneath.

The large man decided discretion was the better part of valor. He sat.

"Billy, when did you first get the idea to steal the dog?" I asked, fixing him with my full gaze. "Was it when Mr. Keyes refused the security, or was it before? Were you jealous of his wealth? Did you think he owed you?"

"You're talking nonsense. I never—" Billy began.

"You're the mastermind behind it all," I said, cutting him off. I turned to the others and said, "Billy realized he had a great opportunity to make one big score with the Derby Dog. Here's how it worked.

"Gloria likes expensive things," I said. "New cars, new clothes. But she doesn't like paying the bills. In fact, she's not in school. She's defaulted on student loans and wasn't making ends meet as a vet technician." I had done a little checking after I recalled Shaun's question to me about being a bill collector.

"Billy knew Gloria before she came to watch the statue since she worked for your vet, Keyes. Billy's a good judge of people. He knew she was hurting for money. Once he came up with the idea to steal the Derby Dog, he approached her to help."

The girl said nothing, her mouth clamped shut.

"Gloria recruited Shaun for the heavy lifting," I added, glancing at the football player. "But her main job was to find the right fall guy. In waltzes George Ablow with his gambling habit. Gloria already knew, or George let it slip; either way, she and Billy decided he was a perfect patsy. Billy even gave George horse tips to encourage his gambling jones. Almost like handing a drunk a bottle of tequila.

"George lying to the police about going to the convenience store wasn't part of the plan, but it helped. It was dumb luck."

"When Gloria and George had coffee, she did the pouring," I continued, pacing back and forth. "She slipped something into his cup to knock him out. Since she works at a vet's office, she has access to all kinds of drugs. When George passed out, she called Shaun to tell him the coast was clear. They put the statue in Shaun's GTO. George doesn't know cars, but he described the car leaving as having a rumble, like an old '60s muscle car."

All eyes were on me. Center stage. I liked the feeling. "Here's the bit of genius. Shaun peels rubber and wakes up George. When he tells his story to the cops, he fully expects Gloria's story to match his. Since she was at the end of the lane, the car had to pass her. But she denied seeing a car." The dog that didn't bark.

I could see that Keyes and Kristi were listening to me, but they were staring at the three culprits. The thieves were getting nervous.

"But once the cops searched the cars, it was a cinch. Here's where Billy's planning paid off. After George was knocked out, Shaun dragged the statue in the dirt to George's car to leave tracks. Originally, everyone thought there would have to be more than one person moving the Derby Dog, but a hefty football player like Shaun could have managed moving the statue all by himself. He pried out an emerald and planted it in the trunk. It would be easy to do in a car like George's, since the trunk release is inside the door. There was one thing that struck me as wrong." I tapped a finger against my skull. "The police said the tire tracks led right up to George's car, yet if he stole the statue before leaving the barn at midnight, when he returned it's doubtful the tracks would line up with his car. The other thing that didn't make sense is if George was stealing the emerald eyes and diamond choker, why not just pry them out and be done with it? And why was a thief so careless as to lose one of the two emerald eyes. That's a third of his take. Doesn't make sense."

I had Keyes's full attention. Now came the tricky part. "Didn't that bother you, Gloria? Shaun? Why leave one third of the pay-off behind?" I nodded dramatically. "Because it wasn't one third. I bet Billy didn't tell you about the rest of the jewels. Did you guys ever wonder why he wanted the statue? I bet he was adamant about the statue. There were more jewels."

All three glanced at each other, with Billy's grimace pleading for the other two to be quiet.

"Oh yeah," I said, pressing on. "There was more than the diamond choker." I directed my attention to Keyes. "You told me that no one knew about the Derby Dog's secret compartment, but that wasn't true. Leigh Van Meter told me that Billy helped unload the statue into the barn. I bet you were so enthralled with the statue, you didn't remember your manager standing alongside listening as you impressed Van Meter with how lavish a gift you were giving the Foundation."

Shaun and Keyes were both staring daggers at the jockey, who chose that moment to make a break for the front of the barn. He hadn't gone twenty feet before Marlowe was on him. Bull mastiffs were bred in England to run poachers to the ground. My partner bowled over Billy, sending him sprawling through the barn door into the sunlight.

On cue, Officer Danny Neher came out from the horse stall, where he had been hiding during my pontification, and quickly cuffed the three thieves.

"Book 'em, Danno."

I've always wanted to say that.

Lucky or Not

by Elaine Munsch

The horseshoe has long been considered a symbol of good luck, a belief that has many components. Originally the horseshoe was made of iron, a substance stronger than other metals and able to withstand fire. It was formed by a blacksmith, a man whose trade involved working with the powerful elements of iron and fire. Even the blacksmith himself was considered a lucky man, a healer. He was the man who worked with the majestic horse, an animal prized not only because of its necessity for travel and farming, but also because of its beauty. Not only did the blacksmith care for the horse but he also was the one who molded and shaped the necessary tools for farming.

Seven nails hold the horseshoe in place. The magical number seven, with all its implications—seven planets, seven colors of the rainbow, even seven deadly sins—adds to the mystique.

The real question is not whether the horseshoe brings good luck, but how to hang it to contain the luck. One tradition says if you hang it so that the ends are pointed up, you can hold the luck, stopping it from leaving you and your home. But another tradition says if you hang the horseshoe over your door with the ends pointed down, the luck from the shoe will flow over those who step across the threshold, protecting them and preventing evil from entering the home.

You choose. After all, it is only a superstition.

Isn't it?

IF THE HORSESHOE FITS

by Elaine Munsch

Elaine Munsch, a native of Cleveland, Ohio, graduated from Nazareth College of Kentucky, a school that was located near Bardstown about an hour south of Churchill Downs. During her freshman year in 1965, she and assorted other Derby neophytes took the old blue school bus to the Kentucky Derby. As beginner's luck would have it, she picked her first Derby winner that year. Using the age-old and time-proven method of "I like the colors of the silks," she chose Lucky Debonair. However, since then, her cat Murphy has won the family's Derby pool more years than not.

"So, who do you like in the fourth?"

The voice sent shivers down her spine, but long ago she had schooled herself to show no emotion. Her oversized hat shadowed her face, so she turned her head slightly to see him. "Are you following me?"

"No, ma'am. I follow the four-legged beauties." He gestured with his racing program to the big screen in the infield which showed the horses now being loaded into the starting gate. "Keeneland closed last Friday, so I had no choice but to move on to Louisville and the Downs. You just happened to do the same, that's all. Kismet."

"Kiss something else, my boy. That night was a mistake. Too much bourbon and a whole lot of lust. Don't think it will happen again or that you can blackmail me."

"Whoa, lady! You've got it all wrong. This is just a friendly hello, nothing more."

The hesitation in his voice told her there was something else to follow. Just what it was would soon unfold, she was sure. She studied his face as he looked toward the track. He was a handsome man, black hair and deep sea-blue eyes that surely had more than one woman drowning in them.

He felt her watching him and turned to smile; that's when he had her. His smile was a crooked one that echoed the mischief in his eyes. What woman could resist the invitation to find out just what he had in mind?

Their eyes locked for a moment. Lily Bennett—dubbed Lovely Lily by the Hollywood press—turned back to the track.

"Do you remember much of what we talked about last Friday night?" he asked.

"No, I barely remember leaving with you. What we did or said after that is a bit of a blur. Like I said, too much bourbon and lust with too little sense. Do you want to get to the point? The race is about to begin."

Just as he was about to reply, the loudspeaker roared, "And they're off." For the next minute, all they could think about was the race. By the time the horses galloped past, they were shouting encouragement at the top of their lungs. As quickly as the race started, it ended. Neither held a winning ticket.

"Come with me to Silks for a drink," he said. "I need to tell you something you should know. This won't take long, and then I'll be out of your life forever . . . if that's what you want."

"Okay. One drink and a little conversation. That's it."

Lily and the blue-eyed gentleman walked from the rail toward the paddock, turning left to enter Silks, a lounge equipped with betting windows and TVs for race viewing to keep the patrons interested. They chose a table in the far corner. Daisy, the hundred-year-old waitress, came to take their order.

"A virgin strawberry daiquiri for me," Lily said.

"I'll have Maker's Mark on the rocks."

She raised her eyebrows and said, "I guess I'm buying if you're drinking from the top shelf."

"No, no. I insist. After what I have to say, you may not stay to finish your drink."

Lily raised her hand. "I'm embarrassed to even ask this, given our night of passion, but . . . your name?"

The man threw his head back and laughed. "Boy, I deserved that. Thomas Mallory at your service. Or is that a bad choice of words? Last Friday, you seemed to think we'd make a hell of a team. I'm a bit blurry on what we were going to do, but you said you had the brains and I had the talent. Though you might have been talking about another one of my talents."

This time Lily laughed out loud. *It must have been quite the night,* she thought. *I should've stayed sober.*

The drinks arrived on a teetering tray carried by Daisy. "Are we running a tab, Miss Lily?"

"No, Daisy. Put it on the card. We're having just one for old times' sake."

Daisy nodded toward Thomas. "I wouldn't mind having an old time with that one." She picked up Lily's card and headed back to the bar.

"Okay, Mr. Mallory. What is going on? I told you I will not be blackmailed! My husband has his flings; I have mine. I know he's no saint, and I don't think he expects me to be one either."

"I read the papers, Miss Lily. What I have to say is . . . well . . . bizarre if it's not true . . . and difficult if it is. When I saw you today, I was surprised. Not that you were here but that you're still alive."

She almost dropped her drink. "Alive? Why would I be dead?"

He sighed. "Last Friday night I heard your husband ask a man to kill you. And to do it quickly, the sooner the better. If I hadn't been stone-cold sober at the time, I might have blown it off."

"Where were you that you 'heard' this? Scotty may not have always been discreet, but somehow I doubt he would casually announce that he wants to murder someone."

Thomas started to speak, but Lily stopped him. "And why would Scotty want me dead? We are hardly the loving couple—haven't been for several years—but I thought we worked well together on the racing stable. I know he's all excited about Impertinent Lad running in the Derby this Saturday. You're not making any sense. Scotty has divorced three other wives. Sandra, his fourth, died of cancer. Why bump off number five—me?" She slammed her hand down on the table. "And, most importantly, why didn't you tell me this Friday night, if you really thought that was what you heard?"

He folded his arms onto the table, leaning toward Lily. "You through? Here it is. I'm taking a break from the party, trying to avoid an overblown intoxicated woman who has designs on me. I'm tucked away in a dark corner of the balcony when I hear it. Scotty was rambling a bit. I think he needs you dead to pay off some gambling debts. I'm not sure I understood everything, but your husband has apparently taken out a rather large insurance policy on you."

Lily looked thoughtful. "Scotty once talked about how we needed to make sure we had enough insurance on each other. This was right after we got married. He was going to check with our attorney so that, in the event of either of our deaths, the racing stable, my production company, and God knows how many of his little ventures would still be able to operate. But we have money. At least I do. Why didn't he just ask me?"

"I suggest you find Scotty and ask him that question. He mumbled on and on about wanting to have his name engraved on the Derby trophy. Seems to be some sore point with him."

"Why that piece of horse excrement!" Lily fired back. "I'm the sole owner of Impertinent Lad, and I know that really irks him. Just wait till I get him cornered. We are going to have a few words about all this. I'll engrave something on his 'trophy' all right."

Then as quickly as she angered, she calmed down and said, "Gambling debts, huh? Scotty has been spending quite a bit of time in Vegas. I figured he had a piece on the side, but maybe he's been losing more than usual. For a supposedly great businessman, he's sure a lousy gambler. But why didn't you tell me all this last Friday?"

He shrugged. "After we met and started to get cozy, I decided I must have been hallucinating. I don't know. The time just never seemed right. This kind of news is a real mood spoiler."

Lily laughed and nodded her head in agreement. She leaned into the table and covered Thomas's hand with hers. "I have to go now. I think there is a husband that I have to see."

"You're going to ask him about this? Is that wise?"

"Yes, it's the only way. Scotty can't lie to me; he turns bright red and stammers. Hit him straight on. He's not used to that in the business world, but I have a few buddies who play in the NFL; they're always talking strategy. 'March on down the field. Best way.' Thomas, if you're right, I'll owe you. And I always pay my debts."

Before she stood, she reached over to his tie pin. It was a golden horseshoe. "I gave Scotty one of those. He's very superstitious." She righted the horseshoe so the ends faced up. "This is so your luck doesn't run out. We can't have that now. You may be my lucky charm, and I have a feeling I'm going to need every bit I can get!"

As she walked to the door, she waved to a couple seated at a corner table.

Someone shouted, "Good luck with the Lad!"

She stopped and said, "You don't need much luck when you've got the Lad running. Y'all just remember that come Derby Day and you're at the betting window."

Lily headed for the elevator that would take her to Millionaire's Row and her racing stable's private box. It would be filled with her friends and some of Scotty's business associates, as he had few real friends; to compensate he always mixed pleasure with business. She schooled her face to reveal her best smile and winked at a few of the gents as she scanned the room to see whether Scotty was there. He wasn't, so she made her way across the room to Verna Lee, her trusted aide and long-time friend.

Verna was talking to a man and a woman. The three turned as she approached, and the collective look they gave her started butterflies fluttering around in Lily's stomach. She asked, "Hey, anyone seen Scotty lately?"

* * *

"Dead? Murdered?"

The quartet had adjourned to the private office space within the box, where Detective Cokie Charles from the Louisville Metro Police informed Lily that one of her stable hands had found the body of Scott Schultz in the Golden Lily horse van. Foul play had been confirmed. He died of blunt force trauma to the head; the weapon was probably a crowbar found nearby, spattered with blood.

Grasping at straws, Lily asked, "Are you sure it was my husband?" She reached for Verna's hand.

"Yes, ma'am," the detective replied. "The stable hand and the guard at the gate both identified him."

Lily put her face into her hands, trying to put the pieces together. *Ten minutes ago I learn Scotty wants me dead, but now he is and I'm not. Have I stumbled into a B-grade movie?* She shook her head to clear her thoughts.

"I'm afraid there is more," said Detective Charles.

Lily looked at her and then at Verna. *What more can there be?*

"The person or persons who murdered your husband left a sort of message."

"Message? What sort?" asked Lily hesitantly.

"A horseshoe was nailed to his chest."

"Holy Josephine!" Lily shuddered. As an afterthought she added, "Was the open end of the horseshoe up or down? I guess it doesn't really matter, as Scotty's luck finally ran out." She closed her eyes and saw a golden horseshoe on a blood-red tie.

The gentleman seated across the table from Lily cleared his throat. She looked up, and he said, "Miss Bennett, as a representative of Churchill Downs, I have asked several security guards to escort you to your car. The usual media circus is about to erupt into a feeding frenzy. We would like to spare you that. If you'd like to leave now, I can have your car brought around immediately."

Lily seemed to be in a daze, so Verna spoke up. "Thank you. I think you are right. Lily, we'd better leave now."

She jumped up. "Yes, yes. Now would be good."

Lily gave a nonchalant wave as they walked from the box. As they moved across the brick walkway behind the paddock, she spotted Thomas Mallory. She stumbled as their eyes met. *What in blue blazes is going on?* she wondered.

The limo pulled up and Detective Charles opened the door. Verna and Lily entered. The detective got in, too, causing Lily and Verna to exchange looks.

"Okay if I ride along with you, Miss Bennett?" Charles asked. "My partner has a few loose ends to tie up and will meet us at the hotel. Then we can get all the little details cleared up."

"That's fine, Detective. I've been in enough murder-mystery movies to know that the wife or husband is always the prime suspect. Do you want to talk now or wait until we get to the hotel?"

"This is just routine. You're not a suspect but, as we say now, a person of interest. We're just trying to put some pieces of a puzzle together."

The rest of the ride to the hotel was in silence. Verna shrunk back into the cushions and wrung her hands, constantly glancing at the detective. Lily sat stone-faced, looking out the window.

The driver pulled around to the back of the hotel after he noticed a gathering crowd at the front. The passengers were discharged into the kitchen and made their way to the fourteenth floor, Derby-week home for the Golden Lily Stables group. Detective Sam Murphy, the other half of the homicide team, was waiting for them outside the suite.

As soon as they closed the door to the suite, Lily threw down her purse and flung her hat across the room. "Who the devil would want to kill Scotty? What did he get himself mixed up in? Geez, Louise, why now?"

Detective Murphy had more pointed questions. "Miss Bennett, when did you last see your husband?"

"Friday night. We attended the Fosters' party to celebrate the end of the Keeneland meet. They hold it every spring. Scotty had been in Lexington for the whole month, but I'd just gotten into town from the wrap up of my latest movie. Filming had run over, and I flew back to Lexington, arriving about eight. I was scrambling to get to the party before it ended. When I got there, Scotty was in full party mode—rather drunk and very congenial. He had a young 'thing' on each arm, drooling all over his Armani suit. I said, 'Hello, carry on,' and went to get myself a drink. A few hours later he sauntered by, telling me he was going to Louisville. The horses, including Impertinent Lad, had been moved over in the afternoon. Scotty wanted to be at the track first thing in the morning. Even though he seemed a bit more sober, I asked if Randall, our driver, was taking him over to Louisville. He said yes and that Verna was going along as a chaperone. I said good-night. I told him I was going to our farm outside of Lexington, and I would see him today, Monday. I assumed he left. I stayed and partied on."

"Did you speak with him after that?'

"Yes. He called me several times Saturday afternoon and evening. Again on Sunday. He was just calling to see how I was and to tell me how the Lad was feeling. A lot of small talk. Rather unlike him."

Lily realized now that Scotty was checking to see if she was alive. *All this is giving me a headache.* She began to rub her temples.

"When did you arrive in Louisville?" asked Detective Charles.

"Randall had come back to Lexington on Sunday afternoon, and he drove me over this morning. We dropped my luggage off at the hotel and went to the Downs. I made the rounds in Millionaire's Row. I thought I'd run into Scotty but wasn't surprised when I didn't. He loves being around the horses, driving Jim Holland, our trainer, crazy. Scotty is always in the way."

"What do you think he was doing in the horse van? Any idea?"

Lily shook her head. "For all I know, he had decided to muck it out. He probably was planning on giving a tour to his buddies and wanted it clean. I don't know."

"Didn't it bother you that your husband wasn't here or there to greet you?"

"Detective, the success our marriage—if you could call it a success—was due to the fact that we rarely spent time together. We rushed into marriage, forgetting how long 'till death do us part' can be. Sorry, bad choice of words. We were just too lazy to hassle with divorce. A modern-day marriage between two wealthy middle-aged people."

When Lily saw the reaction she had from the detectives, she added, "Hey, this ain't your parents' marriage. We may not have been madly in love, but we weren't plotting to kill one another either." *Or at least I wasn't,* she thought. *Unfortunately, Scotty can't answer that question anymore.*

Before the detectives could ask another question, Verna stepped forward. "I know I'm speaking out of turn. I haven't been asked my thoughts or opinions, but I am volunteering this information. Mr. Schultz might have been in trouble with some gambling types in Las Vegas."

Lily looked at her, startled. "What are you talking about?"

"I'm sorry, Lily. I didn't think it was important until now. The way Mr. Schultz was killed and all." Verna turned back to the detectives and continued. "I overheard a snippet or two of a phone conversation that sounded like Mr. Schultz was trying to 'get more time,' and he told someone, 'Believe me, I'm good for it; I've covered all the bases.'"

"Vegas!" Lily exclaimed. "Why didn't I hear about this sooner?" Then she realized that she had, just a few hours earlier, from the lips of Thomas Mallory.

"You were too busy with the filming project," Verna explained. "I just happened to overhear the one-sided conversation one night when I was looking for some files in your office and Mr. Schultz's office door was open a bit. You know how his voice can carry. *Could* carry."

The detectives looked at one another. Charles said, "I guess we'll check out the Vegas connection."

Lily stood up. "Why kill him? Dead men aren't known to pay their debts."

"But they still had the Golden Lily—you—alive," said Murphy, a little too enthusiastically. "Maybe they would try to put the muscle on you."

"I need to get an aspirin or something. Please excuse me." Lily left the room.

Verna asked the detectives if she could get some coffee or any other refreshment for them.

Both declined, but Charles asked about her relationship with Lily.

"We met while in acting school. It soon became evident which one of us had talent. By that time we were best of friends. Lily doesn't have any family, so she was 'adopted' by mine. I became her manager of sorts. My skills are organizational and Lily's definitely are not. When my father suffered a stroke and we almost lost the horse farm, Lily stepped in and bought the farm from my parents at a very generous price. She built them a small but comfortable home on the property. My brother still manages the farm for her and Mr. Schultz . . . well, now just Lily. She is a wonderful person, has always been there when I needed her, and I hope she would think that I have always been there for her. Isn't that right, Lily?" Verna added as Lily entered the room and caught the tail end of the story.

Lily went up to Verna and put her arms around her. "Yes, I couldn't make it without her. Always by my side. Do or die. Now, detectives, is there anything else? I need to make some phone calls. Scotty's other wives will need to be told so they can break the bad news to his children. I guess I'd better start with our attorney."

The detectives rose to leave, and Charles said, "We'll stop by later this evening. If you think of anything else we should know, here's my card. Don't hesitate to call."

"Thank you. I'll do that."

The police had no sooner caught the elevator down when the second car door opened, depositing Thomas Mallory on the fourteenth floor. Verna still stood at the door, having watched the detectives leave. When Thomas approached, she straightened up and started to shut the door to the suite.

He just pushed her aside and said, "Thomas Mallory of Mallory's Mortuary to see Ms. Bennett. She called, you see. I must speak with her privately about the funeral arrangements."

Verna sputtered. "What are you doing here? Scotty's not around to pay you, so you just get out of here. There is no need to kill her now."

"You!" exclaimed Lily when she saw Thomas. But before she could say anything else, he crossed the room and grabbed her by the arm and led her into the bedroom, firmly shutting and locking the door behind them.

Verna began pounding on the door.

Still holding onto Lily's arm, he said, "Don't say a word. Just listen to me. Who is that woman out there?"

"Why? She's my manager and friend. Are you drunk again? What's going on? First you come to me with some cockamamie story about Scotty wanting to kill me—then *he* turns up dead. What did Verna mean? 'No need to kill her now.' What is going on? Spit it out, or I call those officers back."

He sat her down on the bed's edge and knelt in front of her, holding her hands, looking directly into her eyes. "Remember what I told you about hearing what your husband said about killing you. Well, I was the one he was talking to. I do the 'odd job' for people. But, Lily, I swear I am not a killer. I told him that. I was never going to hurt you. All Schultz said was he would find someone else and then he left. I thought if I stayed close to you, you'd be safe. Then you woke up before me and skedaddled. I figured you were okay, but when you didn't show up yesterday, I got nervous, thought maybe he did find someone else. Maybe cocktail parties are rampant with hit men masquerading as waiters or whatever. I don't know. "

"Kind of playing it fast and loose with my life, weren't you, blue eyes?"

"But that woman—Verna, you say—I'm pretty sure she overhead the conversation Scotty and I had. Maybe she decided to kill him before he got to you. What are the chances she killed him?"

"Okay, so you think five-foot-two, hundred pounds soaking wet Verna killed Scotty, a two-hundred-pound-plus, six-foot-three man. What did she say? 'Hey, Scotty, step into this van and, oh by the way, please turn around so I can bash your head in.' And why did she nail a horseshoe to his chest?"

"I have no idea wh— What did you say? Nailed a horseshoe to his chest?"

"Scotty was not only murdered, but the killer wanted to make a statement: Your luck just ran out, Schultz."

Thomas grimaced, touching the golden horseshoe on his tie.

"None of this makes sense," Lily said. "You say he was going to kill me, and then he turns up dead. You say you overheard the conversation, but it turns out you were party to it. Now Verna is the one who overheard the conversation. This is ludicrous. Horseshoes and luck."

"What would stop Verna from getting someone else to do the dirty work? I've seen some of those giants that hang around you. Old football buddies. One glance at how they look at you. I don't know a word to describe it. *Adoring* just begins to cover it. They'd kill for you in a heartbeat."

Lily was just about to argue with him when the lock to the door was shattered. Verna and a nasty-looking gun filled the space. Both Thomas and Lily jumped as she entered the room.

"Mr. Schultz always called you his luckiest charm." Verna's voice was menacingly calm. "But he never understood how right he was. He never appreciated you like the rest of us do. You always said that you would take care of us, and you have. Favors need to be returned."

Lily shrunk back on the bed.

Thomas stood very quietly. "Just what are you saying? That you killed Scotty?"

Verna stood silent.

Lily quietly spoke, "What were you thinking, Verna? "

Verna pointed the gun at the golden horseshoe on Thomas's tie and whispered, "That the best defense is a good offense."

Derby Trains

by Beverle Graves Myers

Getting to the Derby can be as much fun as the race itself. Cars and airplanes are today's preferred modes of travel for the out-of-town Derby guest, but in the first two-thirds of the 20th century, luxury trains were the way to go. Besides the regularly scheduled passenger trains, Kentucky Derby Specials from all points of the compass pulled into Louisville's Union Station at Tenth and Broadway or the Seventh Street Depot on the Ohio River on Thursday or Friday and stayed through the weekend. Participating railroads included the Louisville & Nashville, Pennsylvania, New York Central, Chesapeake & Ohio, and Illinois Central. These lines filled local spur tracks with coaches and private cars.

With hotels booked far in advance and bursting to capacity, many Derby goers slept right on the trains. Their rolling accommodations were just as cozy as Louisville's finest hotels. Compartments and berths provided comfortable beds, and dining cars of the era were famous for their fine food. The railroad lines competed to offer signature dishes, such as the Louisville & Nashville's famed "Country Ham Breakfast" that featured ham from Duncan Hines, eggs, biscuits, and redeye gravy.

With the coming of Amtrak in the 1970s, the various railroads gave up their passenger trains including those for the Derby. However, one vestige of this golden era remained. It became a tradition for the governor of Kentucky to bring a Derby Special full of dignitaries from Frankfort. Of late, a CSX train has dropped the governor's party on Central Avenue near Churchill Downs and made the return trip to Frankfort after the governor presented the trophy to the Derby winner's owner. For Derby 2004, Governor Ernie Fletcher made news by interrupting the many years of Derby trains. His guests instead traveled to Louisville by chartered bus. To the delight of Derby goers and rail fans alike, the Governor's Derby Train resumed its journey in 2005.

The True Story of the Whirlaway Café

by Beverle Graves Myers

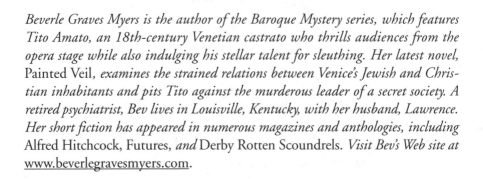

Beverle Graves Myers is the author of the Baroque Mystery series, which features Tito Amato, an 18th-century Venetian castrato who thrills audiences from the opera stage while also indulging his stellar talent for sleuthing. Her latest novel, Painted Veil, *examines the strained relations between Venice's Jewish and Christian inhabitants and pits Tito against the murderous leader of a secret society. A retired psychiatrist, Bev lives in Louisville, Kentucky, with her husband, Lawrence. Her short fiction has appeared in numerous magazines and anthologies, including* Alfred Hitchcock, Futures, *and* Derby Rotten Scoundrels. *Visit Bev's Web site at* www.beverlegravesmyers.com.

A man who's been collecting his social security check as long as I have ought to understand a few things. Like when to let the past rest in peace.

I thought I'd learned that lesson good enough. But last Derby Eve, I let my guard down. Donnell and I were taking a break out back of the Whirlaway's kitchen door with a couple of cold beers, watching stringy clouds drift across the moon while the clink and rattle of dish washing went on inside. My bones were tired, the air was as mellow as only Louisville in May can be, and dang if I didn't let my slick-tongued nephew drag the past smack-dab into the present.

"Uncle Wave, tell me about that horse." Donnell's brown face glowed slick with sweat in the flash of the neon sign on the café's roof. The annual Derby hoopla was in full swing, and the crowds wanting barbecue and burgoo had nearly run us off our feet.

"Horse?" I answered, knowing full well he was fishing for the details of how I'd managed to buy the café that had graced a busy corner just west of downtown Louisville for more years than I cared to remember. Every year around

Derby time, he asked the same question, and every year I played dumb. "What dang horse you talkin' 'bout, Donnell?"

"You know . . . Whirlaway. The horse you named this place after. How'd you decide to bet on him? Was he a sure thing?"

"Sure thing nothin'. That chestnut colt was as nervous as a long-tailed cat in a room full of rocking chairs. He could run all right, but not in a straight line. The Derby favorite that year was Porter's Cap."

"Then I don't get it. Why'd you bet all the money you'd saved on one squirrelly horse?"

I tipped my beer back and took a long pull. Donnell had good sense about beer. He'd grabbed us the right kind. Longnecks, malty, with ice crystals sliding down the glass. My nephew waited patiently, wondering if this was the year I'd give him a straight answer.

I smiled slowly. "Man gave me a tip."

Donnell snorted so hard, beer almost leaked out his nose. "A tip, huh? I could walk back in the restaurant and get twenty tips on tomorrow's Derby. All different."

"This was a guy in the know, not some jive talker."

"Okay, Uncle Wave, so you got a tip. How much did a railroad cook make in 1941?"

"Chef," I said quickly. "I was the youngest head chef the Louisville & Nashville Railroad ever had."

"So, how much did you make?"

"What you gettin' at, Donnell?"

"I've been thinking. You always told us you bought this café with the money you won on Whirlaway in the '41 Derby. But even if that horse went off at fifty to one, you would've had to bet a nice piece of change to win enough to buy a restaurant."

I tipped my chair back and stared down my longneck at my nephew. "Whirlaway paid two dollars and ninety cents on the dollar."

Donnell raised a thick eyebrow. He wasn't going to push, but he wanted the real story behind the café that would someday be his. Maybe it was the balmy Kentucky air. Or the good beer. Or maybe it was what the doctor told me when I went in for my check-up last week. I'm not sure why I told it, but I figured it was time Donnell got the truth.

Louisville was a different place back then, before the big war. A black man couldn't get just any job. I was busting with pride when the principal handed me my diploma at old Central High School, but that gold-stamped paper didn't seem to count for much in the white world. I worked a lot of day jobs, penny-ante stuff, before I got hired on by the Louisville & Nashville. The country traveled on the rails then—goods, coal, lumber, people—and the L&N ran freight and passenger trains all over the South.

I started as a chop boy, peeling apples and potatoes by the bushel, but by Derby 1941, I'd worked my way up to head chef on one of their luxury trains that ran from Cincinnati, through Louisville, down to New Orleans, and back. The Pan-American: twelve-olive green coaches, plus mail, diner, and baggage cars pulled by a big, black steam locomotive. We just called it the Pan.

Except for the two-day layovers when the dining car crew could go home, we spent every minute of our lives on that train, up each morning at five, firing up the wood ovens to roast meat and bake pies. Didn't get to bed until dinner was long past and the kitchen counters had been polished till they gleamed. We cooked three hundred meals every day in a kitchen not much bigger than the Whirlaway's meat locker. And I'm not talking about some hamburger joint on wheels. It was three full meals, made from scratch, as good as any high-class restaurant that wasn't rolling over the rails at sixty miles an hour.

Except for being hot as Hades, kitchen work wasn't really that bad. I liked feeding people. The only real downside was working under the dining car steward, an old Butchertown boy who'd given up the bloody work of the stock-yards for riding herd on a bunch of hungry passengers. Franz Kersting was this big white guy who always hunched his shoulders like his steward's jacket was one size too small and lined with steel wool.

"You're going to have to cut another slice, Wave. The lady wants it pink, running juice," Kersting griped as he squeezed around the charcoal broiler to place a plate of nicely browned prime rib on the steam table. The steward's pasty white cheeks were as red as the T-bone steaks I'd just tossed on the grill.

"That's the last piece. It went quick, what with the extra coaches hooked on for Derby. If the lady wants prime rib, she'll have to eat it well-done."

"She won't have it. What else you got? She wants something ready right now. The rest of her table's already eating."

"Lemme see, I could slice her up some turkey. It's nice and juicy, and we got plenty of dressin' and gravy."

"It'll have to do." Drawing his heavy chin into a frown, Kersting eyed the cleavers and carving knives hanging over the turkey carcass on the cutting board. He chose one and handed it to me with a stony stare.

"Yessir. Gettin' right to it." I shook seasoning salt onto the steaks and put the shaker down with a thump.

"Come on, snap it up, Wav-er-ley." Kersting said my name real slow, making each part into a word all its own. Needling me even more than usual. When I'd been promoted to head chef, I'd asked him to call me Mr. Johnson, but he'd made it clear that Sonja Henie could figure skate in Hell before he'd call any black man "mister."

I thought of some things I could say but just swallowed hard and went to carving turkey. I needed that job, see? I had special powerful motivation to save up some cash—Lonnie Mae Goodloe. Lonnie Mae and I had been sweethearts since high school, and if we were ever going to get married, we had to have money for a place of our own. Only thing was, hanging on to my paycheck was never my strong point. Let's just say that the neighborhood bookie and I were on better than speaking terms. I loved the idea of making a quick bundle, and he loved taking my money.

After Kersting had carried the turkey and trimmings away, I grabbed one of the waiters as he dropped off an order at the "hole," the window between kitchen and pantry where orders and food changed hands. "What's eating the boss this evenin'?" I asked.

Jimmy Odell was a loose-jointed teenager with straightened, oiled-down hair. He rolled his eyes. "Fat Franz worryin' 'bout his woman. Wessel's been fillin' his ear with tales."

L. B. Wessel was the conductor, another Butchertown boy who'd chosen the railroad over slaughtering hogs. He and Kersting were real tight. After the passengers settled in for the night, they played cards with some of the other white crew. On layovers, they were drinking buddies.

"What? That blonde Kersting is always braggin' about? The Jean Harlow look-alike?"

Jimmy flashed a toothy grin. "That be the one. Her name's Opal. Wessel say she playin' around while Kerstin' on the road. Guess she tired of bein' a L&N widow."

"I seen her once, when she came to meet the train. How'd that slob get such a good-looking woman?"

Jimmy shrugged as another waiter elbowed him aside. I shoved a plate of shrimp gumbo through the hole and went back to my cooking. Flipping the steaks with one hand, I stirred a bubbling pot with the other. Through the steam, the wall clock showed 7:20. In a few minutes, Kersting would carry his chimes through the coach and compartment cars, striking a mellow triplet to announce the last dinner seating. For the passengers, he could really turn on the charm. I wondered if Wessel would take the opportunity to rag the steward about Opal, but only for a minute. When one of the boys dropped a ketchup bottle that exploded a red, sticky mess all over our crowded work space, all I had on my mind was cleanup.

We finally got the kitchen swabbed down and all those hepped-up Derby passengers fed, but I can tell you, it was a job I wouldn't want to repeat every day. For four seatings of thirty-six diners, with the ovens, ranges, and grills all going at full blast, we might as well have been cooking in a furnace. I could have wrung a gallon of sweat out of my shirt and apron that night. The only thing that kept me standing was the steady flow of air created by the ventilators. Thank the Lord, there was one of those exhaust fans right over the range. Every few minutes, I'd splash water on my face and tip my head back to take advantage of the air being sucked up through that fan.

The fires were out and the waiters were stripping the tables of soiled linen when Jimmy stuck his head through the pantry hole. "Wave, where are you? We got a situation out here."

"What you say?" I straightened up from scraping leftovers into the garbage.

"Man wants a meal. We told him the kitchen done close, but he won't leave. He been drinkin' mint juleps in the club car, and he 'bout half lit."

"Why you tellin' me? Get Kersting to take him back to his compartment." It was the steward's job to deal with the passengers, not mine.

"Kersting takin' a smoke out in the vestibule. I went up to get him, an' he just tell me to shove it. I ain't gonna argue wit' that man. He in a mood!"

I wiped my forehead on my arm. Through the steel floor, I could feel the train slowing down. I figured we were approaching Baxter Avenue Station, the little urban platform that was the last stop before the busy Union Station that stood at Tenth and Broadway in downtown Louisville.

From behind the partition that separated the pantry from the dining area, a hoarse voice bellowed, "Hey, what's a fellow got to do to get some food around here?"

"What I'ma gonna do, Wave?" Jimmy's voice rose to a nervous squeak. "Ain't you got sumpin' I can give him?"

Jimmy wasn't fussing over nothing. The railroad brass bragged on the Pan's topnotch service. On the L&N, the passengers were always right, and a complaint, even an unfair complaint, could get a man fired.

"I wanna speak to the management," the voice slurred. "Where is everybody, anyway?"

I sighed. The other waiters must've made themselves scarce.

Jimmy grimaced, ebony face framed by the polished steel of the pantry window. The waiter was a raw kid, on the job just a couple of months. He didn't know how to pacify a rowdy drunk.

Damn Franz Kersting, anyhow, I thought. If he wanted to fret over his round-heeled wife, he could do it on his own time. Right now, he was needed on the job. "Stay back here, Jimmy," I said, untying my filthy apron and throwing it in the corner. "You can start sortin' linen."

I came out of the pantry, made two quick left turns, and barreled down the narrow corridor that ran between the kitchen and the outside wall of the car. In the dining area behind me, the drunk launched into an off-key version of "My Old Kentucky Home."

The bell on the locomotive clanged as the train moved slowly alongside the raised platform at Baxter Avenue Station. I opened the door at the front end of the dining car passage. The vestibule was empty, but the smell of cigarettes hung in the air and there were several fresh butts littering the metal floor plate. I knelt down. One was still warm at the tip.

I scratched my jaw as the screeching brakes brought the Pan to a full stop. There were only two places the steward could have got to. Either Kersting had moved forward, into the coaches between the dining car and the locomotive, or he'd jumped from the slow-moving train as soon as the dining car had reached the platform.

I braced my hands on the lower half of the outside door and leaned out of the open top. The crowd on the platform was larger and more excited than usual, mostly white folks from the east side of Louisville greeting their Derby guests. I didn't see the steward, but if Kersting had jumped to the platform, he could've already run down one of the enclosed stairways that led to Baxter Avenue.

Stepping to the other side of the vestibule, I looked over the barricade and across the sloping roofs and wooden pens of the Bourbon Stockyards. The setting sun had sucked the blue from the sky; the twin steeples of St. Joseph's Catholic Church stood out as sharp spears against the canvas of a flat, colorless twilight. A neat grid of streets lay just beyond the stockyard pens. The old pike that farmers had once used to herd their hogs and cattle to market was now lined with neat homes and small businesses. For a running man, feet fueled by jealous suspicion, Butchertown was only five minutes away.

Kersting might be headed home or he might be two coaches up, jawing with Wessel. Either way, I had a hungry drunk to deal with. I went back along the passage and entered the dining area. A middle-aged man in dark-rimmed glasses and plaid sport coat sprawled in a chair.

"Well, finally." He sat up with a hiccup. "Man could starve to death in here."

I trotted out a respectful smile along with my schoolroom elocution. "You missed the last seating, sir. The train will pull into Union Station in about fifteen minutes, just as long as it takes to get across Broadway and back the train up to the passenger platform. You can get a sandwich at the coffee shop in the terminal."

"No time." He tried to point to his wristwatch and ended up poking the air. "Gotta meet a jockey at the Brown Hotel . . . Eddie Arcaro. I'm a sportswriter for the Cincinnati *Enquirer*. I don't need a four-course dinner. Can't you just whip up an omelet or something?"

I shrugged my shoulders. "No fire in the stove."

Rolling onto one hip, he dug in his back pocket and came up with a fat leather wallet. "Look, boy. Here's a five-spot. Get me something to eat and some black coffee before we get to Union Station, and you'll get another."

Ten dollars for a bite to eat when he could've ordered a sandwich in the coffee shop for a quarter? Crazy. But what did I care? As the train lurched into motion, I pocketed the bill and hightailed it back to the kitchen.

I rescued the coffee urn from the counter by the sink just before the dish-washer was about to plunge it beneath the bubbles. The liquid in the bottom of the pot was strong enough to get up and walk on its own, but for the tipsy sportswriter, it'd be just what the doctor ordered. My next stop was the meat locker. I located the remains of a ham, shaved off a stack of paper-thin slices, and married those to a kaiser roll slathered with creamy mayonnaise that I'd made that morning. I tossed the roll onto a china plate, but the sandwich looked a little lonely surrounded by nothing except the L&N's signature ivy border. One of my assistant chefs came up with the perfect accompaniment—a slice of pecan pie topped with a scoop of vanilla ice cream.

When the sportswriter saw our creation, his bleary eyes snapped to atten-tion. His first bite took out half the sandwich. He was soon alternating spoon-fuls of pie with gulps of tepid coffee. I swear, the guy sobered up with each passing second. With only crumbs remaining, he sank back into the chair, lit a cigarette, and handed me the rest of my tip.

"Good, real good," he said through the swirling smoke. "Really hit the spot. I might make it through that interview after all. Hey, you play the ponies, boy?"

"Yes, sir," I answered cautiously.

"Then I got something else for you. Hot tip." His head bobbled a bit as he picked at his teeth with a toothpick. The bourbon from the juleps was still battling the sandwich and coffee. "Bet on Whirlaway. To win."

I shook my head. "No, sir. My money's on Porter's Cap. Whirlaway blew the Bluegrass Stakes by runnin' wide. Same with the Derby Trial. Nag can't stay on the rail. He's all over the track."

"Not anymore." He leaned forward. "I spent a couple of days at Calumet Farm last week. I been pals with Whirlaway's trainer ever since I worked the city desk at the Lexington *Herald*. Ben Jones has got that crazy horse running straight, and when Whirlaway makes a beeline for the wire, no horse can touch him."

I must have looked skeptical, because he nodded his head, gesturing with his cigarette for emphasis. "It's these special blinkers Ben had made—with the left side cut away. Keeps the horse on the rail. I watched him put Whirlaway through his paces. Ben sat on a stable pony while Pinky Brown rode Whirlaway through the gap between the pony and the rail."

I bent over to take his empty plate. "It's a sure thing, huh?"

"Watched 'em do it twenty times or more. No more shying away, and he's running like greased lightning." The man got to his feet, surprisingly steady, and clapped a hand on my shoulder. "Put your money on Whirlaway, boy, and you can't go wrong."

I scraped the crumbs from the tablecloth into the plate, already planning to find a pay phone as soon as the train hit the station. The Pan had reached its switching point and was now backing up on the track that led to the passenger platform. I was calculating how much cash I could afford to put on Whirlaway when I saw a familiar figure through the window.

Kersting was stepping out of a cab at the corner of Ninth and Kentucky. He had a black suit jacket over his white uniform and a wide-brimmed hat pulled low to hide his face, but I'd know those butcher's shoulders and bowlegs anywhere. Darting nervous looks right and left, he hopped over several sets of track and disappeared around the curve of coaches rolling slowly toward the station.

My stomach sank to my knees, and I began to have a very bad feeling about Opal Kersting. I thought about the steward's little lady all the while I helped the crew make the kitchen gleam, getting it ready for Kersting's inspection. The steward finally walked in the dining car as the Pan rolled under the ornate ironwork roof at the back of the station. He'd lost the dark coat and hat and looked like a man who'd just swallowed a dose of salts.

"Where've you been?" I asked, without any attempt at ceremony.

He hunched his powerful shoulders. "In the crapper. Not that it's any of your business."

"On this train?"

"Hell, yes, on this train. Where else would I be using the toilet?" He poked me in the chest with a fat finger. "That gumbo of yours I had for supper must've been off, Wave. You better hope it don't do any of the passengers like it done me."

"Uh-huh," I muttered, wondering if anybody else had seen Kersting get out of that cab. I kept wondering while we left the steward to inspect the kitchen, while we folded the tables in the dining car into berths, and while we pulled our bedding out of the "possum belly" under the floor of the car. I was dead certain he had left the train at Baxter Avenue Station and run home. What would he have done if he'd found Opal entertaining another man when he burst through the door?

I was wondering and worrying so much that calling my bookie slipped right out of my mind. After the train dropped its Derby passengers and headed south toward Nashville, I folded into my berth and gave myself a serious talking to. Why did I want to get mixed up in white folks' troubles anyhow? I had enough of my own. I was missing Lonnie Mae something fierce, and I knew she was getting tired of waiting for me to get settled. I pounded my pillow and ordered myself to fall asleep to the coach's familiar sway, but it was a no go.

In my mind's eye, I saw a lady so blonde she was almost white-headed, wrapped in a satin gown, lying on a bed with her face twisted to the wall. Opal's gown would be pink, I thought. Pink and smooth like the inside of a seashell. I snuggled down in my pillow and soon dreamed of a blood-red stain spreading in a circle around the hilt of a knife buried in her stomach. That jerked me awake with every nerve tingling. Man alive! I needed to calm down. Moving quietly, trying not to wake the rest of the peacefully snoring crew, I headed to the kitchen for a cool glass of buttermilk.

I stood there a good long time, my back against the counter, empty glass in my hand. The kitchen was quiet except for the whirr of the exhaust fans. *Thump-thump-a-thump* they went, playing background rhythm for my tumbling thoughts. I pushed the vision of Opal aside and considered the tip about Whirlaway. Maybe I could get my bookie on the phone at the next stop. Lonnie would sure be happy if I had some money to give her. Then I stewed about seeing Kersting get out of that cab. Should I tell somebody? Or not? I couldn't decide. Something was bugging me. A sound at the back of my mind. A sound disturbingly out of place, like the rumble of thunder in a clear blue sky.

Glass clinked on concrete as Donnell set his beer on the Whirlaway's back step. He wrapped his arms around his knees and waited. Finally he said, "Go on, Uncle Wave. What happened? Was Opal dead or not?"

I sighed. "Cops met the train at Flomaton, Alabama, the next day. They delivered the bad news during the second lunch seatin'. Early that mornin', the milkman found the bodies after he noticed the kitchen door of Kersting's house standin' open."

"Bodies? Two of 'em?"

I nodded. "Opal Kersting and her lover, Pete Schmidt . . . young guy that worked on the line at Oertel's Brewery. Cops told Kersting a burglar must've broke in and cut 'em with his shiv when Pete came charging out of the bedroom. Kersting cried like a baby, I seen him."

"They catch this burglar?"

I shook my head. "Never was no burglar. Cops figured there must be, 'cuz nothin' else made sense. Way they saw it, Opal's husband was away on his run,

Pete wasn't married, and no one else meaned either of 'em any harm. So it had to be a burglar."

Donnell frowned and said, very quietly, more a statement than a question, "But you told them, didn't you, Uncle Wave. You told them that Kersting got off the train."

I didn't want to say, but I figured it was time I came clean. I swallowed the last drop of beer to wet my throat. "No, I didn't. That sound I heard in the kitchen, it was the exhaust fan over the range, making a clunkin' noise like it never did before. I got a flashlight and climbed up to take a look-see. There was somethin' stuffed up in there—somethin' white that was hittin' the tip of the fan blade. I eased it out with my long grill tongs."

"What was it?"

"A dinner napkin . . . wrapped around a knife. It was a steak knife from the car, with 'L&N' embossed on its wooden handle. I can still see it just like it was yesterday. Blood—sticky and dark—all over the blade and soaked into the seams of the handle."

"The murder weapon?"

"Right. That knife had taken two lives." I nodded several times. "But I just saw it as my ticket off the railroad and into a good life with Lonnie Mae. Kersting been on the train a long time. He'd bragged about saving his money to retire down to Florida with his hot little wife." Through the gloom, I strained to look my nephew in the eye. I needed to know what he thought of his uncle now, but Donnell was staring at his shoes.

I went on. "I hid the knife in a different place and went to find Kersting. We made a deal. His nest egg for the knife and my silence . . . money and knife to change hands the minute we got back to Louisville."

"So the money you bet on Whirlaway . . . it came from Kersting?"

Nodding, I whispered, "Called my bookie from the station in Bowling Green. He nearly lost it when I told him how much I wanted to put on that horse, but we'd done business for a long time, so he took the bet."

More words rumbled up from some deep dark place. "I bought the Whirlaway Café with blood money, Donnell. I had Kersting right in my hands. I could've put him in the electric chair where he belonged, but I didn't. I made a bargain wit' the devil and let a murderer go free. There's not a day passed I haven't beat myself up over it."

"What happened to Kersting?"

"He went out to California and got a job on the Union Pacific. Heard he got shot over a card game. Cheatin', prob'ly."

"Why're you telling me now, Uncle Wave?" Donnell was still staring at his feet. Would he ever be able to look me in the eye again?

"I'm not gonna be around much longer. It's true . . . doctor done told me."
I nodded as Donnell's chin finally came up. "An' that's okay, 'cuz I got Lonnie Mae waitin' on the other side. But I got to do somethin' and want you to promise you won't undo it when I'm gone."

Donnell didn't speak. His eyes were hard disks, unreadable.

"I'm changin' the name of the restaurant. It's a little enough thing, but I wanna do it." I jerked my chin toward the blinking sign on the roof. "That's comin' down. We'll get a new sign. From now on, this gonna be Opal's Place. Really been hers all along, not some dang horse's."

I held my breath. Nothing Donnell could say would wash away the sorrows of the past, but I was aching for him to say something. Just anything to let me know he understood and would respect my wishes. He didn't speak, actually, just got to his feet and swooped me up in a big bear hug. But that was plenty.

I should've told him the true story years before.

Author's note: Because of Ben Jones's special blinkers and jockey Eddie Arcaro's deft handling, Whirlaway galloped into history as a Triple Crown winner. The Pan-American made its last run on April 30, 1971, just over ten years before the L&N Railroad ceased to exist by merging into the new Seaboard System Railroad. Today, the tracks leading to Union Station have been pulled up, but the majestic Romanesque structure still stands as the headquarters of TARC, Louisville's mass transit company. The remains of the Baxter Avenue Station, at this writing a boarded-up, tumbledown wreck, are just visible from the intersection of Lexington Road and Baxter Avenue. Special thanks to Jim Herron of Herron Rail Video and the L&N Historical Society for providing a wealth of detail about railroad dining cars in the 1940s.

The Fillies

by Cheryl Stuck

The first evening of the Kentucky Derby Festival kicks off with a fabulous ball produced by the Fillies, a club originally formed in 1959 by Frances Askew Davis. In the beginning, the group of seventeen women had three membership rules: All the ladies must volunteer to work on the Derby Ball, further the fame of Kentucky, and place a bet on any filly entered in the Derby.

Since those early days, the club has grown to a maximum of 250 active members. The women still adhere to those original rules, but they also hold fund-raising events, build a float for the Pegasus Parade, and above all, care for the Kentucky Derby Festival Queen and her court of princesses. A panel of three out-of-state judges narrows the field of applicants to five princesses, based on personality, intelligence, values/civic activities, appearance, and their general knowledge of the Kentucky Derby Festival and current events.

Up to 1,100 people now attend the Fillies Derby Ball, which has a different theme each year with extravagant decorations. Attendees enjoy cocktails, a gourmet dinner, and entertainment. The highlight of the evening is the coronation of the Derby Festival Queen, determined by a spin of the wheel by the current Fillies president. The first official duty of the queen is "knighting" two outstanding Kentuckians, chosen for their community or Derby Festival involvement. Throughout the two-week festival, the queen and princesses serve as ambassadors, attending more than 70 events.

Dying to get in? A new member must be nominated by a current Filly and endorsed by two other members, then voted in by the membership committee.

ORINOCO

by P. J. Robertson

P. J. Robertson has studied psychology, history, and education, as well as sociology. After teaching sociology for several years at a Midwestern university, she returned to her first love, the mystery novel. She is now working on her second full-length mystery featuring C. J. Sutherland and her Bouvier des Flandres dog, Oliver. P. J. lives in southern Indiana with her husband, three Bouviers, and one miniature schnauzer.

By the time the shots rang out, Lieutenant Jake Carter and I were halfway down the first set of stairs, headed for the track.

We'd watched the start of the race from the grandstand seats high above the track at Churchill Downs. My first ever Kentucky Derby, and in my spring suit and flats, I felt a bit like Cinderella before her godmother's visit. Jake hadn't warned me that people, woman especially, went all out on their Derby attire.

A gasp had arisen from the crowd as the sleek Thoroughbreds leapt from the starting gate. Orinoco's rider, lime-and-black silks flashing in the afternoon sun, swayed in the saddle. People jumped to their feet in front of us, pointing toward the crowd favorite slowing and drifting toward the outside rail as the rest of the horses swept on.

Jake grasped my elbow and pulled me to my feet. My head swam and my world tilted.

The jockey shook his head as though to clear it and then raised his crop. As it descended, the three-year old chestnut colt leaped forward and sped after the receding pack. Several times the rider seemed to lose his balance and then regain it, each time losing ground. And each time, groans from those betting on the favorite could be heard over the cheers of those betting the lead horse. At last the jockey seemed to gather himself, and the whip fell again, spurring the horse into a sprint that carried it past the last two laggards in the field.

The most exciting two minutes in sports were quickly passing, and the favored winner was running third from last on a fast, dry track. Orinioco's jockey seemed to be ill, but he held on, urging his horse ahead.

They drove past one more horse, and Orinoco gained the rail, joining the mass of horses maneuvering for position behind the leaders. His way was blocked; he had to pull to the outside in order to pass. A big gray moved to cut him off, but Orinoco pushed by. Lengthening his stride, he left the pack of horses behind. Just three horses stood between him and the winner's circle.

For a moment, the jockey's head lolled to the side. With a visible effort, he straightened his body, hunkered tightly over the horse's withers, and gathered the lax reins. Orinoco fought to gain ground; they inched past the third-place horse.

"C. J., let's go," Jake said. "There's something wrong with that jockey. He may just be sick, but I'd better check it out."

I tightened the leash on Oliver, my assistance dog, and held onto the handle rising above his harness. I could relate to balance problems since I'd been having such difficulties myself for several months. One nasty little virus affecting the nerves leading to the inner ear, and wham, my view of the world was turned upside down. But my Bouvier des Flandres buddy was always there to support me until the dizziness passed; the jockey had no such support.

Grabbing Jake's arm to slow him for a moment, I asked, "Who's the jockey? I can't understand the announcer."

He glanced back. "Rafe Martinez. Rumor is, he's been having some personal problems lately, and it's been affecting his riding. I'm surprised the Elliots put him up on Orinoco for the Derby, but he's done some good riding for them in the past."

Oliver pressed firmly against my leg as we struggled to get through the crowd lining the railings. The cheers and race commentary made it difficult to hear much, but we heard the crack of a shot, saw the horse swerve. A second shot threw the rider sideways, out of the saddle. For an instant he hung from the stirrup, but the bucking action of the frightened horse dislodged him and he hit the track, a pall of dust settling over him.

As we raced for the track, Jake's words tumbled into his cell phone.

Two men spilled from the horse ambulance as it stopped beside the downed jockey. One checked the rider as the other grabbed screens from the vehicle and began erecting them. A silent ambulance pulled up, medics jumping out as it slowed.

We lost sight of the track as we raced down hallways and more stairs. Jake grabbed a security officer by the arm and flashed his police ID in front of the man's face. I couldn't hear what Jake said over the screams of startled racegoers, but I was sure it had to do with securing the gates before the sniper could escape. The guard yelled into his radio as we swept on.

By the time we came out of the building, the race was over. A pony rider had caught Orinoco and led him off the track. The winner and his jockey, trainer, and owners paraded to the winner's circle, but the spectators' eyes were divided between the winners and the area now obscured by screens. Some crowded the fences, trying to decide which was the better show.

Two security officers stood guard at the entrance to the track. Again Jake flashed his identification and was waved forward. He pushed me in front of him, and the officers stood aside somewhat hesitantly, especially when they noticed Oliver trotting alongside me.

Before disappearing behind the screens, Jake said, "C. J., you'll have to keep Oliver back so he doesn't contaminate the evidence—not that the medics haven't destroyed most of it already."

"Oliver, down. Stay."

He reluctantly sank to the ground, nostrils flaring, and I edged closer to the opening between screens.

The medics had straightened Rafe Martinez's body, turning him on his side, cutting off his sweat- and blood-drenched shirt, and raising the thin sleeveless turtleneck worn underneath. I didn't need binoculars to see the puckered edges of the bullet wound against the sallow skin under his armpit. Dark blood pooled under him. Stains spread over his ribs and back and showed up again on his elbows. My enhanced olfactory sense took in blood, sweat, and horses, but there was another odor, one I recognized. *What is it?* I wondered. *Tobacco! That's it. Do jockeys smoke?*

Jake, who had been kneeling beside the body, stood up.

"Jake," I hissed.

He glanced at me and shook his head, but I motioned him closer and said, "What are the brown stains over his ribs and back? There're more on his arm."

He returned to the body and pointed out the stains to the heavyset medic crouched over the body.

The medic bent closer, sniffing. "Liniment."

Jake turned to see if I'd heard.

I nodded. "What about the tobacco odor?"

The medic sniffed again and shrugged his shoulders. "Must be the horse liniment you're smelling."

Liniment could contain a lot of smelly ingredients, camphor among them, but I knew nicotine wasn't one of them. Not if the animal it was used on was to live, anyway. As every weekend gardener knows, nicotine can be as deadly on the skin as when ingested.

With their sirens blaring, every city and county police car in Louisville and the surrounding areas must have wheeled into the parking lot. In moments, an army of police officers erupted onto the track. Oliver's ears lay flat, but he held his position as I watched the swarming anthill that the homicide scene had become. A black Mercedes drove directly onto the track and disgorged a small man gripping a black bag. The medical examiner, I presumed. Technicians carrying photo equipment followed.

I needed to get Oliver into some shade, and my own face and arms were tingling from the slanting afternoon sun. I wondered how to get Jake's attention. Hands in his pockets, he reeled off information to the stout man who stood beside him, swiftly penning directives into a small notebook. A woman in a business suit occasionally interjected comments.

Jake's dark hair, touched with glints of silver where the sun struck it, hung over his forehead. Finally, he started my way, accompanied by his note-taking partner. Despite the noise, I could hear their conversation.

"So, who's the broad?"

Jake shook his head at the smirking man. "She's a friend, okay? She's the sociologist who's helped me on a couple of cases. Does a lot of research into family interactions."

"Oho, she must be some help. You bring all your helpers to the Derby?" Luckily he didn't know I was spending the night in Jake's guest room.

"What's that supposed to mean?" Jake's face slightly flushed, and he stopped and turned to his co-worker. "She's married—notice the wedding band?"

On cue, I held up my left hand, wiggling my ring finger. Oh, yeah, I was married all right, but my husband, Matt, was in northern Alberta with his supposedly sick mother while I was teaching sociology at a nice little community college in southern Indiana. I'd be more sympathetic, except I'd require a doctor's written diagnosis before I'd believe his mother was really ill—more like trying to keep her baby boy from leaving the area. Matt was pretty naïve when it came to his mother.

And ever since I'd met Jake Carter coming out of his sister's classroom after his presentation to her introduction to criminal justice class, I'd wondered if absence really did make the heart grow fonder. The lieutenant was one attractive policeman—and single. *Unlike me*, I thought.

Jake reached my side. "C. J. Sutherland, meet my partner, Dennis Flaten." Once we'd exchanged appropriate greetings, Jake continued detailing his plan. "Dennis, I want you to talk to the security guards and ushers. See if anyone saw anything suspicious. Question the vendors as well. We'll have to question the crowd—must be close to 150,000 people here today. Send the uniforms out to help take information at the gates—the guards will be overwhelmed.

No one leaves without showing proof of name and address, in case we need them again. And we need to know where each was seated. Anyone with any information, take them aside and we'll question them as soon as we can. Ask the security chief where to have them wait." He gestured toward the woman still hovering over the crime scene. "She knows what she's doing. And get some of the men to search the stands. Looks like the shot came from there rather than the infield or the backside, but if they don't find anything, have them cover it all."

"Gotcha, Lieutenant. Where will you be if I find anything interesting?"

"In an office near the dressing room, questioning the other jockeys. Then I'll be talking to Orinoco's owners and trainers. Someone needs to question the pony riders, valets, and grooms . . . find out if anyone had it in for Rafe Martinez. Or maybe just wanted his horse to lose."

As his partner hurried off, Jake turned to me. "Want to hear what the other riders have to say?"

"Need someone to take notes?"

He grinned. "That too."

"Sure. I need to get out of this sun and give Oliver a drink. Then I'm ready for anything."

"Not exactly the day I had planned for your first Derby."

I took his arm. "Well, it's definitely one I'll remember."

The small, barren room reeked of sweaty bodies, as we sat on metal folding chairs around the long table that centered the room. Flaking paint showed that the concrete floor had once been painted, but the color was impossible to detect—somewhere between dirty gray and brown, I figured.

Jake looked around and laughed. "Guess I should have asked to use one of the luxury boxes. This is pretty. . . ." He shrugged.

"Basic?" I suggested.

"Good word."

Facing the door, I sat at one end of the table, holding the ballpoint and notebook Jake had requisitioned. Oliver sat at my side, chin on my knee. Jake and a thin Hispanic man in jeans and a cotton shirt faced each other across the width of the table near the other end. The jockey kept glancing at my black dog, obviously uneasy with his presence. Oliver kept dark eyes focused on the sweating man.

Jake cleared his throat and said, "So, Morales, how well did you know Rafe Martinez?"

"What?" the jockey almost spat. "You think we're both Hispanic, we gotta be amigos? You bring me in here first, the others will think I'm a suspect, man."

"I brought you in first because you were the first one out the locker room door," Jake said. "Some days it doesn't pay to be first."

The stories told by the jockeys were much the same. Most of them agreed Orinoco's rider had seemed ill, but no one thought it important enough to point it out to the officials. They rode, sick or well, broken bones or whole, if they could stick on a horse. And Rafe was known as a user, popping pain meds as well as drugs to combat his tendency to gain weight—the kiss of death to a jockey's career. He chain-smoked and on occasion had been heard emptying his stomach before an important race—or after an indiscriminate gorging. A couple did comment he seemed worse than usual, pasty-faced and sweating, and a bit off-balance. Oh, and he spit a lot, but then they all did.

Three riders admitted seeing Rafe at one of the local bars the evening before the big race, hiding out in a back booth with a known bookie. None of them had been close enough to overhear their conversation, but no one was particularly surprised at the association. According to the jockeys, the bookie, one "Stogie" Wilson—nicknamed for the cigar he was never without—associated with some bad characters. And the scuttlebutt along the circuit said Martinez would throw a race if the money was right; he was just looking for the proper incentive for retirement. A bit of a pension fund, if you will.

My hand was cramping long before Curt Langley, the next-to-last jockey, sat down in the hot seat. I wondered how I'd last through more interrogations when Dennis knocked on the door. He stuck his head inside the room and said, "Lieutenant? Can you spare a minute?"

Jake asked the jockey to wait, and I massaged my fingers while the chance presented itself. Short, of course, and slight, with close-cropped hair and a freckled complexion, Curt looked more like a schoolboy than a well-known jockey. He appeared tired and obviously just wanted the interview over so he could leave.

"Curt," I said, just to make conversation, "I noticed Rafe had liniment on his sides and back. Is that unusual?"

He relaxed at the apparent stupidity of the question. "No, ma'am. We all use it—we have more than the usual amount of aches and pains in this job, ya know."

"Yeah, I guess you would. Do you all use the same kind?"

"I guess. We just pick up the liniment that's around the barns. Someone makes it up and sets bottles around—not sure it's something you can buy at the store. Probably at least one bottle in everyone's kit."

"It doesn't happen to smell like tobacco, does it?"

"No'm. It stinks, but nothin' like that. Why?"

"Just wondered." Changing the subject, I asked something that had been bothering me. "Was Rafe married?"

"Last I knew."

"Was his wife here to watch him race?"

"Doubt it. The wives don't follow us around much; they mostly watch on TV like everyone else."

Aghast, I asked, "You mean she might be sitting at home wondering what's happening here? I hope Lieutenant Carter has had someone contact her."

"She lives a few miles from here—across the river, up in Indiana someplace. Has a couple of little kids."

"Did you ever associate with them outside the track?"

"Not really. My ex-wife used to work with Linda—that's the wife's name— Linda Martinez. My ex said she used to walk into a lot of doors, if you know what I mean." He kept his voice low and looked everywhere but at my face.

And yes, I did know what he meant. Like many careers, racing was hard on relationships: the separations, the injuries, the fear. As I knew from my research, abuse existed everywhere, so why not among jockeys and their families? "Was Rafe pretty hard to get along with—at the track?"

"He wasn't sweetness and light, if that's what you mean, but we're all just here to do a job, and we pretty much ignore each other and get on with it."

I nodded. *Not much different than faculty meetings.*

Jake returned, obviously no longer interested in the jockey who shared the table with me. His mind on overdrive, he sent Curt on his way. The only jockey not yet questioned was Kit Andrews, rider of the day's winner, Tailspin, and it didn't look as though Jake was in any hurry to interrogate him.

I stood, balanced by fingertips on the tabletop. "What's the news?"

His eyes gleaming, Jake explained that searchers had located a high-powered rifle, complete with scope, hidden under some vendor supplies at the top of the grandstand. "The shooter must have assumed everyone would be watching the track. Had to be good to hit Martinez at that distance. A moving target, at that."

"Not to mention not hitting anyone standing between him and his target," I said, shuddering to think what could have happened. "A professional?"

"Probably. We're pretty sure ole Stogie's employers bet heavily on Tailspin—the figures show *someone* did—and wanted Rafe to keep Orinoco from winning. It looks like Mr. Martinez wasn't being as accommodating as he usually was. Guess he hated to give up a big win like the Derby. And we've got a nice description of the gunman. Little old lady in one of the top tiers wanted a drink. This guy had been selling drinks from a tray all afternoon. She turned those old-fashioned opera glasses around and caught him in the act of shooting. She wasn't sure what she was seeing at first. Good thing he didn't notice her."

My mouth dropped open. "She was looking for a drink in the middle of the race? Of the Kentucky Derby?"

Jake shrugged. "A jury's gonna love her, though, all dressed up in her pink suit with a matching straw hat mashed down over her white curls. Must be in her eighties, but sharp as a tack. Gave a great description. We're pretty sure we know who was ordered in for the shooting. And there's a chance he hasn't left the grounds."

"So the nicotine smell was a red herring."

Jake shrugged. "Maybe not. The autopsy should tell us whether someone added a bit of nicotine to Rafe's liniment. We've taken all the bottles from the dressing room and Rafe's bag. They'll be tested if nicotine shows up on his skin. Maybe the gamblers doped his liniment, hoping to make him sick enough to lose, but when it looked like he had a good chance to win, they finished him off. Only time will tell." He smiled and added, "It was a good call on that odor. Not sure I would have noticed, with that bullet wound there in front of me."

"Thanks," I said. "I should get out of your way. Do you suppose I could find a taxi to take me back to my car?"

"That won't work, not today. I'll take a few minutes and run you home so you can get your bag from my place. I'm sorry to put our plans on hold. Rain check?"

"Of course. I can't hold you responsible for the change in plans. I doubt you arranged this for my benefit." I chuckled. "Besides, this has given me a chance to watch you work."

"C'mon. Let's find my car."

On the way I remembered to ask about Linda Martinez.

Jake said, "I sent a team over to her house to notify her and make sure she had someone to stay with her, but I've not heard back. She lives just outside Salem—you go through there on your way home, don't you? Do you want to stop by and check on her?"

"Yes, I'd feel better knowing that she was doing okay. She might not have family or friends nearby."

After checking his notes, Jake copied something on a blank sheet and handed me the paper. "Here's her address and phone number. If you find out anything you think I need to know, leave a message on my cell phone. I don't suppose I'll see my apartment or my office anytime soon. We've got a hell of a job ahead of us gathering enough proof for a jury."

* * *

On I-65, thousands of cars moved like tortoises, nose to tail, not helped by the eternal roadwork going on north of Louisville. Luckily for me, I had only to travel a few miles into Indiana before I could exit. Unluckily for me, a large number of other people had the same idea, but I had time to admire the soft spring greens of trees and fields, vivid in the setting sun, and to inhale the heady bouquet of lilacs gracing nearly every homestead along the way. All scents tempered, unfortunately, by the noxious fumes of gasoline- and diesel-fueled vehicles.

By the time I reached Salem, my neck and head ached and I almost convinced myself to go home without stopping to see Linda Martinez. Almost. But I'd also had time to think on the slow drive northward, and I wanted to ask the new widow some questions.

A man at the first gas station I came to gave me directions to her house. Sipping a Diet Coke and sharing a package of cheese crackers with Oliver, I drove the few blocks to their home. No cars were parked in front of the two-car garage, and only dim, bluish light shone through the sheers masking the large front window.

I brushed the orange crumbs from Oliver's beard before we traversed the brick walkway and gracious landscaping between the street and the house. Colorful woodland flowers spilled casually from irregularly shaped flower beds flowing around the foundation and surrounding the massive maple trees. As we walked under the weighty limbs arched over the path, we were plunged into sudden dusk. I hurried to the porch, Oliver close to my side.

The door was painted a soft lilac shade that complemented the wildflowers blooming so abundantly. Ivy cascaded from a wire basket stuffed with moss and attached to the door.

There was no sound from the television lighting the room, and no response to the doorbell's cheery ring. I knocked and called softly, hoping it would carry through the closed window. "Mrs. Martinez, the Louisville police sent me; please open the door."

A shadow passed between the bluish light and the window, and Oliver cocked his head at the sound of footsteps approaching. The door swung inward a few inches. A soft, Southern voice invited, "Come in, then."

"This is my service dog, Oliver. Is it a problem if I bring him inside?" If she mistook him for a police dog, it didn't really matter.

The voice became more animated. "I didn't see him there. Do bring him in." She opened the door more fully, and for the first time, I could see the person behind the voice. Even in the subdued light I could make out a face swollen with tears, eyes and nose red and streaming.

"Mrs. Martinez, could I fix you some coffee or tea or something?"

She scrubbed at her face with a wad of tissues. "Please, call me Linda. Who did you say you were?"

I gave her my name and told her my connection to Jake, explaining that he was in charge of her husband's case.

"Let's go into the kitchen so I can wash my face, and I'll put on the coffee—I need something to do. Would you like a cup?"

"Yes, thank you. It's been a long day." Then I realized it must have seemed an even longer day for her. Following her down the hall, I noted the family pictures lining the walls, while Oliver just looked for a cool tile floor to lie on.

After washing her face at the sink and dabbing it dry with paper towels, she reached toward a Snoopy cookie jar on the counter. "I have some dog treats. Is it okay for your dog to have one?" Not waiting for an answer, she took a handful of tiny, bone-shaped treats out of the jar, looked at Oliver's eighty-five pound body, made larger by his shaggy coat, and gave a small laugh as she offered them to him. He glanced at me, and when I nodded he chowed down.

"What kind of dog do you have?" I asked, noting a small blue bowl filled with water and a matching food bowl, empty, arranged neatly against the wall beside the back door.

Her body stiffened as she turned toward me. With a few pounds off and some care taken with her makeup and hair, she could be the beauty portrayed in her wedding pictures hanging in the hallway.

She gestured awkwardly toward the bowls. "A Yorkie named Peanut." Hesitating, she added, "He's away, with my boys, right now."

She didn't seem sure of that, but we could come back to it later.

When the coffee was dripping briskly into the carafe and ceramic mugs were arranged to her satisfaction, Linda sat opposite me at the small wooden table. The room was cozy—not overly large, but with adequate storage space and a generous side-by-side refrigerator-freezer that had plenty of door space for the colorful pictures adorning it.

"Your kids' artwork?"

Nodding, she smiled. "They're at my sister's house this weekend. She has boys nearly the same age as my two."

Once the coffee was poured and cream and sugar had been offered and refused, she sat fiddling with the handle on her cup. At last she looked up at me from red-rimmed eyes. "Did Rafe suffer?" she asked quietly.

"It seemed quick, so I don't think so."

Her look of bewilderment was replaced by a small smile. "That's good."

I sipped my coffee and fondled Oliver's ears, giving her a minute to grieve. Breaking the silence, I said, "Tell me about the abuse."

She didn't look surprised. "There's not much to tell. It's the same old story, and don't I know it. I'm a nurse, an RN. I've seen it all, but that didn't mean I knew how to handle it when it happened to me."

She took a sip of coffee, made a face at its bitterness. "Things were fine for years, I thought, except that Rafe was pretty controlling. But after the boys were born, he became even more possessive."

I nodded. In some cultures, the man still considered himself the patriarch, with unquestioned authority over the family. The birth of children, especially sons, often exacerbated the situation.

"He didn't want me to work after the kids were born. Robert is seven and Jamie six," she added in response to my unasked question. "We moved away from Louisville so the boys could grow up in a small town. And I could get work here—a good nurse can always find work. But we fought over it." She shook her head. "Hell, we fought over everything."

"When did he start hitting you?"

"While he was out on the race circuit, I took a part-time job at the hospital and found a really good woman to stay with the kids—it's not like they were dropped off at day care every day. But when he found out, that's the first time he hit me. Before, he'd twist my arm, or push me, but this time he left big bruises; nearly broke my arm. After that, anytime he was displeased, he'd take it out on me." Her hands trembled as she lifted her cup, sloshing coffee on the table.

"Why didn't you leave?" I asked, already knowing the answer.

"He threatened to kill the kids, and then me," she whispered. "I could stand dying—then it would be over—but he had it all planned, how he'd make me watch him strangle the boys and then kill me." She turned frightened eyes to me. "How could he even say those things? He loved the boys and they loved him; he never so much as spanked them!"

"I don't know," I replied, my voice cracking. I moistened my throat with a sip of coffee and I continued. "I'm assuming this went on for some time, with you afraid to leave and afraid to stay."

"He'd gotten worse. He was thirty-seven, you see. His career as a jockey was about over, and he'd never made it really big. And there was the weight problem . . . always the weight problem. The violence increased, and I was becoming afraid he'd go after the boys." She turned her face away. "He threatened to hunt us down wherever we'd go, and I believed him. We'd never live without fear, never know when he'd find us. I knew we had to get away eventually. I've been sending money to my sister to save, trying to think of somewhere to run, somewhere we might be safe." Her voice sounded flat.

I got up and poured us both more coffee. Standing over her, one hand on her shoulder, I asked the hard question. "When did you decide to kill him?"

Sobbing, she pointed to the dog's bowls. "Earlier this week, right here in the kitchen. He'd come home angry; I've no idea why. The boys were playing . . . a bit noisy, but they're just kids. All of a sudden he grabbed up Peanut and threw her against the wall. I snatched her and started to run out with her, but he grabbed my arm and threatened to do that to the boys, just to show me he meant it." She turned to look up at me, her eyes full of tears. Her voice rose. "How could he *do* that? He loved that dog. We'd raised her from a tiny pup, and she's so little and. . . ."

I shook my head and walked around the table. Again she wanted answers I couldn't give. "What happened to Peanut?" I asked grimly, sinking into the seat across from her.

"I raced to the vet. I wanted to take the boys, but Rafe forced me to leave them here. Hostages, I guess. And he was right—I'd have taken them and not come back. I guess I shouldn't have left them with him, but I couldn't stand by and watch Peanut die. He'd never laid a hand on the boys. . . ." Linda looked at me, her eyes beseeching.

I touched her hand lightly and nodded so she'd know I understood and, as a dog lover, agreed.

"Peanut has internal injuries and a broken leg, but she'll be okay. The vet is keeping her and promised not to release her to anyone but me. She knows what happened—she'd like to get Rafe in her office, alone. Said she had some blue juice. . . ."

Nodding, I urged her to continue. "So, why the nicotine?"

If she was surprised, she didn't show it. "The horse gave me the idea. Rafe'd gotten this last big chance to ride the favorite in the Kentucky Derby. Orinoco." In response to my raised eyebrows, she explained. "Orinoco is a type of tobacco, mostly grown for pipe smokers. I come from south-central Kentucky, and my folks raised tobacco. Even as kids, we knew all about GTS, or green tobacco sickness. My daddy warned us that if our skin touched the wet tobacco leaves, it could make us real sick or maybe even kill us. We had to watch each other and the other workers for symptoms. And of course, as a nurse, I've seen quite a bit of nicotine poisoning, especially in children. People don't think about their toddlers eating cigarette butts, but it happens. And people forget that nicotine spray can kill more than bugs."

I nodded my agreement. "What are the symptoms?"

"The first things are sweating, dizziness, sometimes excessive salivation. Wasn't always easy to tell whether we were getting too much sun or GTS."

"I can see that it would be a problem."

"The only way we were ever going to get away from Rafe was if he was dead, so I figured using tobacco to kill him would be appropriate." Tears poured down her already sodden cheeks.

Oliver whined and shifted uneasily by my feet, so I reached down to scratch behind his ears. His eyes were fixed on Linda.

"Go ahead," I whispered to him.

He walked over to the weeping woman and placed his head gently in her lap. She touched his neck, and he lifted his front feet into her lap, raising his furry head to face level. When he licked the tears from her cheeks, she threw both arms around him and nuzzled her face into the thick fur of his neck.

After several minutes, she looked up. Oliver slipped to the floor and settled his head onto her knee. She stroked him mindlessly, waiting for the next step.

But what's the next step? I wondered. I didn't want to think about what I'd do to someone who hurt Oliver or my daughter. "Where'd you get the nicotine you added to his bottle of liniment?"

"Distilled it from tobacco. It isn't hard, and it's easy to find out how on the Internet. But I already knew, from when I was a kid."

"Do you use nicotine as an insecticide on your plants?"

"No. No poisons."

"Is there any way to prove you made it?" I probed.

Her eyes met mine, opening wide. "What are you asking?"

"Did you leave fingerprints on the bottle of liniment?"

She shook her head.

"Did you make the liquid here?" At her nod of assent, I asked, "Is there any way traces could show up—in the pan you used or in the sewer lines?"

She mulled it over and said, "I suppose so, but the pan is full of dirt and flowers, out on the back patio. It's in amongst a dozen others. I didn't rinse it in the house, so there shouldn't be a trace in the lines. Plus I cooked it down on the camp stove out in the garden shed. I dumped the leftover tobacco and cigarette papers into a wastebasket at one of the rest stops on the Interstate. Someone could find it if they knew where to look. I just wanted the mess away from here so the kids couldn't get into it. I mean, I wasn't trying to hide anything. If I have to go to prison for killing Rafe, the boys will still be better off. My sister will make sure they have all the love and attention they need."

"Wait a minute! Didn't you hear any of the news coverage? Rafe was shot while gaining on the lead horses. Your nicotine made him sick, and yes, maybe it would have killed him. I suspect since he was a heavy smoker, he didn't react as quickly to the nicotine as a nonsmoker would have. The medical examiner will find nicotine in the liniment, but at the moment, they suspect that some of his gambler friends put the poison in it to make him sick, to keep him from riding Orinoco to a Derby win. And when that didn't seem to be working, they went to Plan B. All along, the marksman was poised to shoot Rafe if it looked like he could win. And that's what happened."

Linda's features registered her relief. "You mean I didn't kill him? But I did try to; the nicotine might have killed him if he hadn't been shot, right?"

I nodded.

"You aren't going to turn me in?"

"No. But can you keep from turning yourself in if the police question you about Rafe's death? I don't think they have a clue you were involved, but you might find it hard to bear up under the questioning."

"For my boys, I can do anything!"

And for Peanut, I added silently. "Then start acting like the mournful widow. Don't overdo it; just keep in mind that you have two boys to raise. Go stay with your sister for a few days, in case the reporters come looking."

Linda gave me her sister's phone number.

"And here's my phone number." I pressed my card into her hand. "Feel free to call if you need any help."

She hugged me, but this time she was smiling.

"Your call has been forwarded to an automatic voice message system. After the tone, please record your message."

"Hi, Jake. It's C. J. I stopped by the Martinez house and spoke with Linda. She's shocked by her husband's death but is coping. I suggested she and her boys stay at her sister's home for a few days. I have the phone number if you need it.

"She suspected her husband was involved in something illegal, but since he didn't talk about his work, she wasn't sure. Anyway, the only thing of consequence she told me was that he really wanted to win the Derby before he retired. Guess like most of us, he wanted to go out a winner.

"Sorry I don't have more to report. Don't forget that you owe me dinner. Congratulations on the quick solution to the crime."

Superstitions

by Sheila Shumate

Breeding, training, a jockey's skill, and a little luck all contribute to a winner. Still, there are those who hedge their bets with superstitions they feel will guarantee a win in the first jewel of the triple crown, the Kentucky Derby.

Churchill Downs has 47 barns, but you'll not find a barn number 13. Above some of the doorways to the barns are horseshoes, which are pointed upward to keep the luck in. Racing lore states if a horseshoe is turned downward, the luck will run out. Until the 125th Run for the Roses in 1999, the horseshoe on the Derby trophy turned downward. Other than jewels added for the 75th, 100th, and 125th Derby anniversaries, no other change has been made to the original design of the gold trophy, first commissioned for the 50th anniversary in 1924.

Everyone has heard the superstition about a black cat crossing your path, but Skank, a black cat who lives in barn 18 at Churchill Downs, crosses the paths of jockeys, trainers, and horses every day without causing any bad luck. To the contrary, a large sign above barn 18 reads, "Home of 1992 Kentucky Derby Winner, Lil E. Tee."

Trainers are not immune to superstitions. D. Wayne Lukas, a trainer with four Derby wins, feels the jinx is in and there is no way he can win if he has a favorite and someone tells him he can't lose. Nick Zito, one of the most superstitious trainers, has a whole ritual of where everything must be done from the right side. Shug McGaughey would not allow any brooms around his 1989 Derby entry, Easy Goer, believing it would sweep away all the good luck. Unfortunately Easy Goer didn't sweep to victory.

Jockeys have their own superstitions that they feel help them ride to victory. Patricia Cooksey, one of only four women to ride in the Derby, was convinced her lucky underwear helped her win several consecutive races. She wore the same pair for three months—she washed them every day, of course—but eventually they wore out and she had to get a new lucky pair. No one knows where or how the superstition of laying new silks on the floor and having all the riders walk on them started, but the jockeys feel that it makes them less likely to fall off their mounts.

Another superstition of unknown origin says that walking around the backside with a bag of peanuts in their shells will bring bad luck. And no one wanted a gray horse until Native Dancer started racing. Known as the Gray Ghost, he won 21 of his 22 races, with his only loss at the 1953 Kentucky Derby.

A LITTLE BITTY TEAR
LET ME DOWN

by Brenda Robertson Stewart

Brenda Robertson Stewart has a Bachelor of Arts degree in English from Indiana University. In addition to writing, she is a painter, sculptor, and forensic artist, specializing in facial reconstruction for identification purposes. Her first published short story, "Anonymous," appears in Derby Rotten Scoundrels, *and her first mystery novel,* Power in the Blood, *was published in July 2005. She grew up in southern Indiana and resides near Indianapolis.*

It was disconcerting to see a tree drifting down the Ohio River with a dead body dressed in a dark blue suit stuck to one of its limbs and floating in the wake. As a matter of fact, when Mr. McMahon's fishhook caught in the clothing of the bloated carcass, he wet his pants.

Back in Louisville at the accounting firm of Jackson and Evans, the employees were discussing the disappearance of one on their fellow workers. Josh Haskins had been missing for two weeks and two days.

Delbert Jackson, senior partner of the firm, smoothed his hand over his bald head in a practiced manner and patted his considerable paunch. "Okay, I saw Josh at the Derby as those of you did who sat in the clubhouse with me. Did anybody see him after he collected his winnings? Did he tell anyone how much money he had won?"

Bill Simpson spoke up. "The last time I saw Josh, he and Jeff were walking toward the payout window."

Trish Winters agreed that she had seen the two men walking away together and added, "I wonder how big he won. I took home about twenty dollars myself."

Jeff Mayer rubbed his hand through his blond curly hair. "It was big, all right. Josh asked me to stay with him and walk him to his car. He had this crazy idea that he wanted to be paid in cash. The Derby people kept telling him it would be safer if they simply transferred the money electronically as they do with most large betting payoffs, but Josh insisted. I think he had about $250,000 coming after the IRS took its share."

"You mean he collected that much money in cash?" asked Del.

"I told him it wouldn't be safe," Jeff replied. "The racing officials contacted a bank to get the money ready and send it in an armored car to Churchill Downs."

"Wow!" Trish said.

"The racetrack officials told Josh repeatedly that their responsibility ended when he accepted the money," Jeff continued. "It was quite a wad of dough. He stuffed the money bag into his shirt and we walked to the parking lot. He got into his car and drove off. I followed him to I-65, where he turned south. That was the last time I saw him."

"Wow is right," said Bill. "He really won that much? I'm shocked." His left eye began to twitch. With his dark hair and bushy eyebrows, he reminded Jeff of Groucho Marx. All he needed was a cigar and glasses.

Trish said, "I can't believe I turned him down for a date." Her red face matched her hair.

Jeff's coworkers turned suspiciously toward him, and he said, "Hey, I'm telling you he got in his car with the money and drove off. I never saw him again!" Seeing his workmates shake their heads in disbelief, he sat there with his head in his hands. Surely, if they suspected him of having something to do with Josh's disappearance, it was only a matter of time before the police, who had already questioned members of the firm several times, would arrest him. He was so upset, he shut down his computer, locked his desk, and headed out of the office, looking at nothing but the floor.

As he drove home, Jeff mulled over what he knew. The police suspected foul play because of the amount of cash Josh was carrying. They had found his car outside his condominium, which showed no signs of forced entry. A Derby racing form lay on the kitchen table. Since there were no signs of a struggle, no bloodstains, or other evidence of a crime, the authorities thought it unlikely Josh had left against his will. He must have known the perpetrator. That much information had been published in the newspaper.

Jeff arrived home and, once inside his living room, curled his lanky frame into a fetal position on the couch and clicked the TV on with the remote. He dozed off but awakened with a start when he heard the beep from a news alert. Missing most everything except "full details at six," he called his aunt Phyllis, who watched soap operas all afternoon.

She finally answered after five rings. "Lo, Jeffery," she gurgled, obviously .

with a mouthful of food. "Sorry, but one of my friends brought me a box of Godiva chocolates."

In his mind's eye, Jeff could see the elderly, overweight woman with snowy white hair sprouting from her head like a Brillo pad.

"Aunt Phyllis, did you happen to see a news alert on Channel 3? I missed it, but I thought I heard the word *body*."

"Yes indeedy. I heard it right before Crystal told Cameron that he's the father of her baby. You know, we thought it was Michael. That scoundrel—"

"Aunt Phyllis, please, the news alert."

"Oh, right. It seems a fisherman found a body floating in the river this morning. It hasn't been identified. When are you coming to see me, Jeffery? You've been neglecting your old aunt."

"I'll come by this weekend and take you to lunch. Okay?"

"Maybe Sunday brunch?" she prompted.

"Sunday brunch it'll be. Get dressed in your finest, and I'll pick you up about eleven."

"Oh, I'd better get my nails done and my hair reconstructed before then."

Reconstructed was the right word, Jeff decided. Her hair always had so much hair spray on it that it appeared to be lacquered. He sighed as he hung up the phone. Prone to eccentricity, Phyllis Mayer, his father's older sister, had never married. When she wasn't watching soaps, she was reading mysteries and bugging the police with her theories. She had helped them solve a few crimes, however, so they tended to indulge her. And it wasn't detrimental that she was the police chief's godmother.

Suspecting the worst, Jeff stayed glued to the TV. Probably just coincidence, he thought. The story of the body found by the fisherman led the news. With the recent rain, the river was up and the tree with its horrifying parcel had been moving at a good clip. After losing his fishing pole in the river amid his excitement, the old man had run to his pickup truck to go call the authorities. But it wouldn't start, so he walked the two miles home. By the time the police got there, the tree and body were gone. They took off in a boat they had brought along on a trailer, and had about decided the old man was making up the story when they spotted the tree floating along with a body attached like another limb. The body had not been identified according to the newscaster, but the victim was a young male. If anyone had any information, there was a number to call.

Jeff wished they had shown the body. He might have recognized the clothing if it was Josh's body. No, he thought, his friend was sitting on a warm beach sipping mai tais.

The next day passed in a blur. Everyone at Jackson and Evans felt confident the body was not Josh's since the police were conspicuously absent.

Wednesday, it was raining buckets. The wind turned Jeff's umbrella inside out, and he was dripping wet. Deathly silence met him when he walked into the office. Looking up, with water cascading over his blue eyes, he saw a stranger sitting at his desk.

"We've been waiting for you Mr. Mayer," said the police lieutenant.

After issuing Jeff an invitation he couldn't refuse, the lieutenant led him back out into the driving rain. When they arrived at the police station, a detective led Jeff to a rather stark, barren room for questioning.

There must have been a sale on gray paint when this place was built, Jeff thought. "Do I need to have an attorney present," he naively asked the detective.

"Why would you need an attorney?" the stone-faced man replied. "All we need is for you to answer a few simple questions."

"Was the body Josh's?" asked Jeff.

"You're here to *answer* questions, not ask them," the lieutenant responded as he joined the detective in the interrogation room. "Now sit your wet butt down and let's get started."

The pair asked Jeff the same questions over and over. *When did you last see Josh? Did you follow Josh home? What time did you get home? Can anyone verify where you were?* Jeff answered them as accurately as he could, but he felt like a wind-up toy after about an hour, and the policemen didn't seem happy with his answers.

"Come on, Jeff, where did you stash the money after you dumped ole Josh into the Ohio?" said the lieutenant with a smirk on his face.

Feeling a chill in the room as well as in the lieutenant's voice, Jeff refused to answer any more questions. After four hours of grilling by the two policemen, they allowed him to leave.

Jeff drove to see Phyllis. If the soaps were over, maybe he would have a chance to talk to his aunt before "Oprah." Normally he loved the long curving drive that led up to her enormous stone house, but he sent only a cursory glance to the turret he had played in as a child.

Charles, Phyllis's ancient butler, opened the door. "Jeffery, what a surprise. Your aunt will be delighted to see you. Tillie just went to the kitchen to fix her a snack."

As he was led to the drawing room, Jeff wondered how many snacks his favorite relative ate in one day. Charles, ramrod straight and wearing his funereal black suit as always, announced him to Phyllis, who was lying on the sofa in front of a giant-screen TV. Dressed in a red sweat suit, she reminded Jeff of Mrs. Claus.

"Oh, my dear boy, you decided to surprise me. I wasn't expecting you. Tillie will be here shortly with tea. It's hard to break old habits, you know. I did live in London for a time."

"Tea is great, Aunt Phyllis, but I need to talk to you about a potential problem I've got."

"Surely it will wait until we've had some food. We need to keep up our strength."

"I don't want to interfere with your TV schedule."

"Nonsense. I have TiVo, so I can watch 'Oprah' later. Wonderful invention. You don't even need a tape. Do you have it?"

"No, I heard it's complicated."

"Not at all. Charles will set it to record for me. Now, why are you so nervous? Please stop your pacing and talk to me."

"Do you remember Josh Haskins—my friend and fellow accountant?"

"Yes, quite a handsome young man with dark hair and brown eyes, as I recall."

"Well, we both went to the Derby with Del. Two other people I work with were there as well. Josh won quite a bit of money and foolishly made them give it to him in cash. Later that night, he disappeared, and the police have been questioning me. They think I killed him in order to steal his winnings."

"Where did they get such a ridiculous idea?"

"I was the last person to see him at Churchill Downs. He asked me to wait with him, and it took some time for the officials to get the cash to the track." He quit speaking when Tillie rolled a tea cart into the room.

"Oh, here's our snacks," Phyllis said with enthusiasm. "Just put the tray over here by me, Tillie, and I'll serve. You and Charles just relax and have your own tea. We'll have a late dinner."

Tillie rolled the cart over by Phyllis, and after removing the empty candy boxes from the coffee table, she transferred the filled tray to the table. As she hurried across the room to the door, she said, "Let me know what time you want your dinner, ma'am."

"Thank you, Tillie," Phyllis said. "Now, Jeffery, I want you to describe your entire day at the Kentucky Derby. Don't leave anything out, no matter how trivial you think it is."

"Okay. As far as I know, each member of our party drove separately. We met at the gate, and Del took us to the clubhouse. It was a normal Derby Day—you know, eating, drinking, and betting on the horses. Del seemed a little subdued. I've heard rumors the firm may be in financial trouble, but if that were true, surely he would have invited some potential clients instead of his lowly employees."

"I don't think Delbert Jackson has any financial worries."

"How well do you know him, Aunt Phyllis? He gets a gleam in his eye whenever I mention you."

She laughed while patting the right side of her hair in a nervous gesture her only nephew was familiar with. "Now Jeffery," she said, while patting some more and rolling her eyes, "a lady never tells. I'll say no more on the subject."

Speculating that maybe they were better friends than he thought, he continued his story. "Trish Winters, another accountant in the firm, was a guest as well. I don't think you've met her. She's fairly new—a looker to be sure. Red hair, green eyes, freckles—an All-American, scrubbed look and a figure that won't quit. Sorry, I guess that's not relevant."

Phyllis smiled. "What was she wearing?"

"Wearing? Oh, one of those flowered dresses with a full skirt—you know, the ones that swish with each step. And of course the required picture hat. I think women wear those big brims so men can't see what devious thoughts are flitting through their brains. There was a lot of green in her dress that matched her eyes."

"Too bad you didn't pay close attention to Trish. There might have been some clues."

Recognizing sarcasm when he heard it, Jeff looked at his aunt rather sheepishly. "The other guest was Bill Simpson, the newest member of our firm. He's kind of a smart-aleck—nice enough, but a know-it-all."

"And what was he wearing?"

"A blue pin-striped suit with a paisley tie. He looked like an ambitious, wannabe executive, and acted a bit stuffy, but he was cordial enough. Josh, on the other hand, was bubbling with excitement about betting on that long-shot horse, Anonymous. None of us thought such an unknown could win the Kentucky Derby, but it goes to show what we know about horse flesh. Del, Trish, and Bill say they left Churchill Downs as soon as they could get out after the big race, but Trish won a little money, so she must have stayed long enough to cash in her ticket. I didn't see any of them after Josh and I left the stands."

"I guess we'd best turn on the news," Phyllis said, munching on another cheese salad sandwich.

Jeff was stunned when the newscaster confirmed the worst, reporting, "The body found downriver earlier this week has been positively identified as Joshua Haskins, an accountant with the firm of Jackson and Evans. He had not been seen since picking up his considerable winnings at the Kentucky Derby. The cause of death was blunt force trauma to the head."

"Josh was a great guy, Aunt Phyllis. Why did they have to kill him?"

"I'd guess he knew his robber, and he—or she—was afraid Josh would identify him. You said the police found a racing form in Josh's house. I'm sure it was checked for fingerprints. We'll need to examine Josh's house and driveway to see if any clues have been missed. I do love a mystery." Phyllis enthusiastically rubbed her hands together.

Jeff drove home. He couldn't bear to stay at his aunt's house for dinner. Besides, he had eaten so many tea sandwiches, he wasn't hungry. Dinner at Aunt Phyllis's was always a long, drawn-out affair, and he wanted to go grieve for his dead friend.

He decided to take the rest of the week off. Since tax season was over, he could afford some time to help his aunt work to solve Josh's murder before he got himself arrested. The next morning, he drove Phyllis to see the police chief, whom she intimidated shamelessly. He was the son of one of her closest friends, and she had changed his diapers when he was an infant.

After placing a phone call, the poor man sent them off to meet the lieutenant and detective at Josh's house, where Phyllis thoroughly inspected the house and grounds. She found three synthetic red hairs—the kind from a cheap wig—caught up in a shrub, and gave them to the detective to send to the lab.

"You about done here, Ms. Mayer?" he asked as he placed the hairs in an evidence bag.

"Just a few more minutes please," trilled Phyllis, surveying the postage-stamp-sized yard at the condominium for the third time.

As Phyllis and Jeff walked back to the car, they overheard the detective say, "We checked Josh's cell phone records and know that he received a call about 9:00 p.m. on the night he disappeared. It seems that—"

"What! You say Josh got a call on his cell phone at nine o'clock?" Phyllis said a bit too sharply. "Who did he talk to?"

"I'm afraid we can't divulge that information to a civilian, Ms. Mayer," the lieutenant answered with a Cheshire cat grin.

"Come on, Jeffery," Phyllis said with an indignant look on her face.

Jeff saw the two policemen roll their eyes at each other, and guessed that they wished they hadn't spoken of the cell phone call where his aunt could overhear.

At her insistence, Jeff took his aunt to the accounting firm offices to question Del and the other Derby guests. Phyllis looked intimidating even if she wasn't asking questions, and Jeff thought his workmates weren't going to be happy to see the pair. On their way inside, he said, "But you're not really going to question Del, are you?"

"Of course, but I'm quite sure he had nothing to do with this affair."

"How can you be so sure?"

"Del and I go back a long way, and there probably isn't much I don't know about him."

"But what about those rumors that the firm is in trouble financially?"

"I don't believe them, Jeffery. And besides, $250,000 would be a paltry sum to Del Jackson. He has his own family money and wouldn't need to kill for more. At least I don't think he would," she added hesitantly. "Anyway, we'll invite him to lunch and find out what he knows."

Jeff knew the subject of food would come up somewhere if his aunt was involved.

"Jeff, my boy, I noticed you didn't come to work today. Is there a problem?" asked Del after Jeff and his aunt had stormed the offices.

Before Jeff could answer, Phyllis said, "Of course there's no problem, Del. The boy needed a few days to help me. We've come to take you to lunch."

Del looked at the woman suspiciously but then grinned like a dog that has just been caught with his paw in the cookie jar. "Sounds like a plan, Phyl. You don't get out often enough. We miss you at the club. Let's have lunch there."

"Okay, Del," she crooned. "Whatever you say."

Jeff thought he might upchuck. He'd never seen his aunt simper before, and he didn't want to see it again. On their way out, Del told the receptionist he would be at the Pendennis Club. During the meal, Jeff could tell that his boss and his aunt had a past together, but to be totally ignored was downright embarrassing—almost as embarrassing as his two elderly companions playing footsie under the table. Once in a while he got kicked by mistake.

Thankful the interminable lunch was over, Jeff was grateful to get back to the office for the inquisition. Del loaned Phyllis the conference room for her little tea party. And it was a tea party, in fact. Charles—her butler, chauffeur, and all around dogsbody—arrived with enough food to feed a hungry Derby crowd.

"It's too early for tea," Jeff sputtered. "And besides, we just had lunch."

"Now Jeffery," Phyllis said, "food puts people at ease."

She invited the entire office staff to their party. No office worker ever refused a party with free food. After an hour of small talk, Phyllis got to work. Her first victim was red-headed Trish.

"Now Trish, I'm helping the police out with their investigation into Josh's murder."

"Most likely you're trying to keep Jeff out of jail. He was the last person to see Josh alive."

"I think not, Trish. The killer was the last person to see him alive. And," she stated emphatically, "Jeffery is not that person. Now, Del has given me permission to question his Derby guests. Would you like for me to call him into this meeting?"

"No, I'll answer your questions. I have nothing to hide." She grimaced.

"I've told my story to the police and every worker in this office, but I'll tell it again."

"That would be nice, dear. Now, please start from the time you arrived at Churchill Downs."

Trish repeated her story of what she had witnessed at the Kentucky Derby. "I didn't have any idea Josh had won so much money. 'Winning big' could have meant fifty dollars, for all I knew."

"Did you bet on the races, Trish?" asked Phyllis.

"I bet my normal two dollars, but I won in one of the other races—not the Derby. I had already cashed in my ticket."

"Are you sure you didn't decide to spend a romantic evening with Josh to get your hands on his money?" Phyllis prodded.

"I told you. I had no idea he had won so much money. I didn't see Josh again after he and Jeff left to cash in the ticket."

"That will be all for now," said Phyllis, "but I might want to speak to you again later. Jeffery, do you have any questions?"

He refused to question Trish, and Phyllis sent him to get Bill. The man was obviously not happy about being questioned by Phyllis, but he reiterated his story about what he remembered from the Derby.

"What did you do after you left Churchill Downs?" she asked when he finished.

"I went home."

"Thank you, Bill. I think that's it for now, but I may need to talk to you later."

Jeff drove his aunt home, and after she made several phone calls, she told him, "I think we can wind up this investigation tomorrow, Jeffery."

"Does that mean you know who murdered Josh?"

"Well, I'm almost positive I know. I've called Del and set up a time for us to get everyone together tomorrow, and the chief of police assured me the detectives in charge of this case will meet us there as well."

"But how do you know who the killer is? I didn't hear anything incriminating this afternoon. Where did you get all those telephone numbers? I'll bet while I was in the bathroom you called the police chief and he spilled everything in his desperation to end the conversation."

"Don't let it trouble you. I'll reveal everything tomorrow morning. Right now, it's time for 'Oprah,' and I don't want to miss it twice in one week."

"I thought you recorded it yesterday."

"Oh, Charles thought he did, but I guess he didn't set that danged equipment right. Anyway, we missed it."

"Sorry about that, Aunt Phyllis. I'll head on home then."

"Tillie's bringing some snacks. You might want to eat first."

"Thanks, but no thanks," said Jeff, fighting back nausea.

Jeff picked up his aunt promptly at 9:30 the following morning, and they drove downtown in virtual silence. The elderly sleuth was giving away nothing in advance. As soon as they arrived at Jackson and Evans, Del rounded up Trish and Bill, and they were joined by two bored-looking police detectives in the conference room.

Phyllis said, "Lieutenant, were there any fingerprints on the racing form?"

"The crime lab found only smudged prints—nothing usable."

"Thank you. According to Trish's roommates, she arrived home in what seemed like a timely manner from the Derby, confirming her version of the events of that day."

The lieutenant nodded, agreeing that her story was consistent with police findings.

Phyllis turned to Bill and said, "You told us you went home directly after the Derby, but when I spoke to your girlfriend, she said you didn't get home until after she went to bed around midnight."

"I can explain that. I'm a clown and I work children's birthday parties and the like. I worked a party after I left Churchill Downs. I didn't want Serena to know because she would have wanted me to give her part of the money. I stopped at a service station on my way to the party and changed into my clown clothes. I was afraid people would make fun of me if I told them about being a clown."

The lieutenant spoke up. "We checked Josh's cell phone records and found that you called him about 9:00 that night." He smiled smugly at Phyllis.

"That's right," Bill said smacking the side of his head. "I completely forgot. I called to congratulate him on his big win. He had been out to eat and was almost home, so I just talked to him a minute or so."

"According to the phone records," the sergeant said, "you talked for fifteen minutes. Is your memory a little vague?"

"I guess so. I sure don't remember talking to him that long. Maybe he forgot to hang up right away. Yeah, that must be it. He forgot to disconnect the call."

"Who else did you call that night?" Phyllis asked.

"I didn't call anyone else."

"Perhaps I asked the wrong question, Bill. Who else did you talk to that night?"

"I don't remember talking to anyone but Josh."

She persisted. "Bill, do you have a cousin named Hank Dodd?"

"Why, yes, I do. That's right; he called me after I talked to Josh."

"Are you sure it was *after* you talked to Josh?" asked Phyllis.

"Oh, yes, I'm sure it was after."

The lieutenant chimed in. "What does your cousin do for a living, Mr. Simpson?"

"I believe he drives a truck. At least, that's what he used to do."

"According to our investigation," said Phyllis, "Hank drives an armored car for Brink's here in Louisville."

"I wouldn't know anything about that," said Bill.

"I think you know a lot about it, Bill," she said. "I think he called you and told you about a delivery he made to Churchill Downs on the evening of the Kentucky Derby. I think you put two and two together. Hank didn't know the name of the big winner, but you called Josh to see if it was him. Unfortunately for him, he told you the truth."

"You can't prove anything. I don't have a clue what you're talking about. I never killed Josh."

"The police have confirmation from Hank that he called you and told you about his delivery. They also have a witness that places Hank in a bar all Saturday evening. I believe you called Josh and asked if you could stop by. Some red hair from your clown wig snagged on the bushes. Here's your killer, Lieutenant." Phyllis pointed her finger at Bill.

Jeff turned to the detectives and said, "Couldn't you get a search warrant and check his clown wig against the hair you found at Josh's place?"

"We certainly could," said the lieutenant.

Bill jumped out of his chair and headed for the door. Phyllis stuck out her foot, and he tripped and went sprawling across the floor.

"I think you broke my leg, you cow," he cried. "Somebody get me an ambulance!"

"Shut up, Bill," Trish said. "You're a jerk."

The detectives helped Bill into a chair, where he kept sputtering. "That little girl at the party made me do it. She had these big tears rolling down her cheeks because she didn't get the PlayStation she wanted for her birthday. I heard her mother tell her she couldn't afford the game after she hired the pony and the clown and bought the food the daughter wanted to serve her friends. Her tears got to me. I remembered my own little girl when she was dying from leukemia. I couldn't afford to buy her what she wanted either. It took every cent I could scrape together to pay her medical bills, even with insurance. I used to find her crying, mostly at night. Those little tears would trickle down her cheeks like heavy dew dripping off a rose. That poor little girl couldn't have the present she wanted for her birthday—just like my little Jenny. The words from that old Burl Ives song kept ringing in my head: 'a little bitty tear let me down, spoiled my act as a clown.'"

As Bill sobbed, everyone else looked at each other in disbelief.

Jeff said, "You never told us you had lost a child, Bill."

"I can't talk about that anymore. It hurts too much. I snapped."

The lieutenant said, "So what did you do, Bill?"

"After Hank called and I talked to Josh and found out he won that money, I thought of all the poor children who couldn't have the toys they wanted. Josh wanted to spend the money on a dumb boat. I told him I knew where he could get an almost new one cheap. I had been out on a boat with an acquaintance and knew he was in Europe at that time, so I showed Josh his cruiser. I didn't intend to kill him, but when he wouldn't give me the money, all I could see was my poor Jenny. When he turned to go, I picked up a rock and slammed it into the back of his head."

After a brief silence, Phyllis said, "So you gave the money to poor children?"

"I haven't yet, but I intend to." He looked down at his Rolex watch. "I need to get out of here on time today. I'm entertaining at another birthday party tonight!"

Jeff and the others shook their heads as the detectives led Bill away.

Phyllis said, "You won't need to take me home, Jeffery. Del has invited me to his place for the afternoon."

"All right, Aunt Phyllis. Have fun. I'll see you for Sunday brunch." Jeff thought it would be a good thing if his aunt became obsessed with something besides food.

Top Ten Reasons to Love the Derby

(with apologies to David Letterman)

by Beverle Graves Myers

10. Mint and bourbon—what a concept.

9. Another opportunity to wear that hat you bought for Aunt Millie's wedding.

8. What other sporting event has its own chocolate nut pie?

7. Might bump into Anna Nicole Smith on her way to Millionaire's Row.

6. So much fun watching your friends try to figure out the racing form after four mint juleps.

5. Crying like a baby while they play "My Old Kentucky Home."

4. Hard to get bored during a two-minute event.

3. Features four-footed athletes you'll never see on Court TV.

2. Did I mention the bourbon?

1. Two words: winning ticket.

THE SHOE MUST GO ON

by Laura Young

Louisville native Laura Young is the author of the Kate Kelly mystery series published by Silver Dagger Mysteries. Killer Looks *and* Otherwise Engaged, *nominated in 2003 and 2005, respectively, for the Kentucky Literary Award for Fiction, feature the comedic sleuthing of reporter Kate Kelly, who has a nose for news and murder. Kate Kelly also appears in "Win, Place, or Show Up Dead," a short story in* Derby Rotten Scoundrels. *A former journalist, Laura has covered many Kentucky Derby Festival events and has spent more time nosing around the press box at Churchill Downs than she should probably admit.*

Everyone loves a party. Everyone really loves a party when fantastic stories spill out of the event. And when the gossip is good, the memories are often outstanding. I'm never one to turn down a good party. In fact, I can honestly say it's part of my job.

My name is Kate Kelly, and I write for *Travel Adventures* magazine, based in Washington, D.C. It's a great job that allows me to travel nationwide, soaking up some of the wondrous events that make this country special. In my estimation, the Kentucky Derby ranks as one of the best events ever. Where else does an entire city nearly shut down for weeks on end simply to celebrate a rite of passage? Since I'm not a Kentuckian, I needed a few trips to Churchill Downs over the years to learn that the Derby is much more than one day of horse racing. It's a month-long celebration featuring hundreds of events and thousands of revelers who plan their year around the four weeks between early April and that magical first Saturday in May.

That's why I was excited when the invitation arrived. The amount of postage alone was impressive on the oversized, die-cut invitation that folded out into a veritable origami design of a dozen roses. The Glenview Gala promised Derby Eve fun amongst the rich and famous. Black tie was required, and the price of admission was hefty—practically a mortgage payment. But, since it was also a blatant beg for media coverage, the invitation was accompanied by a flow-ery handwritten note from one Brianna P. Woodford, event planner, graciously offering a complimentary admission in return for a story in *Travel Adventures.*

I get similar invitations all the time. Since I'm not an investigative journalist or hard-news scribe, I tend to let shameless efforts at payola slide a bit on the journalistic ethics scale. Besides, I write for a travel magazine, so I need to attend functions like Derby parties. At least that's what I was telling myself when I received an eerily timed phone call from none other than Brianna P. Woodford.

In a breathless, husky Southern drawl, she flew right into her pitch, assured that I had "probably just received" my invitation. Psychic, now, was she? As she rambled on about why hers would be the party to end all parties, I rapidly clicked on several Internet Derby sites—admittedly, a bad and annoying habit, but one that's a handicap of being a reporter. I prefer to think of it as a talent that allows me to think quickly on my feet.

"So," I interrupted, "this is the party on the hill in the park with all the dancing kids on the sidewalk."

"No," she clipped. "It's not that one."

Mouse click, mouse click. "Then it's the gala for cancer?"

Her irritation was apparent. "We're *much* more impressive than that."

"Which disease is it then?" I asked halfway to myself.

Her intake of breath hissed in my ear. "We're the benefit for—well, it doesn't really matter. What does matter is our event. You simply must not miss it. It's hosted by the Cockerels of Glenview, so that should tell you something."

Well, it didn't tell this D.C.-area reporter squat, but I was game.

"You realize this is *the* party this year," she said authoritatively. "Those other ones are wearing thin, with B-listers at best—second-string actors from '80s sitcoms, who no one remembers, and losers from reality shows. Please believe me when I tell you this will be the Derby party to remember."

As a journalist, I've had my share of run-ins with the great and near-great several times. It's often not as exciting as you might think. Celebrities fall into a few categories. There are the true superstars—those rare gems who have sliced a part of history and put it in their pockets. Then there are the hot, fifteen-minutes-of-fame types. They're often exciting and have a buzz around them that makes for a memorable encounter, but while they think they're the center of the universe, you usually can't remember their names a year later.

Then, of course, come the B-listers that she mentioned—usually the "worst" celebrities. They are overly demanding, ask for the green M&M's in their dressing room, and vainly hold on to any sliver of recognition they can get. They are also usually colossal bores. I'd dealt with my share of them before, so I pushed for evidence of a good guest list.

She was eager to comply. "Completely A-list. You won't be disappointed. And, of course, there's the ultimate part."

She succeeded in catching my attention. "What's that?"

"I'm talking about the Ferregiacomos. It's what everyone will want to see."

I was at a loss. "Is that a new boy band?"

I pictured her counting mentally to three and poking an irritated hole through her notepad as she drew nasty doodles of me. "No. The Ferregiacomos. The shoes? Surely you've heard of them? Not only are they created by the hottest designer in Italy, they are on the feet of everyone who is anyone in LA, Hollywood, and New York. Even in DC," she dripped somewhat acidly, in a minor-league slam of my hometown. "But *these* Ferregiacomos are one of a kind. They are gloriously covered in 350 miniature rubies and hundreds of diamonds. The shoes are insured for one million dollars."

I dropped the invitation in my lap, and my girlish fetish for great shoes overtook my brain. "You're kidding. Who's wearing them?"

I felt the smile come through the phone. She knew she had hooked me. "Elizabeth Magness . . . you know, the supermodel?"

Of course I knew who she was. You couldn't swing a box of Twinkies in the grocery store without hitting a magazine whose cover she graced. I wasn't that interested in a six-foot-two, 110-pound waif who made millions more than I ever would, but I wanted to see the shoes.

I talked my way into a one-on-one interview with the model and agreed to attend the party. "Look, why don't you send me a full press kit?" I asked politely. A thought hit me and I added, "And an all-access media credential."

My visit was set. Derby parties are year-round planning affairs, so it didn't faze me that the invitation arrived in early March, to snow falling outside my window. That gave me nearly two months to toy with the idea of how I'd cover the party for my magazine and what on earth I'd ask a supermodel during an interview. And more importantly, I had to decide what to wear, since black tie was also required for the journalists. Shopping was part of the fun. I found a bargain of a gown at a boutique in Union Station and promptly put it on my expense account.

As I packed my bags for Louisville, I felt almost as if I were heading to the senior prom again. Once I'd entered the wealthy Ohio River view enclave of Glenview, I parked my rental car in the designated lot—which was really a well-groomed field—and raised my emerald satin skirt a bit as I crossed over to the guard. I flashed my pink credential and was not thrilled to hear that the house was a substantial hike up a steep hill. Normally, that wouldn't bother me, but the air was warm and thick, and rain clouds threatened overhead. "Isn't there a shuttle bus for media?" I asked.

The guard laughed. "Uh-unh. Not unless you're a network anchor. You've got a pink pass. Walk that way."

As I trudged up the hill, I worried a bit about the "pink pass" comment. I remembered from my previous visits to Churchill Downs that Kentuckians are savvy about their media credentials, particularly at Derby time. For the most exciting two minutes in sports, an enormous amount of thought is put into the specific colors on credentials that either allow access or completely shut you out of where you want to be. Surely that wouldn't be the same way at a simple society party. I glanced at the rose on my pink media credential and hoped it was top tier.

I made my way to the small white tent marked "Media" at the end of a long and winding drive lined with red carpet. Hollywood had arrived in Louisville. A grand stone mansion was lit up like Christmas, with blazing lights inside and twinkle lights dotting every conceivable spot outside. The "beautiful people" mingled outside on the red carpet, slowly making their way past a large crowd of run-of-the-mill spectators and autograph seekers politely corralled behind white fencing.

Feeling a little like Cinderella, I ignored the far-off rumble of thunder and entered the media tent filled with chaos. Arguments reigned, and the credentials were the cause. Exasperated PR girls in black gowns and up-dos tried to explain the color system (or lack thereof) that included all access, tent only, house only, driveway only, and the most important part—whether you had bathroom credentials, porta-potty passes, or "you're really out of luck, hold it" tags.

Fingering the laminated card hanging from my neck, I turned to the television reporter standing beside me and said, "I was told I'd have all access."

"Hmmph. Honey, that's pink, not fuchsia. Join the color-blind world, because that's apparently the problem—all the colors are different from what was on the original request sheet. If that woman thinks we're going to stand around and be treated like this, she's nuts. We'll head over to the other parties."

Brianna P. Woodford—that woman, I assumed—flew into the tent seconds before a full mutiny erupted. She was diminutive in stature but huge in dress. Dramatic, long, frizzy black curls crowned an enormous black-and-white-checked satin gown. Wearing enough crinolines and skirts to impress Scarlett O'Hara, she swished when she walked. A jugular vein that probably wasn't part of the ensemble plan popped out for view as she shouted, "PEOPLE! Quiet, please! This is a party, not the State Fair. Manners, please."

From the looks on the gathered media, that wasn't the best choice of words. She flew to the table, screamed bloody murder to her assistants, whipped the sheet from one's trembling hand, and began summarily dispatching assorted media out of the tent. She scribbled furiously on the credentials with a Sharpie pen, her method and pasted-on smile directly proportionate to whether or not she recognized the reporter or photographer.

Feeling doomed, I made my way toward her and smiled widely. "Hi, I'm Kate Kelly. You said I'd have all-access, plus a one-on-one with the Ferregiacomo model?"

Her chin folded into her neck. "I don't know you. What, are you with the alternative weekly? Dear, I'm very busy right now. You have a pink credential. Go wait in the back."

Not a chance. "I came from out of town for this. You invited me."

Her entire demeanor changed. She was all sweetness and hospitality. "Oh, I'm sorry. Are you national? *People*? *Vogue*?"

I gritted my teeth. "National. Glossy. *Travel Adventures*. You promised me a one-on-one with the Ferregiacomo model?"

She yanked the pink credential so fast from my neck that the elastic lanyard snapped. I held in a squeal and calculated the medical costs for whiplash. Handing me a dark fuchsia pass, she said, "Please head up to the house. I'll see to your interview in a while."

I followed her advice and sprinted out of the tent. I made my way up the red carpet and briefly enjoyed the fantasy that the stares and flashes going off were for me. However, in reality, the stares were accompanied by the unfortunately audible "Who's she? A nobody?" and the flashes were restricted to bolts of lightning that had begun to sear the sky.

Once inside party central, my senses set afire. The enormous mansion was spectacularly decorated with riots of red roses everywhere. Music thumped through the thick stone walls and called guests through the house toward a tented backyard. Outside under the tent, a band was belting out the latest hits, and an honest-to-goodness megastar commandeered the stage to sing his most recent chart-topper. As I was jostled through the well-dressed crowd, I began to pick out the stars scattered at little bistro tables. I was really beginning to enjoy myself when I remembered that I was there to do my job.

I wandered through the house again and found the supermodel in the front foyer. Statuesque, blonde, and stunning, Elizabeth Magness was beyond a Barbie doll. She was a near goddess among the mere mortals and stars gathered. I heard later that Janet Jackson had a wardrobe malfunction of a different sort when she knocked over a plate of food into Jessica Simpson's lap while trying to get a good glimpse of her.

A white sequined gown clung skimpily to the model's every nook and cranny and tapered to a slim pencil at her knees. The line of the gown nearly pointed toward the shoes, the main attraction. Tiny ruby flowers in the shape of miniature rosebuds colored her feet, and diamonds laced up her porcelain skin and wrapped around her ankles. Three-and-a-half-inch stilettos were smothered in the reflected glow of dozens of diamonds. The mesmerizing shoes made Dorothy's ruby slippers seem like worn Wal-Mart house slippers. Whoever had said she looked like a million bucks wasn't kidding.

Reaching for the reporter's notebook in my handbag, I angled my way through the crowd, only to watch her be engulfed by a mob of spectators who washed her through to the next room.

A beefy security guard stopped me. "You can't interview her. She doesn't talk to reporters. Take a picture of the shoes."

"But Brianna Woodford arranged an interview," I argued.

He blocked my entrance to the room. "Sorry. It's only about the shoes tonight."

We engaged in a staring contest, which I lost. I turned on my inexpensive high heels and headed the opposite direction. All my time arguing out front about my credentials had caused me to miss dinner, which irritated me, but there were still plenty of high-end munchies on silver trays being passed by tuxedoed servers, and I was delighted to wander into a brightly lit room and discover a wide selection of desserts. The evening was saved.

I was glad to be inside, because the goopy humidity outside had morphed into quite a rainstorm. I glanced out a window at the sightseers scattering in the night, while Brianna's assistants danced around the late-arrival celebrities with huge golf umbrellas. I briefly wondered how the massive tent out back was holding up and sensed the volume increase as revelers made their way into the house. Lightning illuminated the window, and all the lights in the mansion flickered. I was pretty sure a power outage wasn't on Brianna's party schedule plan.

I sampled some petit fours and discovered Joan Rivers in the corner chowing down on a piece of Derby-Pie. Before I could go over and say, "Can we talk?" I spotted the model walking past the door. I shoved what was left of a miniature cream puff into my mouth and followed her toward the tent.

Rain pelted the tent, and the flaps on the side shivered in a stormy wind, but the music was so loud the thunderclaps were a memory. The model danced into the center of the crowd, her shoes sparkling on the dance floor.

Brianna appeared, and I made a beeline toward her. "Brianna, about my interview with Elizabeth Magness—"

"That will have to wait. I can't be bothered right now. I have a party to run. Have you no consideration for the stress I'm under right now? The future of my company depends on tonight. I'll take care of providing some written statements later for you."

My jaw dropped. I came all this way to do a story, not have it provided by some PR person. I could write my own story, thank you very much. I saddled up my argument and almost missed Elizabeth and the shoes dance past me back into the house.

Brianna interrupted my plea with an icy smile. "I have to go. You'll figure something out."

I stood in my spot and sputtered and fumed momentarily but never worked myself up to full indignation. Maybe I should have listened when the band started playing the old INXS hit "Suicide Blonde." Brianna wasn't a blonde, but in short order, she turned nearly suicidal.

The party went downhill quickly.

The tent lit up in a flash, and a bone-shattering pop exploded around us as lightning sliced through an enormous oak tree that literally decided to crash the party. As the surge of electricity sent sparks flying from the amplifiers onstage, the venerable oak tore through the side of the tent and collapsed the entire far side of the structure. Mud poured into the tent from where the tree was uprooted. Musicians leapt from the stage, and partygoers—myself included—headed for the house. Several people ran into the glass-enclosed swimming pool area, and in their rush, a few fell directly into the water.

The noise level of laughter, shrieks, and shouts inside the house was deafening. The lights went out, and a blood-curdling scream erupted from the front foyer. When the lights returned seconds later, Elizabeth Magness lay sprawled on the staircase, unconscious and bleeding. A bloodstained silver tray nearby seemed to be the weapon of choice.

As several doctors who were in the house jostled each other to provide aid to the supermodel, I noticed the piles of chocolate-covered strawberries that covered her limp body. Oh, the chocolate tragedy. Why did her assailant have to use a tray full of chocolate? What a waste. And how would I ever get an interview now?

While I was busy mourning the chocolate, others noticed the more important part. Elizabeth was barefoot. The Ferregiacomos were missing.

Security guards swarmed the room a little late, and the tuxedoed police chief busily barked orders on a cell phone in the hallway. Brianna appeared, her hair wet and her skirt splattered in mud. She looked like she'd been hit by a train, and her expression didn't get any better when the off-duty officers—who suddenly found themselves very much on duty—sealed off the house. The chief ordered that no one could leave the premises, and the world's most expensive game of hide-and-seek began in earnest for the million-dollar shoes.

Separating the celebrities from the local hobnobbers, the police lined everyone up in assorted rooms for questioning and searching. The catering staff was sequestered in the kitchen. Brianna flew to and fro, frantically demanding that staff couldn't be questioned because they needed to continue to serve drinks. The media, in their enthusiasm to shoot everything in sight, overtook the police and spent an equal amount of time lining up guests to conduct their own who-done-it interviews.

Meantime, the groggy and stunned model sat on the staircase, fending off the help of the several doctors preening around her. Sporting a bruised goose egg on her pretty forehead, she seemed unaware that the golden eggs were gone. She was more concerned about permanent scarring and which makeup would best cover the bruise, as opposed to the fact her bare tootsies were now the source of an insurance agent's worst nightmare.

I did my obligatory interview with a handsome officer named Bobby, and when I proved that the shoes weren't in my humble possession, I moved over to a corner to watch the spectacle unfold. Unfortunately, it took a while. The novelty wore off fast for the revelers, who were anxious to resume the party or move on to the other star-studded gala over in Cherokee Park. The police, however, remained less than hospitable, demanding that everyone stay put, despite well-heeled and snobby protestations that it was "obvious" a server or maid probably stole the shoes.

I didn't necessarily buy that argument. But I heard it so frequently, my enthusiasm faded for playing the guessing game. Instead, I made a sport of watching Brianna to pass the time.

On one level, I felt extremely sorry for her. After all, the party planner was probably out of a job now. I actually overheard someone intone, "She'll never work in this town again," and I didn't doubt that. She'd need all the help she could muster. Her best-laid plans had been washed down the drain by the storm and a thief with sticky fingers. But the more I watched her poise and mental stability deteriorate by the moment, the more I started to wonder about her physical deterioration as well.

Her checkered gown was not to my taste, but as I played fashion police, I noticed that the puffy skirt seemed strangely puffier on one hip vs. the other. I knew she was a bit battered and stressed out, but I didn't think she was developing a widow's hump further south than usual overnight. I'd heard about getting your nose out of joint, but your hip out of joint? I watched her closer for a while, and a troubling thought bubbled in my mind. Surely not.

A great buzz erupted when word spread that two servers had slipped out the kitchen door into the dark and stormy night. I had a hunch their escape had more to do with green cards than ruby shoes, though, so I decided to make my move.

I walked over to where Brianna stood and said, in my most gentle and caring tone, "I'm so sorry everything has gone wrong tonight." Comforting person that I am, I put my hand on her hip and added, "Is there anything I can get you?"

My adrenaline surged when I felt more than a hip under the skirt, and her adrenaline surged as she spun around and violently shoved me away. I flew backwards and slammed into a sidebar table, hurtling a crystal bowl full of spiked punch into the air. The sticky liquid splashed onto several guests' clothes, my poor gown included. The scene grew wilder when I yelled, "They're under her dress!"

Brianna's eyes were on fire as she screamed back, "You media wench!" and turned to run away. She slipped in the spilled punch and sprawled on the floor. Her skirt flopped up, and there were the Ferregiacomos, hooked to an industrial-strength granny garter belt that probably hadn't seen the sunshine since the Eisenhower administration.

If she thought stealing the shoes would save her company after this disaster of a party, she was sadly mistaken. How could she even contemplate trying to fence such notable stolen goods? It never would have worked.

Gasps echoed in the room, camera flashes exploded, and the police descended. In very short order, the master PR planner sorely needed her own crisis-management expert. Or, at the very least, a very good lawyer.

So I never did get the interview I came for; instead I ended up being the one interviewed—both by the police and assorted media. It wasn't what my editor had in mind, but it worked eventually as a bird's-eye view of what Brianna herself had called the "party to end all parties."

In fact, someone from E! Entertainment Television was interviewing me when the police chief finally led Brianna to a squad car in handcuffs. An officer followed, gingerly carrying the Ferregiacomos, now tagged "evidence."

The cameraman's sixth sense picked up on the parade, and he immediately swung his camera away from boring old me. In his haste, he stumbled into a closet door, which popped open a second later. A well-known hard rocker who'd made his millions in the late '90s rolled out of the closet with a young, disheveled intern from one of the local television affiliates. Given the bottle of Maker's Mark that thudded onto the floor and the smell of a controlled substance, it seemed the old mantra of "sex, drugs, and rock and roll" was alive and well.

The rocker pushed his long locks aside, along with his clingy and red-faced appendage, who was consumed with reconstructing her dress. Bleary eyed, he looked up and shrieked, "Awesome party, dudes!"

Awesome party, indeed.